Earth on Fire

Mark Cole

This is a work of fiction. All characters and events portrayed in this book are fictitious, and any resemblance to real people or events is purely coincidental.

EARTH ON FIRE

Edited by Jennifer Cole and Summer Rodrigue
Cover art by GoOnWrite.com

ISBN: 0692258167

ISBN-13: 978-0692258163

First edition: September 2014

10 9 8 7 6 5 4 3 2 1

To my grandmother.
You have done more for me than I could ever repay.
Thank you, Grand Lottie.

Table of Contents

Prologue – The Fire is Lit

Max Gilroy looked over at the kid he had brought on to help him five months ago. Joshua Hrynkiewicz had looked half-drowned when he tried robbing the small electronics store, but Max had seen something in him. The younger man had turned twenty last week, and Max had treated him to a gourmet dinner of pizza and soft drinks. *I had the extra room in my apartment for him to stay in anyway. I'll save money with him paying half the rent.*

"Everything's done and ready for us to open, Mister Gilroy," Josh said.

Max let out a sigh. "If you call me Mister Gilroy again, I'm going to rip off your arms and beat you to death with them." The retired Marine was certainly large enough to perform the feat, but he had threatened the boy with dismemberment many times before to no avail.

Josh laughed at the statement like he always did. "Whatever you say, Boss." The kid unlocked the door and sat back behind the counter, all puffed up and proud. It was the first time Max had let him open the store by himself. Max trusted the young man to perform all of his duties with meticulous attention to detail. After the recent business sale Josh landed increased their annual sales by a significant margin, Max decided to give him the combination to the floor safe.

"It's always a bit before the first customer rolls in, Josh, let's turn on the news and see what's going on in the world." The young man picked up the television remote and pushed the power button.

A found-footage style horror movie was on. "Run!" the woman on the screen screamed. "Oh, God, what is that thing!" An eight-legged monstrosity that Max couldn't describe any better than a cross between a man and a spider leaped from the side of a building and landed on the woman. Blood and gore splattered everywhere as the thing feasted upon her.

That looked extremely realistic. Crazy special effects these days. "Come on, kid, put it on the news." Max looked at Josh and saw his face was white as a sheet. "What?"

"I never changed the channel yesterday. This should be the news," he said just as the image changed to a woman and man sitting in a newsroom. The blonde woman's hands were shaking, and the man looked like he had just vomited off camera.

"We apologize for those scenes of graphic violence," the woman said, her voice hardly louder than a whisper. A hand from off-screen tried handing her a paper, but it took her a moment to steady herself enough to reach for it. "The President has ordered an immediate evacuation of the following cities: Seattle, Washington; New York City, New York; Los Angeles, California; Houston, Texas; and Atlanta, Georgia. If you live within one-hundred miles of these cities, gather what non-perishable items you can, and evacuate to the northern central United States."

Everything began to shake as if an earthquake struck the city. The power went out, dust fell from overhead, and the two men hunched down next to the wooden counter. The light from the windows was cast into shade as something enormous thundered by outside. "Did you see that thing?" Josh shouted. "What the hell was that?"

Max shook his head. "I saw it, but I've no fucking clue what it was." He reached behind the counter and pulled out his Mossberg shotgun. *I wish I had the 50 cal with me.* Max set the shotgun down on the floor and grabbed the Remington Josh had tried to use to rob him. He handed the cheaper shotgun to the kid. "You know how to use that?"

Josh shook his head, his face still white.

"Kid, look at me," Max said. Josh tore his wide eyes from the window and slowly turned his head to look at Max. "I need you to keep it together. I don't know what's going on. I won't let anything happen to you, but you have to stay in the moment. Don't worry about what you don't see. Just do what I tell you, and everything will be fine. Do you understand?"

"Y-yeah," Josh stuttered out.

"Come on, Josh. I need you to do better than that. You can do this. Do you understand?"

Josh took a deep breath and some color returned to his face. "I understand. How do I use this?" he said, lifting the gun a little.

Max took it from him and showed him the basics. "This is the safety, push it through to engage the trigger. There's a round in the breech already. Pump it after each shot. Other than that, it's a simple point and click interface." Max held the gun out to Josh. The younger man put his hands on the shotgun, but Max didn't release it. "Rule number one: do not point the gun at anything you do not intend to destroy."

"I got it," Josh said as he nodded. Max let go of the shotgun just as the windows shattered. The retired Marine snatched his larger shotgun from the floor, and his left ear rang when Josh's gun fired.

Max swung his gun forward, but Josh's shot had obliterated the monster's head. It's eight legs spasmed for a moment and stopped. "The floor safe still open in the back?" Max asked.

"Yeah."

Max glanced over his shoulder at the young man he had come to respect. "Good, get the cash, shells, and our lunches. We need to stop by the apartment and pick up a few things."

He watched the Outsider ships fly through the endless night of the Void. They had long ago learned to fear him and would have taken more care to avoid his sight had they known he was there. The amorphous shapes of the vessels gave a them a sinister air as the Outsiders surrounded the Thoolian settlement.

William was a Nephilim, the child of a half-demon and half-angel. His mother had been killed in the Purge along with his brothers almost twelve billion years ago, but his half-demon father had recently died a few thousand years ago in a battle that turned wrong. Ever since the Nine Realms had been created to protect the sentient races from the Outsiders, William and his father, Xorn, had taken it upon themselves to help defend the developing life forms in the Void.

Although the Void was a nearly barren emptiness, there were teeming pockets of life that clung desperately to existence. One of those pockets held the Thoolians, a species of creature that looked more like a ball of pale white vines than anything else. They communicated with a basic language of chirps and whistles and could hardly be called intelligent, but the Thoolians had a sense of community and eked out a hard life on the otherwise inhospitable floating islands of the Void.

William clung to the small rock that floated above the Thoolian's home. The patrol of Outsider ships paused between his perch and the island of life. The Nephilim scanned the cluster of four ships, trying to figure out which held the resonance amplifier the Outsiders needed to exist in the Void.

The Outsiders were from some place beyond the Void. They needed a complex machine to root themselves in the Material Plane, or else they would fade away like wisps of smoke. William wasn't sure how the invasion had begun, but he did know one thing. The Outsiders abhorred all life, and what they couldn't enslave, they destroyed.

<You will submit to the Nether,> William heard one of the Outsiders say using telepathy.

Running out of time. Which one is it? The

Nephilim glared at the four ships and demanded that they give up their secret. He noticed the second ship began to change in shape and color a split-second before the other three. *Found you.*

William wrapped himself in a shell of demonic energy, and he launched himself at the center of the ship. He streaked across the Void like a black comet and crashed through the hull of the vessel. The passageways of the Outsider craft warped and changed direction as he stood within the ship, but William had seen the same effect many times before and was not distracted by it.

He sensed the resonance amplifier a deck below him and slammed a hand into the deck plate. With a sound like ripping meat, the Nephilim tore the floor open. He dropped down to the lower deck and was surrounded by Outsiders. They brandished weapons that consisted of several pieces of black stone orbiting a rod embedded in the Outsiders' appendages.

Before they could attack him, William launched a devastating blast of demonic energy at the large black crystal. The black stone shattered. All of the Outsiders faded away, but not before one got a shot off. The pulse beam tore through the Nephilim's bicep.

William looked down at the wound and moved his arm, testing it. *It's fine*, he thought. The ship faded away around him, and William used his black feathered wings to fly down to the Thoolian village.

A group of the vine-like beings gathered around him. The largest mass of tentacles, half as tall as his seven feet, chirped at him, "Safe now?"

"Safe," he chirped back in the ponderous language. William understood all of the Thoolian language, but he was only capable of sounding out sixteen words. "More, I fight."

"Thank you," the biggest said. It held a tentacle out to his arm. "Hurt."

William closed his eyes and focused his body on repairing the damage to his bicep. A few seconds passed, and when he opened his eyes, there was a small scar where the wound had been. "No," the Nephilim chirped.

"Good. Stay and eat," the Thoolian chirped.

The fungus the Thoolians cultivated was tasteless, but there was little food to be found in the area, so William accepted the offer. *That was the first Outsider raid in this region of the Void in years. They came much more often when Father was alive. Something is afoot, and I need to know what it is. I told them when they created the Nine Realms that I would help keep everyone safe. It's what Mother would have wanted...*

William dwelt upon the past while he consumed the fungus the Thoolians brought him. He had never seen any other Nephilim than his brothers, and William knew he was alone, the last of his kind. But he had no way of knowing a Nephilim named Jessica had been born to Alex and Terra Zane.

Chapter One – Back Home

"Daddy," Jessica Zane said. Alex looked down at his newborn daughter in his arms. She had been sleeping, but now her mismatched hazel and green eyes stared up at him. The half-demon wasn't sure how he felt about the baby's ability to speak, but he did know one thing. Alex loved his daughter fiercely.

He smiled at her. "Good morning, little one. Are you hungry?"

"Yeah. Mommy?" the little girl asked with bunched together eyebrows.

Alex fought to maintain the smile and shook his head. Terra Zane, his half-angel wife and a powerful sorceress called the Nexus, had almost bled to death after giving birth to Jessica last night. Only Caitlyn and Hanna's fast thinking had saved her life, but she was still unconscious in the other room.

"No, Mommy is still sleeping, but I walked to the store while Hanna and Caitlyn were watching you and bought some baby formula. Do you want to try that?" he asked. *This is so weird! Babies aren't supposed to be like this.*

"Yeah!" Jessica said as she kicked her legs. She was swaddled in a pink blanket Alex had also picked up from the baby section of the supermarket. *That was a relief*, he thought as he walked to the kitchen. *It seems like Max did what I asked him and had me not declared dead. All of my accounts were still working. Can't believe Terra kept my wallet after I died.*

Alex had given his life to heal his wife and his

friend, Caitlyn Shadowpaw, after a hard fought battle with the Demon Lord Azreal left both of them on the brink of death. But doing so had caused him to violate what had been written in the Libram of Fate, and the angel Eternius had ordered Alex brought back to life to bring fate back into alignment. Part of fate returning to normal had meant Terra had to die, but Alex had destroyed the Libram of Fate before that came to pass, nullifying that part of the tome that controlled the destinies of the Nine Realms' inhabitants.

Shifting Jessica to just his left arm, Alex opened the container of baby powder and dumped a scoop into a small baby bottle of water he had filled earlier. Jessica turned her head and watched what he was doing with rapt attention. *So curious.* Alex screwed the cap and nipple onto the bottle one-handed, and he mixed the powder and water with a thirty second shake.

His daughter stared at the bottle he was shaking with a look of perplexed wide-eyed astonishment. "What that do?"

"Are you asking me what the powder did, or what it is supposed to do?" Alex asked.

"Yeah," Jessica said. *She must mean both.*

His daughter was the first Nephilim born in the last twelve billion years. An ancient wolf that lived inside Yggdrasil, a sacred tree on Caine, the Plane of Order, had told Alex and Terra female Nephilim were beyond rare. Fenris had also told them that they were extremely intelligent and had the ability to use magical energy and demonic power to devastating effect.

"The powder has a lot of vitamins and minerals in

9

it," Alex explained. "It is supposed to be like milk but better for you. When I shook it, the formula mixed with the water and turned into the drink." She stared up at him with her brows drawn together. "Did you understand what I said?"

"Yeah," the infant said.

Maybe I'm taking this a bit too seriously... "Are you just saying yeah to everything I ask?"

Jessica's mouth scrunched up, and her eyes widened. "No."

Alex almost laughed at the offended look on his daughter's face. *It's like she has a little how-dare-you-accuse-me-of-that look on her face.* "Sorry," he said. "Do you want to try it?"

"Yeah," she said and reached her tiny arms out for it.

Does she want to hold it? I thought I was supposed to do that. Alex put the nipple of the bottle into Jessica's mouth. She put her hands on the plastic four-ounce container and sucked on it. The infant pushed the bottle away, and Alex was surprised by the strength in her little arms.

"No," Jessica said as she glared at the bottle.

Alex looked from the formula to his daughter. The sun had just risen outside and a beam of light fell on her hair through the window. Alex saw streaks of red light up in her brown mop. "What's wrong with it? Does it taste bad?"

"No," Jessica said at length. The baby drew down her brows and closed her eyes. A few seconds went by before she opened them again and looked at Alex plaintively.

"Did you warm it up first?" Caitlyn asked from behind him. Alex turned around to see the changeling limping across the small living room. Caitlyn had decided to stay in her human form while they were on Earth, since a woman with golden eyes would be much less conspicuous than a panther with golden eyes.

"What are you doing up? Hanna said you should lay down and give yourself a chance to heal!" Jessica whimpered in his arm, and he looked down at her. "Sorry, I didn't mean to yell."

After Terra gave birth, she began to bleed heavily. Hanna had tried to use a dam of air to stem the flow, but it wasn't doing enough. Because Terra was a half-angel and her physiology was slightly different from the other two magic users, any healing performed would cause the injuries to transfer over to the person casting the healing.

Terra was Caitlyn's adopted sister, and the Changeling of the Fang was not going to allow her sister to die. She partially healed Terra, taking half of the injuries onto herself. Caitlyn's scream of pain was not something Alex would soon forget. He wasn't sure he would be able to ever repay the debt he owed her for saving Terra's life.

"Babies don't like milk that isn't warm. You have to heat it up first," Caitlyn said, ignoring his shout.

"Yeah," Jessica said.

Alex frowned at his newborn. *When did she learn to say yeah?* "You didn't know that either." He looked up at Caitlyn. "Please lay down."

Caitlyn limped past him and picked up the container of formula. She looked at the pictures on the back of it, filled the second four ounce bottle with water from the filtered bottles Alex had bought last night, put it in the microwave, and heated it for thirty seconds. The changeling pulled the bottle out and put two scoops of the off-white powder into the bottle. Caitlyn capped and shook it, then dribbled a little on to her wrist. "Perfect," she said as she took the bottle from Alex's hand and replaced it with the one she had just made.

Alex put the nipple in Jessica's mouth, and she began to suck from the bottle. "I didn't know you knew how to use a microwave," he said.

"Is that, ow, what that thing is called?" Caitlyn said as she limped past him and laid down on the couch.

Alex walked into the living room and sat down in the recliner next to the couch. "Yeah," he said. *Oh, she learned it from me.*

Caitlyn covered her eyes with her arm and said, "Never seen one before. It looked like the one in the pictures on the back of that container. The picture had the same symbol on it as the… microwave did."

Symbol? "That was just a three and a zero," Alex explained. "You pushed the 'add thirty seconds' button."

"Oh, that's what it said. Felt about that long. You'll have to teach me how to read your language some day," Caitlyn said.

Alex was struck dumb for a few seconds.

"Caitlyn, my language is the same as the one on Dae. I've read signs and other things on the Realm of Magic; they are all in English."

Caitlyn lifted her arm and cracked one eye open. "No, they aren't. There are usually in Common, the language the humans invented, but it looks nothing like the runes that make up your language."

Alex laughed and shook his head. "You're messing with me. Next you are going to tell me you don't speak English."

"No, learning to speak the common languages of each of the Nine Realms was part of my training as Warden of the Forest," Caitlyn said.

"Then how did I talk to all of the people on Dae? Were they all speaking Common?"

"You really don't know?" she asked in a bewildered tone. "The Guardian's Blade translates languages for you. Everything you hear is translated to the language you are most comfortable with, and everything you say is in the person's native language."

"What? How?" Alex asked.

"I don't know. You're the Guardian, you tell me," Caitlyn muttered. A few seconds went by, and she started to snore softly.

Alex had been born on Earth to a demoness and a human. His mother had been forced to flee, leaving Alex's father, Daniel Thomas Zane, to raise him. When Alex was a child, his father had been killed, and Alex was put into foster care.

After bouncing from one bad home to another, Alex enlisted in the United States Marine Corps where he served in a division of Force Recon that specialized in urban combat. When bad intelligence had sent them into a massacre, he had gotten out of the Marines and met Terra. She was looking for the Guardian of Balance, a person from Earth capable of wielding the Guardian's Blade.

Being the Paragon of the Plane of Balance had done Alex no favors so far, but he couldn't complain. He had married a beautiful red-headed half-angel and was safe back in his home on Earth.

"Daddy," Jessica said. Alex looked down; the bottle was empty. "More."

"Such a demanding baby," Alex joked. "You could ask."

Jessica's face turned from one of neutrality to one of concern. "More?" she asked, her little voice going up at the end in the imitation of a question.

Alex laughed and kissed her on the forehead. "I love you. Of course, little one. I only bought two little bottles, so I'm going to have to clean one. I'm going to set you in your crib for just a minute, okay?"

Jessica cocked her head to the side. "What love?"

"Yeah," Alex said. *How am I supposed to explain love to a baby?* "Love means that it makes you happy to see a person, and even when you are upset with that person, you still care about what happens to them and want them to be safe."

"Love Daddy," Jessica said with a smile. Alex felt tears well in his eyes. "Love Mommy."

Alex nodded. "I love Mommy too," he said as he placed Jessica on her back in the crib beside the couch.

"Mommy hurt. Mommy sleeping."

"Yeah. Don't worry. She'll be better soon." Alex walked into the kitchen and started cleaning out the two bottles. Jessica kept talking while he scrubbed them, but he couldn't hear her over the sound of the water.

Alex turned off the water and heard, "Want Mommy. Want Mommy. Want Mommy." He walked over to the crib and picked Jessica up. She had rolled over onto her stomach.

"I know you do, Jessica, but Mommy needs to rest. You want Mommy to get better so she can hold you and play with you, right?"

"Yeah. Bottle?" she asked as she looked around for it.

Alex smirked and shook his head. "I still need to make your bottle. Do you want to watch me make it again?"

"Yeah!" she said, kicking her legs again. *She's excited! That's cute.*

He made a second bottle, making sure to heat it this time, and sat down in the recliner to feed her. She sucked down three of the four ounces before falling asleep. Alex lay Jessica down in her crib and winced as a helicopter flew over the apartment. *Please don't wake up. I need to sleep eventually...* She didn't move an inch, and Alex sagged in relief. The sound of a second and third helicopter flying overhead brought Alex to the window.

Black painted attack choppers armed with heavy machine guns and air-to-ground missiles streaked past on a northerly course. *They must be up from Lewis-McChord doing training. I didn't know there was an Air Force base north of Seattle, though...* Alex sat back down on the brown cloth recliner and pondered the helicopters' appearance. *They were flying awfully low and fast.*

A hand touching Alex's shoulder almost made him jump out of his skin. He snapped his head to the side and saw the hand belonged to Hanna, the seven-year-old Changeling of the Wing that had sewn up Terra and Caitlyn last night. The short brunette was both a skilled doctor and healer, and Terra had told him that she picked up new ideas like a sponge. Alex put his finger over his lips and pointed at Caitlyn and Jessica.

Hanna nodded and patted her stomach then pantomimed drinking something. *Hungry and thirsty.* Alex lifted himself from his recliner that seemed to be taunting him with how comfortable it was and walked into the kitchen. He pulled a frozen breakfast sandwich from the freezer, placed it on a plate, and put it in the microwave.

Alex poured Hanna a glass of orange juice while the egg, sausage, and cheese in a biscuit warmed. She accepted the drink and took a sip of the bright orange liquid. Her eyes widened in surprise at the flavor, and she grinned at him. *I guess she's never had orange juice before.*

He glanced at the microwave and saw it only had a second left. Alex yanked the door open it started beeping and sighed. *That was close.* Hanna looked at him curiously, and he shook his head to not worry about it. Motioning her to take a seat at the table, Alex removed the hot ceramic plate from the microwave with a clean, black cloth.

Alex placed the plate on the wooden dinner table in front of Hanna, and whispered, "Careful. It's hot." She nodded and waited a few minutes for the food to cool before gobbling it down. *Geez, she must have been ravenous,* Alex thought as his eyes drifted closed.

Hanna poked him in the arm, and Alex's green eyes shot open. She started communicating with a serious of basic hand gestures. *You look tired. Go lay down in the bedroom and sleep. I'll watch Jessica.*

Alex nodded and got out of the recliner. Hanna climbed into it as Alex walked from the room. He pushed open the bedroom door and looked around in the gloom. *It was a good thing Hanna cast the bed of air under Terra, or there would be blood everywhere.*

He crept through the bedroom and laid down next to his wife, being careful to shake the bed as little as possible. It was hard to tell in the dim light that was being given off by her transparent blue wings, but it looked like Terra had gotten some color back to her face since last night. He wanted to put his arm around her but decided against it. *She needs to rest. I don't want to wake her up on accident.*

Alex closed his eyes and drifted off to sleep.

Caitlyn lay on the couch with her eyes closed, listening to Hanna shift about on the chair. The leather couch smelled like warmth, and the blanket had Alex's and Terra's scents on it. *It seems nice here. Last time... not so much.*

"Hey," a small voice whispered. The changeling rolled her head to the side to look at Hanna, but her eyes were closed.

"Hey."

She gingerly lifted herself and looked at the crib. Jessica was on her side staring at her. Caitlyn suppressed a shudder. *Not even twelve hours. This isn't natural.* "What is it?"

"Want hold," the baby said.

Caitlyn shook her head. "I'm sorry, Jessica, but I can't. I don't think I can lean over and pick you up right now." *Not that I want to.* Caitlyn shook her head and let out a deep breath. *That is Alex and Terra's baby. You knew she wasn't going to be normal. It's not her fault.*

"Want you."

Nodding, Caitlyn twisted around on the couch and reached a hand out to the baby though the crib's bars. She held Jessica's hand loosely in her own. "This is about all I can do right now."

"Yeah," Jessica said. "What name?"

Caitlyn craned her neck so she could look at the baby, and she smiled tentatively. "My name is Caitlyn Shadowpaw, but I'm your mommy's sister, so you can call me Aunt Caitlyn."

Jessica smiled back at her. "Aunt Caitlyn." A

rapid thumping sound filled the air, and they looked around. "What that?"

"I don't know," Caitlyn said. "Earth is a noisy place with all these people and their machina. I'm sure it's nothing."

"I don't like it," Jessica whispered as she squeezed Caitlyn's hand. Caitlyn winced in surprise at the unexpected strength behind the baby's grip.

"It's okay," Caitlyn cooed, and the crushing pressure lessened. "Everything's all right. Don't worry."

"Okay, Aunt Caitlyn." Jessica released her hand and rolled over. Caitlyn couldn't tell if the baby had decided to go to sleep, or if she was just staring at the far wall.

I know she's their baby, but this isn't right. Babies aren't like this. What kind of life will she have? Will any of them have?

Another thumping noise went over them, and Caitlyn glanced on the window. *What is that?*

Josh rode shotgun in Max's SUV as they screamed down 1st Ave South. The young man had his gun in death grip as Max wove around obstacles. People everywhere ran screaming away from Seattle. Josh watched as another one of those spider things flung itself from the SODO building, sail across the huge parking lot, and land on a guy running. Josh grit his teeth and pointed the shotgun out of the window.

Max touched his arm. "Don't waste the shell. We don't have many, and—" An explosion in the intersection just ahead made Max wrench the steering wheel to the right. "Hold on!" The SUV lifted up on just the right tires and threatened to overturn.

"Lean left!"

Josh wasn't sure if he and Max leaning toward the side that was in the air did any good, but they were able to slam back down and keep going, heading west on S Lander Street. "What happened?" Josh shouted.

"Bus exploded," Max growled. Josh watched as the big man looked into the rear view window and gulped.

"Recalculating," the GPS said in a vaguely annoyed voice.

Josh twisted around in his seat to see what it was. A huge monster with tree trunk like legs smashed through the fiery bus and was charging at them. "Max," Josh said, his voice rising.

"I see it." Max pushed down on the accelerator, and the SUV began to shudder.

"Turn left onto Colorado Avenue South," the GPS asserted.

"Max, I don't think we can turn onto Colorado going this fast," Josh said as he glanced at the GPS.

"We aren't."

Josh looked up through the windshield and froze. A wrecker had its bed lowered and at an angle, lined up with the several tracks in the rail yard between

Colorado and Alaskan Way. They were just seconds away from trying to use the wrecker as a ramp to jump an empty flatbed train car. "Max!"

"Only way!"

"Max!"

"Have to!"

"MAAAAAX!" They hit the wrecker, and Josh felt like his spine was going to fuse into one piece as their forward momentum was rapidly converted into vertical motion. He let go of the shotgun and placed one hand on the dash and the other on the handle above the door. They reached the apex of their arc and sailed over the flatbed.

The GPS floated up from the dash and hung before Josh's eyes. "Recalculating." *I didn't even know this thing could go ninety-eight,* Josh thought. The SUV slammed down into the third set of tracks, and there was a loud grinding sound. A stationary train loomed right before them, and Max yanked the wheel to the left.

Josh looked through Max's window to see the big monster crash through the train they had sailed over. The tires caught, and the SUV shot south along the tracks. Max maneuvered past trains and lone cars and got them onto a line that led southeast.

The SUV shuddered as it went over the ties. Josh looked through the rear windshield to see if the monster had followed them. They went under the West Seattle bridge overpass, and Josh wasn't able to see the big thing. Max got them off of the tracks and onto Highway 99.

"We taking 509?" Josh asked as he glanced at the broken GPS. *You put up a good fight, GPS.*

"Yeah, 16th if the bridge is up."

"All right." Josh took a deep breath and let it out slowly. "Good driving, Max."

Max grunted and swerved around a four car crash. There seemed to be less people in this area just a couple streets over from where they were.

"Where did everyone go?" Josh asked.

"Less shops and stuff around here," Max said. "It's more industrial, so there's less people."

"Max. What's going on?"

The big man shook his head. "I don't know. I..." Max glanced over at Josh and saw that he was trembling. "Hey, you've done good so far. We'll be all right. We just need to get to the house and pick up a few things."

Josh took a deep breath and nodded. "Okay." *Why do I have to be so scared?* He glanced over at the unshakable man beside him. *Why can't I be more like him?* Josh wrapped his hands around the gun and grit his teeth. *I will be.*

I can make it this time, Alex thought. *I only need to be a little faster.* This was his sixth time trying to save Terra's life. He sprinted across the battlefield on Caine. *I can make it. Help her run. Keep going*

straight.

"Pop, pop, pop," went the small caliber gun someone was firing nearby. Alex saw his wife's glowing blue wings and screamed at his legs to pump faster. *I'm going to make it.* He grabbed her arm and pulled her out of the way of the laser that was about to fire. Terra stumbled but only for a second before she regained her balance. An explosion blew them apart, and Alex could only see the ruined mass of one of her legs.

"Alex."

The Guardian sat upright in bed like he had been struck by lightning. His shirt was soaked with sweat, and the blanket was tangled around him. Terra had propped herself up on an elbow, and she looked at him. "You were having another nightmare," she said.

"I'm fine. Don't worry about it," Alex said as he got out of bed. "You should go back to sleep. Hanna said it would be another day or so before you were well enough to walk around."

Terra shook her head. "No, you aren't fine, and I am going to worry about it. You've been having nightmares every night since you saved me on Caine. Maybe we should talk about it."

"About what, Terra?" Alex asked, his ire rising. "The fact I saw you die hundreds of times while I was trying to save your life? Did I tell you about the time I tackled you to the ground but was only a split second late? Only half of your body was below me; your torso was a couple feet away."

"Alex," she said as she reached both arms out to

23

him. He walked around the bed to her side, and they wrapped their arms around one another. "I'm fine. You saved me. I'm right here."

"I know," he said with his head buried in her shoulder. "I just... it was horrible, the things I saw. It's just going to take some time to get them out of my head. Will you put up with me until then?"

Terra laughed softly. "Of course I will, you big oaf. Now, where is Jessica?"

"She's in the living room with Caitlyn and Hanna," Alex said. "After you had her, you were pretty messed up. Caitlyn had to partially heal you." Terra sucked in air through clenched teeth.

"Yeah, she's in the same condition as you are, but she lost less blood. You are going to need some more time before you can move around without feeling light-headed." Alex ran his hands through his hair. "There's something else."

"What?" Terra asked.

"Jessica can talk."

Terra frowned at him. "That's not funny."

Alex looked up into her hazel eyes. "I'm not joking. She's learning fast. She picked up a few more words from me in the forty-five minutes or so that she was awake."

"Bring her to me," she said with an iron tone. Alex nodded and walked into the living room.

Hanna was laying on the floor in front of the crib talking to Jessica. "It isn't hard. Just roll onto your stomach, push yourself up to your hands and knees, then move like this," Hanna explained as she crawled

24

around the floor.

Neither of the two girls had noticed Alex enter the room, and the half-demon watched as his daughter struggled to lift herself to her hands and knees. Jessica succeeded for a moment but lost her balance and fell on her side. "It is hard," the baby insisted.

"It is, but don't worry; you'll get it with practice," Alex said. Jessica and Hanna both turned and looked at him.

"Daddy!" Jessica exclaimed. "Is Mommy better? I love her."

Alex smiled. *Wow, already trying to crawl and speaking full sentences.* "Mommy is feeling a little better, but she still is going to need some more time before she's done healing. She loves you too. Do you want to go see her?"

"Yes!" Jessica said as she kicked her legs.

Alex walked over to the and picked her up. "Are you already done saying yeah?" he asked.

Jessica nodded. "Hanna told me yes was the..." The baby had a perplexed look on her face while she searched for the right word. "...not wrong word."

"The word you were looking for was 'right'. Yes is the right word, but yeah means the same thing. Yes is just more proper," Alex explained. He pushed the bedroom door open. "Light," he warned just before he flipped the switch. The overhead fan and quartet of lights turned on, bathing the room in white light.

Jessica saw her mother laying down on the bed and grinned. "Mommy! I love you!"

Terra broke into a wide smile, and Alex couldn't

help but grin. "I love you too, Jessica." Alex walked over and placed the baby in his wife's arms. The two stared at one another without speaking for several seconds.

My girls, Alex thought. He felt something stir deep within himself.

"Hey, there, Jessica," Terra whispered. "I love you." Tears welled up in her eyes, and she grinned. "So beautiful."

"I hurt you," Jessica said, and her eyes welled up with tears.

"No, Baby. I'm just happy," Terra said, shaking her head. "You didn't hurt me earlier either. It wasn't anyone's fault. Sometimes things like this happen when women have babies. Do you understand?"

Jessica nodded. "Daddy loves you."

Smiling, Terra said, "I know he does. I love him too, and Daddy loves you."

"I know he does. I love him too," she said, repeating what Terra had said.

"You are a little sponge," Alex said with a laugh.

Looking at him with a look of confusion, Jessica asked, "What's a sponge?"

Alex explained that a sponge was used to soak up water. "You are soaking up words like a sponge soaks up water."

"I want to be a little one, not a sponge," Jessica complained.

Terra looked at Alex with a raised eyebrow. "I called her 'little one' a couple times earlier." He looked down at Jessica and said, "You can be a little one. We'll go over more abstract concepts later."

Jessica frowned at him but agreed anyway. "I heard you talking," the baby said to Terra.

"Daddy and I were talking about some things a little while ago," Terra said.

"No," Jessica said as she shook her head. "It wasn't light yet."

It wasn't light yet, Alex thought. *What's that supposed to mean?*

"Do you mean it was before you were born? When you were still in my belly is when you heard me talking?" Terra asked.

"Yes. I heard you and the words you didn't say. You love me," the baby said with a smile.

Terra stared at the baby. "Yes, I do. So you read my thoughts before you were born, is that how you can speak so well?"

Jessica thought over what she had said. "Yes. Thoughts isn't words. Words is hard."

Ok, it's starting to make a little more sense, I guess. Alex was going to teach Jessica when to use is and are, but the power flickered and went out. He heard the distant pop, pop, pop of someone shooting a gun. "What's going on?" he muttered.

Hanna walked into the bedroom. "Why did it get dark all of a sudden?"

"Power went out," Alex said. He closed the bedroom door and opened the breaker panel. Nothing happened when he toggled the switches. Alex heard more gun fire, but this time there was a louder shot. *I know this place isn't in the safest neighborhood, but*

I've never heard shooting before. "I'm going to check out what's going on."

"Okay," Terra said. "Be careful."

Alex nodded and walked from the bedroom. Caitlyn was sitting up on the couch. "What's happening?"

"I don't know," Alex said as he grabbed the Guardian's Blade off of the small dining table. "I'm going to go outside and see what I can." Hanna walked into the living room. "Stay here with Caitlyn," he told the young changeling.

Hanna nodded at him and sat back down in the chair. Alex heard Terra and Jessica talking in the bedroom as he unlocked the door. Alex knew something wasn't quite right as soon as he stepped outside.

The smell of smoke pervaded the late summer air, and the light clouds overhead were darker than they should be. Alex heard more gunfire, but it was coming from the north side. *What the hell is going on?* The Guardian jogged around the apartment building and ran up the stairs to the third floor landing so he could see over the trees.

The dark wisps of cloud overhead were from an enormous pillar of smoke rising to the north. The sound of gunfire was coming closer. *Is SeaTac on fire? But why's there a shootout?* Trees a few hundred yards north of him began to sway as something large crashed through the woods surrounding his apartment complex.

Alex hurtled down the stairs and sprinted back to

the apartment. He flew inside and locked the door behind him. "Get everyone in the bathroom. It's in the interior and will be the safest place."

"Why?" Caitlyn asked as she rose on unsteady feet. "What's happening?"

The building shuddered as something slammed into it. "I think we're under attack! Move!"

Chapter Two – Safer

A large chunk of the upper apartment crashed into the living room, flattening the couch Caitlyn had just been lying on. "Go!" Alex shouted. Hanna and Caitlyn rushed into the bedroom to help Terra move into the bathroom with Jessica. The kitchen and dining area were ripped clean off as something large and grey crashed through the wall and kept running.

There was a flash of searing light, and the Guardian held the leather pommel of the Wrathblade in both hands. Any doubts as to what was happening were banished when Alex stepped over the rubble that had been the eastern wall of his apartment. A towering monstrosity with six thick legs supporting a torso that had four muscular arms reared and slammed down into the parking lot, crushing the neighbor's car under its cloven hoof. A horned, three-eyed face stared down at him from at least twenty feet overhead.

The enormous demon roared and stomped like it was about to charge. *I can't let it charge at the apartment.* Alex dove over what remained of his walls and sprinted into the parking lot right at the demon. The centaur-like monster kicked the flattened car at him, but Alex dropped to the ground, causing it to sail over him and crash into the building.

A woman stepped out of the apartment across the lot to see what the noise was about and screamed. Alex glanced her way and saw what looked like an eight-legged monstrosity crawling up the side of the building toward her. She screamed again, and the thing leaped at her, crushing her and tearing her apart.

Looking at the woman getting attacked proved to be a mistake. Alex didn't have enough time to roll away from the charging demon, and it landed a powerful blow to his side. The Guardian's rage flared, and the Wrathblade's flames grew. He launched himself at the demon, swinging his sword in a wide arc. The burning blade bit deep into the monster's torso, and black blood spewed into the air. The demon swayed and collapsed, coming inches from crushing Alex's old Sentra.

The eight-legged thing hurled itself fifty feet through the air at Alex. The Guardian was turning to strike it from the air when the larger demon shuddered and shoved Alex's car at him. The car struck him on the side and threw him off balance. The spider demon landed on Alex and knocked him to the ground. The Guardian's Blade clattered to the ground, reverting back to its wooden form when it left his hand.

Multiple rows of slavering fangs, like the teeth of a shark, snapped at Alex as he pushed against the demon's shoulders in an attempt to keep it from biting him. The things eight legs ended in claw tipped hands, and they tore vicious furrows in Alex's skin. The half-demon's mounting pain and rage unleashed his demonic powers, and the demon exploded in burst of blood and gore.

Alex rolled over to his hands and knees with a groan and stood. He snatched the Guardian's Blade from the ground.

<You know, you really should keep a better grip

on your sword, Wielder,> the Voice of Balance sent into his mind telepathically.

Shut up, the Guardian thought. *I don't want to hear it.*

He patted the car as he walked past it. "Well that was close, wasn't it, old girl?" he asked the Nissan. Alex walked down the steps to his first floor apartment and tried to enter through the front door, only to remember he had locked it. He stumbled over rubble as he entered the apartment through the knocked down wall.

Alex walked into the bedroom and rapped on the bathroom door. "It's safe to come out. I killed it." The door cracked open, and Hanna's brown eyes peeked through the crack. She saw it was him and opened the door the rest of the way.

I have to get them out of here. "Hanna, I need you to open a portal to Dae," Alex said. The young changeling nodded and moved past him. She closed her eyes and stood motionless in the middle of the bedroom. Caitlyn walked past him and sat down on the bed.

"What's going on?" Terra asked as he lifted her from the floor. Jessica was staring at him from where she lay in his wife's arms.

"Demons are attacking Earth," he said. "I'm having Hanna open a portal so all of you can get out of here."

"What do you mean, "all of you"?" his wife demanded.

Here we go. "Terra, you are not fit to fight,

Caitlyn's in little better shape, and someone has to watch Jessica. I need to get all of you back to where you will be safer."

"I understood what you were saying," Terra said with eyes narrowed into slits. Jessica was glancing between the two of them, still silent. "I just want to know why you think you won't be coming."

Golden light filled the room, and Alex glanced over his shoulder. There was a red tint to the portal. The keystone seal that prevented unauthorized planar travel to Dae was still up. "This is my home. I have to help protect it."

Terra's eyes widened. "Your home is with us, Alex. You can't leave me... not after I just got you back." Tears began to well in her hazel eyes.

Alex put his hands on his wife's smooth cheeks. "Hey, you'll see me again, I promise. And I always keep my promises, don't I?"

"You do," Terra whispered.

"Daddy," Jessica said with outstretched arms. Alex picked up his daughter and kissed her on the forehead.

"What is it, little one?"

"I love you," she said with tears in her eyes.

Alex smiled and kissed her again. "I love you too. You grow up big and strong and help take care of Mommy while I'm gone, okay?"

"Yes," she said. "And you take care of you; okay, Daddy?"

Alex nodded and gave her back to Terra. "I will." The red tint disappeared from the portal. "Let's get you two to Dae," Alex said.

A tumultuous riot of emotions flowed across the magical link that connected Alex and Terra. Alex couldn't pick any one of the emotions out, but he knew everything his wife was feeling was negative. He stepped to the golden portal and paused. Darren and Brahm stood on the other side to welcome them.

"I love you," Terra said, her eyes were clamped shut, but tears were still escaping through the corners.

"Hey," Alex said. Terra opened her red-rimmed eyes and looked at him. "Don't be sad, Beautiful."

The Nexus shook her head, making her red hair flail about. "Don't you say that! Just don't... That's the last thing you said to me when you died on Dae. Just tell me you love me and that you'll see me soon."

Alex nodded. "I love you too. I'll see you as soon as I can." He lifted her higher and kissed Terra on her lips. For a second, he closed his eyes and was able to forget about all of the pain and loss that had been crushing him, but it was only for a second. Their lips parted, and before he lost his nerve, Alex passed Terra through the gateway into Brahm's waiting arms. He turned to face Caitlyn.

"I'm not going back. You can't be here by yourself, and I'm staying with you," Caitlyn said.

"You are hurt, Caitlyn. You need to go back to Dae and recover," Alex protested.

"I can't hold this portal open much longer," Hanna said. "It's harder than it looks to maintain a portal without a gateway arch."

Alex gritted his teeth. "I don't have time to argue

with you."

"Then don't. Hanna, I'm staying, go through the portal," Caitlyn said.

The Guardian crossed his arms and sighed. Hanna looked up at him, and Alex nodded. She stepped through the portal, dispelling it behind her. *And if Terra wasn't pissed off at me before, she certainly will be now.* With the portal's closing, Alex was no longer able to tell where Terra was, but he could still feel her emotions, and anger was principle among them.

"So, what's the plan?" Caitlyn asked.

Terra fumed as she bobbed along in the stretcher. *How could he keep Caitlyn with him after he said she's too hurt to stay, but he still made me leave?* she thought. The Nexus ground her teeth, and Jessica touched her chin. *Because the big oaf wanted the two of us to be safe, that's why.*

A feeling of apologetic regret was coming across the link, and Terra did her best to respond by feeling calm and loving. Alex's feelings changed to happiness and calm, and Terra smiled.

"Mommy's not... not happy with Daddy?" Jessica asked. Darren made the stretcher dip to one side almost knocking the two of them out of it when he turned his head about to stare.

Terra gave her head a shake, both at Jessica and

Darren. "No, I'm not upset with Daddy anymore. He's doing what he thinks is right, and I shouldn't be angry at him for that."

Jessica bunched up her eyebrows and started to cry. "I want Daddy."

The half-angel held her daughter close. "I know, little one," Terra said, using Alex's nickname for her. "I do too." Jessica cried until she fell asleep.

"We can't fight against an army with just the two of us," Alex said. He was leaning against the wall shared wall between the bathroom and the closet while Caitlyn changed clothes. "If he still lives in the same place, I can get us to someone we can rely on."

"What's his name?" Caitlyn called.

"Max Gilroy. He's the reason we still had a place to come back to. I was always planning on going around and seeing the world, and I kept telling him that one day I would just pack up and go. He had my Power of Attorney to watch over the place as long as the bills kept getting paid. I had a year of savings, so it looks like we made it back with a couple months to spare," Alex said.

The sunlight coming in from the bedroom window was cast into shadow, and Alex's first instinct was that they were under attack again. He reached for his sword but saw it was Caitlyn.

"I'm ready," she said. Caitlyn had put on a loose fitting pair of Terra's jeans and a short sleeve shirt that had a deep V neck, revealing a significant amount of cleavage.

Alex frowned at her choice of clothing but didn't protest. *Oh, crap. She hasn't fallen completely in love with Darren in this timeline. Terra's death must have been the catalyst that caused their relationship to grow. I'm going to have to straighten this out.* "Come on," he said with a sigh. "Let's see if the car works."

Alex decided to stay in his white t-shirt and denim pants, but he laced up the pair of the tan military-issued boots he had kept when he got out of the Marine Corps and slid the sword's baldric over his head. He wasn't sure keeping Caitlyn with him was the best idea. She was walking slow, and he had to help her over the rubble. *I'm going to have to protect her until she recovers.*

Caitlyn let out a low whistle when she saw large demon Alex had killed. The pair reached the car, and Alex felt about on the bottom for the magnetic box he had mounted onto the undercarriage. After a few seconds of searching, he pried the metal box from where it was and opened it.

A silver key fell into his hand, and he unlocked the doors. "Come on, Baby. You know you love me," Alex cooed as he sat down in the driver's seat and stroked the steering wheel. He slid the key into the ignition, and his hopes rose as the car started dinging. The key turned, and his old car sputtered to life.

Alex let out a victorious whoop, turned to Caitlyn,

and said, "Come with me if you want to live." The changeling looked at him with a confused expression. "It's from... Never mind. Lift up on the handle on the other door and get in; we need to go."

The raven-haired changeling tugged on the latch, but the door wouldn't open. *Stupid demon jammed my door.* Alex got out of the car. "Climb in through my side. Be careful of the gear shift."

"What's that?" Caitlyn asked as she walked around the front of the car. He pointed at the small black lever. The changeling stood for a moment outside the car, trying to figure out how she could climb through without hurting herself. "I don't think I can crawl through there, Alex."

The Guardian ran his hand through his cheekbone-length brown hair. *I really need to get some of this mop cut off.* "Just ride in the back, but on the opposite side from me. That way if we get into a wreck on one side, one of us will have a better chance of surviving." She nodded and got in, sliding across the gray cloth.

Alex sat back in the driver's seat and buckled his seat belt. "Buckle up," he said as he looked over his shoulder and shifted into reverse. He had to show Caitlyn how to operate the safety mechanism, and when she was secured, he released the brake and rolled out of the parking spot. *I'll need to take back roads. The interstate is going to be blocked for sure.* Alex turned on the radio.

A recording of a woman's voice was on the station. "The President has ordered evacuation of the following cities and their outlying boroughs: Seattle,

Washington; New York City, New York; Los Angeles, California; Houston, Texas; and Atlanta, Georgia. If you are within fifty miles of these areas it is advised that you head inland and north. The central United States are still secure. Do not panic and gather what non-perishables you need to survive. The President has ordered evac—" Alex listened to the message two more times to ensure nothing more would be forthcoming, flipped off the radio, and glanced in the rearview mirror at Caitlyn.

"What did she mean?" she asked.

He swerved into the opposite lane to pass the burning husk of a car on 16th Avenue South. It didn't look like there were any survivors around it. "Seattle isn't the only city getting attacked. There are four more, and that was just what was happening in the United States. I wouldn't be surprised if the entire Earth was invaded."

"Why would Azreal attack the Realm of Balance?" Caitlyn asked.

Alex shrugged. "I don't know. He could just want to add a few billion more to his death toll. The Overlord of Hell doesn't need a reason to commit genocide." They rode in silence for a few minutes dodging around obstructions and backing down a blocked road to take another route before Alex spoke again.

"There's something we need to get straightened out, Caitlyn," the half-demon said.

Her golden eyes narrowed, and Caitlyn frowned, staring at him in the reflection of the rearview mirror.

"What's that?"

Alex sighed. *Do it fast, like a bandage.* "Before I started travelling through time to save Terra, the Guardian's Blade showed me everything Terra had gone through. Every battle. Every close call with Jessica. Every conversation."

Caitlyn's face blushed. "Including when we talked about me loving you."

"Yeah," Alex said. *I don't think I should tell her about what I saw between her and Darren. It could color her perceptions and prevent that relationship from developing. Ugh, I'm so glad I can't use Regret anymore. Time travel hurts my head.* "Caitlyn—"

"I do love you, Alex," she interrupted. He glanced up at her in the mirror and saw her shaking her head. "I know I shouldn't, but I can't help the way I feel. I was lost when you died. But that's not—"

"Stop. Stop before you say something you can't unsay," Alex blurted out. "I'm not the man you should be with, Caitlyn. I love Terra with every fiber of my being. You're like a sister to me, and nothing will change that."

"I know," she whispered just loud enough for him to hear. "That's why I never told you and didn't want you to find out when you came back. It's just…"

Please don't make me regret asking this. "Just what?"

Caitlyn sighed. "I just wish things could have been different. That's all. It hurts me to think that you are so close and still so far away, and I would never do anything to get between you and Terra. If all I can be is a sister, then that's what I'll do and be grateful that you still want me by your side."

"Thank you, Caitlyn." Alex turned the car onto South 188th Street and went through the tunnel south of the SeaTac airport. "I'm…" Alex trailed off when he saw a spindly-legged monster hurtling down the road after them in the sideview mirror. "What is that?"

Caitlyn turned in her seat just as the demon belched a glowing green ball of acid at the car. Alex swerved into the other lane, and the acid hit the roof of the tunnel. "It's a devourer larva. They eat anything. I'll take care of it, just don't let it hit us." Alex stomped on the accelerator, and the old car jumped forward.

She closed her eyes and took a deep breath. Rubble began to fall from overhead. A large chunk of stone fell a few dozen yards in front of the car, and Alex scraped silver paint from the passenger side as he dodged around it. The car blasted from the end of the tunnel like a bullet from the barrel a gun. Alex saw the way ahead was clear and risked a glance at the rearview mirror.

A cloud of dirt and dust essayed from the mouth of the tunnel as it collapsed on the devourer. "That will slow it down," Caitlyn said. "It will hopefully get distracted by an animal and go chasing after it. If not, we'll have to deal with the demon when it gets free."

"You mean it's not dead?" Alex asked as he turned onto Highway 509.

"Not by a long shot. The carapace on its back would have prevented any real harm." Caitlyn glanced out of the window and sank lower in her seat. "How can you go this fast?" She put her head in her hands. "Let me know when we get there or if you need me to drop any more tunnels."

Alex snorted a laugh. "Sure." Max's apartment was only a little farther north in a small complex in Renton. "We'll be there in a couple minutes." The closer Alex got to Seattle, the more devastation there was to behold. A pack of zombies feasted upon a family they had dragged from a large van. *Shit,* Alex thought. *We're going to have to deal with a zombie outbreak and a demonic army.*

Alex saw the exit off of the road was blocked by a bus that had been knocked over, but there was a concrete divider blocking him from crossing over into the oncoming lanes to use the other exit. *It's only a half-mile from here. We can walk it.* He drove up the exit and parked the car.

"We have to walk it from here. Can you make it a half-mile?" Alex asked.

Caitlyn nodded. "As long as I don't have to ride in this machina any longer, I'll be fine." Alex didn't have the heart to tell her that she was going to be spending a lot of time in vehicles on Earth.

"Good," he said as he unbuckled his seatbelt. "Let's go." He got out of the car and opened the door for her. After a short explanation, Caitlyn pressed the release for her seatbelt and slid across the seats. The changeling winced as she lifted herself from the car. "You sure you'll be able to make it?"

"I am," she said. "It just hurts to spread my legs."

Alex blushed at that statement, and she frowned at him. "Really, Alex?" Caitlyn let out an exaggerated sigh. "You're such a male. Where do we need to go?"

"That way," Alex said pointing east. He squeezed through the gap between the bus and the guardrails. The smoke was thicker this far north, and neither of them saw anyone living in their ten-minute walk to Max's apartment. Alex focused for a moment on his link to Terra and felt that she was calm, but slightly angry and annoyed. He had felt her love for him earlier, and it had made him feel a little better about keeping Caitlyn with him.

Alex was relieved to see the big man's black SUV idling in the parking lot. It looked like the vehicle had been through the wringer. It was dented and scraped in several places, and both the rear passenger windows were shattered. "Good, he's here. Follow me. We have some stairs to climb, are you going to be able to do that?"

Caitlyn groaned. "Yeah, I'll be fine." The sound of bones snapping came from behind Alex. He glanced over his shoulder to see that Caitlyn had changed into her panther form, and she padded along behind him. "I wasn't sure if it would hurt more or less like this, but it seems easier to walk. And it's not like I need to worry about drawing any more attention than a demon or zombie running about."

"Good, just try not scare anyone." Alex ran up the stairs three at a time and banged on the second-floor apartment.

"I'll do my best," Caitlyn said from a few steps

down.

The sound of a shotgun cocking came from the other side of the door, and Alex stepped out from in front of the door. "Who's out there?" a young man's voice shouted through the metal door.

I know I have the right apartment. "Alex Zane. Is Max Gilroy there?"

"Who is it?" a deeper voice yelled.

"Some guy named Alex. Isn't that the guy that used to work with you?" the young man said.

Heavy footsteps ran to the door, and it swung inward. Max's seven-foot frame filled the doorway, and he looked around the corner at Alex. "Where the hell have you been?" the man roared.

"It's good to see you too, Max," Alex said with a smirk. "It's kind of a long story. Can we come in and talk about it? It's not exactly safe to be outside."

The man glared at Alex. "If I didn't know better, I would say you are somehow involved in all of this." Max stepped into his apartment and beckoned Alex inside.

"More than you know, Tiny. More than you know," Alex said as he patted Max on a thick bicep. A skittish young man with a pump-action Remington pointed it at Caitlyn when she padded into the apartment. "Whoa, kid. Calm down. She's a friend."

"Can you tell him that I mean him no harm and would appreciate it if he didn't point a gun at me?" Caitlyn asked.

The young man fell back a half step. "Did that cat just talk?" he said with wide-eyes.

"Yeah, but her name is Caitlyn Shadowpaw, not cat. The real trick is getting her to be quiet," Alex said as Max shut the door. Caitlyn huffed and bumped against Alex hard enough to knock him off balance.

"Not funny," the panther said.

"What's your name?" Alex said.

The young man pointed the shotgun down and to the side. "I'm Joshua Hrynkiewicz. I work with Max at his store."

"Yeah," Max said. "I had to find someone to pick up the slack after you up and disappeared. You have some explaining to do, Sarge."

Alex sighed but didn't get on to the big man for calling him Sarge. *I started it, and turnabout's fair play.* "It's a long story, so I'll just fill you in on the high points. Terra was kidnapped by a demon. It turns out she's a powerful half-angel sorceress. She rescued herself, and it turned out that I'm a half-demon. My sword here is called the Guardian's Blade, and I used it to kill a Demon Lord named Azreal but died in the process.

"An angel named Eternius told a group of crystalline beings called Life Wardens to bring me back to life, and I created a loop in time so I could keep Terra from getting killed. I had to destroy a book called the Libram of Fate, which governs the destiny of all the major events in history. Eternius, the one who wrote the book, was understandably upset, but kind of conflicted about it all because he was Terra's father. Terra and I just had a baby, a little girl named Jessica, here on Earth, and I had to send Terra and the baby back to the Realm of Magic where they'll be safe." Alex closed one eye and thought for a moment while he rubbed his stubble strewn chin. "That's pretty much all of it."

Max and Josh stared at Alex with the same slack-jawed disbelief. "Sure, if there're monsters running around Seattle, then why can't you be some kind of mystical warrior with a magic sword and talking panther named Caitlyn," Max said.

Alex grinned at his friend. "Exactly."

"You're just going to go with what he's saying? This guy sounds crazy!" Josh shouted.

"Of course he believes me," Alex said. "It was a completely rational explanation. And it helps that there are demons and undead roaming around to back me up." The Guardian looked back at Max. "I'm certain that Azreal, the leader of the forces of Hell, is behind all of this. He's been trying to destroy the Nine Realms for the past six years, but I'm not sure why he's attacking Earth now. We destroyed his armies on the other Realms he had invaded, so it could just be a retaliatory attack against my homeworld."

"So let me get this right," Josh said. "You think this Azreal is attacking Earth because of you."

Alex sighed. "I don't know, but no one holds a grudge like his uncle does," Caitlyn said.

"Uncle?" Max and Josh shouted at the same time.

I was going to leave that part out. "Yeah, but don't you dare try laying the people he kills at my feet," Alex said. Caitlyn growled at the young man, and Josh tightened his grip on his shotgun. "I'm not the one out there killing people; he is. And I'm going to kill that bastard once and for all."

"Sorry," Josh said. "I didn't mean to imply anything."

Max placed a hand on Josh's shoulder. "He knows you didn't, Josh. Alex's trying to convince himself that none of this is his fault, and he tends to get... snappy when he's angry with himself."

Alex glared at Max. "I do not get snappy when I'm angry."

"Yes, you do," Caitlyn and Max said at the same time, and they grinned and each other.

Alex crossed his arms and glared at everyone. His stomach rumbled, and he realized he hadn't eaten since late yesterday. "You have anything to eat before we start plotting how best to kick some demon ass?" Alex asked.

A devious grin crept across Max's face. "Sure, Sarge, I have some MRE's in the truck, because I know how much you love them."

His face went blank, and Alex said, "You have to be kidding me, Max. I hate those things. What do you really have to eat?"

"I'm not kidding," Max said. "I do have about twenty MRE's in the truck, but there's some food in the fridge. I'm just getting the last of my ammo together and loaded up. This entire area's already been evacuated, so there's no one to take the truck."

"Sounds good. Come on Caitlyn, I know you're hungry too." The two of them raided what little bits of food were left in Max's fridge. Alex watched Max walk out of the front door carrying his large fifty caliber machine gun under one arm and two boxes of ammunition for it under the other. Alex had made fun of Max for buying the weapon, but he guessed that it turned out to be a good idea after all.

Max and Josh walked back inside just as Alex and Caitlyn finished eating.

Alex drank a small glass of water to wash down the bread. "So, what's the plan?" he asked as he and Caitlyn walked to the door.

"We need to get somewhere safer," Max said as the four of them walked down the stairs. "I was thinking Naval Air Station Whidbey Island. There's a Marine Corps training squadron there."

Alex stared at the back of his friend's head like he was a crazy person. "Are you insane? You want to go through Seattle then across the Puget Sound in the middle of a war zone, just so you can show up and be told you're useless by some lieutenant that gets to fly an instructor's plane?

Max reached the bottom of the stairs and looked back at him. "I didn't say it was the best plan... Hell, if you can think of a better one then let me hear it."

"We go down to Lewis McChord," Alex suggested.

Max's eyes narrowed. "No." Josh opened the SUV's back hatch and Max put the two more ammo boxes into the vehicle. Alex saw a plethora of boxes for a multitude of guns and a crate of MREs. The black-haired young man shut the hatch and got in the back seat. Alex opened her door, and Caitlyn got in the seat across from Josh.

"Why not?" Alex asked as he shut the back door. He unsheathed the Guardian's Blade and got in the front passenger seat to find Max still glaring at him. Alex placed the wooden sword between his legs and stared back at the big man.

"I hate the Chair Force," Max said. "Bunch of morons that spend more time with their thumbs up their asses than getting work done."

Alex shook his head and muttered, "Wow, tell me how you really feel." He raised his voice. "We can take back roads to JBLM, and there won't even be any traffic. Not as much as is on the interstate, and we can go off road in this if we really need to. It makes more sense, Tiny. You know I'm right, and with the Army there, we have a better chance of getting into the fighting. Especially when I tell them what they are really up against."

Max said something under his breath and looked over at Alex. "Fine, but I have no idea how to get there without taking the interstate, and cell phones are dead, so I can't pull up a map."

"You don't have a map?" Alex asked.

"Why would I have a map if I can just look it up on my phone?" Max retorted.

"Good point." Alex closed his eyes and thought for a moment. *Come on. Come on, I know I remember looking at a map of the Seattle-Tacoma area before all this started.* He had always had a good sense of direction growing up, and Alex had taken to memorizing maps of areas before he arrived there, a skill that had served him well in the Marines. A few seconds of concentration, and directions began bubbling up in his mind.

"We need to take 167 to 512. After that, you turn on to seven, then 507. That will take you to the gate access road," Alex regurgitated from memory. "We just need to hope the east gate isn't closed, or else we'll have to go all of the way around the base to get someone's attention."

Max rubbed his eyes. "Are you sure about this, Alex? There's a Lieutenant General in charge of that base, you'll be lucky if you get within spitting distance of the man."

Alex patted the silver disc on the pommel of the Guardian's Blade. "You just drive and let me worry about what we do when we get there, Tiny."

"Aye, Sarge," Max said as he shifted the black SUV into drive.

Chapter Three – The Means to an End

Hanna frowned at the manacled man sitting across from her. Doctor Sigma Moore's black eyes stared at her without emotion. "So, you're saying the pre-frontal cortex is the region of the brain above the eyes that is in charge of decision making," the young changeling said.

Moore nodded. "Among other things. Risk-reward, logic, that section of the brain handles many different functions." He lifted his hands a little in a beseeching gesture. "Would it be possible to be released from my manacles, now? I have shown every willingness to cooperate."

The little girl sighed. As soon as the doctor started asking to be released from his shackles, he stopped being helpful. *Well, I learned a good deal about the human brain today. I wonder how the brains of changelings differ from base animals...*

"You've cooperated with the questions of a little girl," Darren said. "You haven't confessed to your crimes." The captain of Terra's personal guard had been given charge of the prisoner when they returned to Dae from Caine last week.

Darren glared at the doctor while Hanna looked around the interrogation room. It was all stone and beneath what would become the Nexus's Palace. Moore's shackles had been fed through a gap in the collapsible table, so that if the man tried to stand or strike out at either of them, he would first have to unlock the complex mechanism beneath the table.

"That is because I have committed no crimes," Doctor Moore repeated. "I have nothing to confess. I assert that I was under duress and forced to build the extraction pods or else my life would have been forfeit."

"We're done here," Darren said. He looked over at the armed prison guard. "Take him back to his cell."

As soon as the guard had a grip on Moore's shoulder, Hanna channeled a trickle of magical energy into the table's mechanism. She was careful to not allow the doctor to see what she was doing even though she was confident that he couldn't see magical energy. The table ratcheted open, and Doctor Moore was led away.

"Damn him," Darren snapped as soon as the door closed. "He's not giving us anything!"

The captain's reaction seemed a bit extreme, and Hanna began to ponder the man's recent actions. *It seems like he's been growing increasingly stressed since Jessica was born. I don't think it has anything to do with that though... He does like Caitlyn, so he's most likely just worried about her.* "I think he's given me quite a bit," Hanna said.

"I'm happy for you," Darren said sarcastically. The man stood and walked to the other door that led up the stairs. Hanna fell in step behind him.

"You don't have to be worried about Caitlyn. She's with Alex and will be just fine," she said.

Darren froze with his hand on the latch. "How did you know that is what's bothering me?" he asked as he looked over his shoulder at the seven-year-old.

You just told me. "It's written all over your face. You've been acting differently since you found out she was still on Earth with Alex. They are two of the strongest people I've ever met. Don't worry," Hanna said, trying to reassure the captain.

"You're right," Darren said with a sigh. "I shouldn't worry. There's no one better suited to fight demons on another Realm than those two."

Hanna couldn't tell if he was still being facetious and decided to take his words at face value. "And Caitlyn *does* like you, she just doesn't know she does," she said.

Darren raised an eyebrow at her and pulled open the door. "How do you know?" he asked nonchalantly as he climbed the spiral stairs.

"I've seen the way she glances at you when she thinks no one is looking. Caitlyn's trying to figure out how she feels about you. You just need to come out and tell her how you feel."

"It's not that easy," the captain said.

Hanna sighed. *That's what adults always say. I think this is going to require a different tack.* "What's hard about it? Just walk up to her the next time you see her and say, 'Caitlyn, I love you. I've always loved you. Come run away with me to a place where I can abandon my insecurities about missing a hand and not being worthy of love.'" Darren spun on the narrow steps and glared at her. *Maybe that was a bit much.*

"That is not how I feel about missing my left hand," he snapped. Hanna squeezed past him and continued up the stairs ahead of the captain.

"Yes, it is," she said. *I've already blazed this trail, may as well forge ahead. It makes sense.* "Or else you wouldn't have reacted like I insulted your manhood. It doesn't matter to her whether you are missing a hand or not, Darren," Hanna said, risking use of the captain's first name. "It shouldn't matter to you either. You've obviously overcome your self-perceived handicap." Darren muttered something too soft for her to hear. "What was that?"

"No way in Hell are you actually seven," he said.

I think people would take me a bit more seriously if I wasn't. "When you are at war almost as long as you've been alive, it forces you to grow up quickly." Her father, Aeryn Steelfeather the Winglord of the Changelings of the Wing, apologized to her every day she was with the army healing their injured. "It's hard to keep up the illusion of childish innocence when you watch a man succumb to the undead necrosis and attack his friends," Hanna said.

"Is that why you are working so hard to find a cure?" The topic was of particular interest to Darren. He had been forced to cut off his own left hand after his brother had been turned and bitten him.

"Two men died that day," Hanna said. "Neither should have had to. I just couldn't do what was necessary. The other nurses were all out treating people at the other stations when the two men were brought to me. The first only had an arrow through his lung; I treated it easily. He was exhausted from the fighting and fell asleep.

"No one could figure out what was wrong with the

other man. He didn't have any injuries and was burning up, and his eyes had turned white. I knew the signs of the necrosis, but I tried to save him anyway. It was no use, everything I tried to do just failed. I froze when his heart stopped, but he kept moving... I should have done something sooner... I should have crushed his skull before he reanimated."

"Hanna," Darren said. "You had to try. There's no way of knowing if anything you tried would have helped."

She let out a scornful snort. "Yes, I did. I knew I couldn't save him. I knew nothing would work. I just watched as he rolled over and tore the throat out of the defenseless man next to him. I screamed and some soldiers ran over and destroyed the zombie." Hanna reached the top of the stairs and opened the wooden doors to the outside. The sun lit up her brown hair, and she reveled in the warmth after the cold dungeon. "I think that was when I stopped being a child."

The man reached the top of the stairs and knelt in front of her. Darren wrapped her in a warm embrace. "I'm so sorry you had to see that. You shouldn't have had to." Hanna patted him on the back, and he released her.

"What I saw doesn't matter, now," she said. "It was a long time ago, and the memory fades a little each day. I honestly don't even remember either of the men's faces anymore. I just wish I knew then what I know now. I've been able to isolate the undead necrosis and keep it from spreading to the brain, but without regular dosing of sorcerer's bane and someone to maintain the spell, the men could turn at any time. I'm on the verge of discovering a cure, and I know it rests somewhere in Doctor Moore's head. It's like I'm building a puzzle blindfolded, and I don't even know if the pieces he's giving me fit."

Darren stood and ruffled her hair. "I understand. You'll get it eventually."

"I know, but will it be soon enough to help those still carrying the necrosis? Or will more die because I think I'm better than I really am?" Forlorn depression roared through her, crushing the hope that had been kindling within her. She glanced up at Darren, and for a second, she thought it was Alex there with her.

The sun lit his dark brown hair, making it look like Alex's lighter shade, and with the sun behind him, it was hard to make out his face. "Don't worry, Hanna," he said with confidence. "Those men and their families thank you for every second of every day that you've given them. You will figure this out, and you'll be remembered as the greatest healer that ever lived. Hanna, the girl that healed the unhealable."

Hanna shook her head and laughed, her bout of sadness passed. "That would be nice," she said. "It's time for my lesson with Jessica, Captain. I'll see you at this same time tomorrow."

Darren saluted her with absolute seriousness. "Yes, Ma'am," he said as he walked toward the council chambers where Terra was meeting with Kara.

Hanna watched him go. *I think we helped each other. Thank you, Darren.* She walked the few hundred yards to the small servant's house Terra was living in until the palace was finished being built. The masons had only just finished the foundation, complete with dungeon and cellars, and they were scheduled to begin the first floor soon.

The Changeling of the Wing smiled when she walked in the back door and saw Deidra Belles feeding Jessica in the baby's high chair. The Nephilim's teeth had already come in, and she was eating solids. It smelled like chicken, rice, and corn was on the menu for the baby today.

"Hanna!" the little girl shouted when she recognized her through the glare from outside. "What are we learning today?"

Hanna laughed at the Jessica's enthusiasm. *She's only been alive a day and a half, can already walk and talk, and I think she's grown a few inches. How fast do Nephilim develop? I'm glad Terra is letting me teach her the basics.* "I thought we would go over colors, shapes, and reading. Does that sound fun?"

"Yeah!" Jessica said. "Daddy said it was alright to say yeah, so I want to say yeah."

Hanna smiled. "That's fine. Your daddy is a smart man."

"You're an idiot. You know that, right?" Max asked. They had been driving for six hours on a trip that should have taken less than one. Roads had been blocked, and there was one bridge that had been completely destroyed that had required finding an alternate route. They were close to Joint Base Lewis McChord; there were no other ways they could go from here, and a tremendous pine tree blocked the road.

Alex glared at the man as they tried to figure out the best way to remove the obstacle. "How was I supposed to know there would be trees down on the back roads? And I don't remember you protesting when I said we shouldn't take the interstate."

"You didn't think there would be trees down on the roads that have trees to either side?" Max asked.

"It's not like we had a storm that could have knocked them down!" Alex shouted. "I didn't know demons would have made it this far south to block roads."

There was a loud scream from behind them, and the two men spun to see Josh falling out of the black SUV. "What the hell is she?" he shouted as he pointed at the vehicle. Caitlyn had a large grin on her face as she lowered herself from the back seat.

"You know, I never did warn them about you being able to change into a human form, Caitlyn," Alex said. "You terrified the poor guy." Max looked the changeling up and down and had an approving look on his face. "Eyes back in your head, Tiny," Alex growled.

"Hey, what does it matter if I look. Last I checked, she was a big cat. How'd she do that, by the way?" Max asked.

"Yeah," Josh said. "How the hell did she do that?"

Caitlyn giggled. "I thought your eyes were going to pop out the way you were staring at me change." Alex gave her a disapproving frown, and she stopped laughing. "Sorry. I didn't mean to scare you."

"No," Alex said. "You meant to scare him. Are you going to move this tree or are Max and I going to have to cut it up, because I know that's really why you changed into your human form."

Max's brows drew down, and he looked at Caitlyn again. "How is she going to—" he started to say but lost track of his question when the tree floated into the air and slid off the side of the road.

"Caitlyn is a changeling. She was born a panther, and when she got older, she learned how to change into a human form. In her human form, she is able to use magic. That's how she moved the tree," Alex said. He looked at Caitlyn and nodded.

She turned around and walked back to the truck, swaying her hips an exaggerated amount. The other two men were staring at her while Alex glared. She turned back around as she climbed into the SUV and giggled at the men from Earth's expressions of bewildered interest.

You just think you're being so cute right now, don't you? "Let's go," Alex said. "We are getting close." He started walking back to the SUV.

"You said that an hour ago," Max pointed out.

"And we are closer than we were an hour ago," Alex said.

Josh reached his door and pulled it open. "You

two argue like a married couple," he said as he got in.

"We do not," Alex and Max said in unison as they got into the vehicle. Caitlyn was sitting in her seat, back in her panther form.

She flicked the tip of her tail back and forth, and Alex could tell she was amused. Josh was looking at her through the corner of his eyes as if he was expecting her to change again. "You just think you're so clever," Alex muttered soft enough for only Caitlyn's sharp, feline ears to hear.

"That's right."

Max shifted the SUV into drive and turned the radio on to see if there was any more news. "—ace Needle has been destroyed," a panicked man's voice shouted. "It was there one second, then it was like looking at it through a mirage. A big black tower twice as tall as the Space Needle stands in its place, and it looks like several blocks of the city were destroyed with the black tower appeared. There's some sort of spinning gemstone at the top of the tower, but I don't know what it's for.

"If you are just tuning in, the Space Needle was just destroyed, and a black tower is standing in its place. Horrible monsters are flooding through the streets. I don't think anyone is left alive. I saw a group of people trying to hold out on a roof earlier. Their building was ripped down by this big... thing. I'm sorry, there just aren't words to describe it. It was like a centipede but thousands of times bigger and covered in spikes. I've never seen anything like it before.

"It's an Obsidian Tower," Caitlyn said.

"And what's that?" Josh asked.

Alex put up a finger, imploring them to wait. The man on the radio continued, "I just heard on the shortwave that towers like this are springing up in every single one of the evacuated cities." A quiet voice said something to him. "Yeah. I understand. I... I'm sorry Seattle, but it's just not safe here anymore. I have to go." The channel went silent.

"Yeah," Alex said, agreeing with Caitlyn. "That's what I was thinking. A spinning gemstone on top of an Obsidian Tower though. That's a new one."

Alex surveyed the encroaching woods for signs of enemies as he spoke. "Exactly what it sounds like," he said, answering Josh's earlier question. "It's a tower made from something that looks like obsidian. I'm not completely convinced that what it is made out of, it just looks the same. Azreal can use the Obsidian Towers to bring in reinforcements from Hell or Ignia, the Realms of Evil and Death. They also inhibit any kind of planar travel from the Realm they are on."

"I don't understand what that means," Josh said.

Alex looked over his shoulder at the young man. "It means we have no way of calling for help from any of the Inner Realms. But don't worry, my wife is out there, and she'll make sure we get some help."

"As soon as we have some valkyrie and einherjar to send, we will," Kara said. Terra had requested the leader of the valkyrie to meet with her on Dae so they could discuss what to do about the demonic invasion of Earth. The Shield Maiden had obliged her, and they discussed the affair in the marble hall that the Council of the Free People of Dae met in.

"Thank you, Kara," Terra said. "I left Alex on Earth yesterday morning, and it would set my heart at ease to know he has seasoned warriors at his side."

Kara nodded. "It will only take a few weeks, a month at most for every valkyrie to have two einherjar bonded to her. The war on Earth is severe, and Yggdrasil is ripe with the souls of fallen warriors."

Alex is fine, Terra told herself. *You can feel him on the link; you know he's well.* She checked on her husband. He was so far away on Earth that the bundle of emotions in her head was faint, but she could tell he wasn't afraid or angry, so she felt that he was safe. Darren entered the hall with an annoyed look on his face.

"I'm sure that is keeping all of you very busy," Terra told the valkyrie. "Thank you again for coming to meet with me, and I must apologize for not having more time. I get the feeling I am about to get some news I don't want to hear."

"I understand," Kara said. The valkyrie could be temperamental, but she seemed genuine and ready to return to Caine, the Realm of Order. "I will take my leave now and return to my home. Be at peace until the battle comes."

"And you," Terra responded. Kara gave Darren a nod in greeting as they passed each other on the colonnade. The Nexus waited for the city guards to close the large wooden doors behind the departing valkyrie before addressing her guard's captain. "How did it go with Moore?"

Darren leaned against the dwarven councilor's vacant chair and said, "Badly. He told Hanna everything she wanted to know, which was way over my head, but the doctor is sticking to the story that he was forced to help Azreal."

Terra balled her fist and struck the arm of her chair. "That Fyrian is a liar, all the way down to his rotten core. The Architect is going to arrive from the Plane of Science any day now, and Moore still hasn't given us anything." She closed her eyes and massaged her temples. "What did Hanna ask him about?"

"Like I said, I didn't understand most of it, but Moore was telling her about the different parts of the brain. Something about language centers and decision making," Darren said. He sighed. "Sorry, they started to use medical terms and lost me, Terra. I'm about as much a doctor as I am a harpist, that stuff is lost on me."

"Don't worry about it," Terra told her captain. *Decision making...* "Is Hanna with Jessica right now?" She lowered her hands and looked at Darren.

"That's where she said she was going." Darren stopped leaning on the oak chair and opened his mouth as if he was going to ask a question but closed it without speaking.

Hanna had been upset when Terra had told her that she was going to be attending the council today. The young changeling had told her that she hadn't recovered enough to be walking about the city, but Terra was as stubborn as her adopted sister. *I wonder if Caitlyn got that from me, or vice versa.* "I want to speak with Doctor Moore personally. Can you return to the dungeon and have him brought back out of his cell?"

"I'll be waiting for you down there," Darren said. He saluted and mounted the steps to walk down the carpeted center of the hall.

"Wait," Terra called.

Darren turned at looked at her with a raised brow. "Yes?" he asked.

"What were you going to say just a moment ago?"

The captain looked down and started to pick at his nails. "Hanna said something to me that set me to thinking."

Terra waited a moment for him to continue, but when nothing seemed to be forthcoming, she asked, "And what is that?"

"I know that Caitlyn is your sister, but I was wondering if she had ever talked to you about... me," he said with a hesitant pause.

"Ah," Terra said, trying to buy herself time to think up a response. *Well, she hasn't, but it would do her good to have someone other than Alex to pine over.* "What was it that Hanna said to you?"

"She said that Caitlyn wasn't sure if she felt... attracted to me or not."

Terra shook her head and smiled. "If she didn't feel anything toward you, then do you really think she would have tried to make peace between you and Ell?"

"That's a good point, but, I don't know, she's just acted different toward me ever since we returned from the Plane of Order. I was just wondering if she had said anything to you," Darren said.

You mean ever since we found out Alex was alive and returned with him. I wonder if Caitlyn even knows how much Darren cares for her. "No, she hasn't, but the next time I see her, I'll be sure to ask her about it. And don't worry, I'll make sure she doesn't know the question has come from you."

Darren smiled an easy grin. "Thank you, Terra. I appreciate it. I'll go get Doctor Moore ready for more questioning, but I don't expect him to be forthcoming with any new information."

Terra nodded, and the captain strode from the council chambers. She waited for the doors to close behind him before she rose on unsteady feet. Terra had still not completely recovered from the loss of blood she had incurred during childbirth and still bled a little, but she was determined to continue her duties as Nexus of Magic. She strode from the council chambers and walked home with two of her personal guard in tow.

A few minutes of walking at a leisurely pace, and she arrived at the small two-bedroom home she was living in until the palace was built. Terra had asked for Jessica's crib to be moved into her bedroom so Hanna could have a place to sleep. The young changeling had entered Terra's apprenticeship a few months ago and lived with the half-angel as was proper for a young sorceress-in-training.

Terra opened the door to her home and saw Hanna and Jessica in the living area just past the foyer. "And that's how you multiply and divide," Hanna finished.

Jessica's head darted about and locked on Terra. "Mommy!" she shouted. The baby tried to stand and walk to her, but she fell to her hands and knees and crawled the entire way.

Terra laughed and scooped her daughter up when she closed the distance. "Hey there, little one. Trying to walk already?"

The infant Nephilim nodded with enthusiasm. "Yeah! And Hanna just taught me reading and writing and numbers!"

"Really?" Terra asked. She looked at Hanna with a curious expression.

"Really," Hanna said. "She knows how to read and write now. And how to count, add, subtract, multiply, and divide. I only have to show her something once, and she picks it up. Jessica is amazing."

"I'm amazing!" the baby said with a grin.

Terra rubbed her nose against Jessica's like a cat's kiss. "Of course you are, but tell me this, little miss amazing, what is five times seven?"

"Thirty-five," Jessica said without hesitation.

"Good job!" Terra said. "Fourteen times eleven?"

"One hundred and fifty-four."

"Okay, smarty pants, how about one thousand four hundred and seventy-two times ninety-seven?"

Jessica closed her eyes in thought. After only a second, she said, "One hundred forty-two thousand seven hundred and eighty-four."

Terra was silent for a moment after her daughter's answer. *Carry the three...* "Wow, you're right."

Hanna laughed. "Like I said, she's amazing."

Jessica giggled while Terra said, "Yeah, I can tell."

"Mommy," the baby said, "I love you. I want Daddy to come home."

"I know, Jessica, I want him to come home too, but he has a very important job. He has to keep everyone safe from the people that would hurt them."

Jessica's brows drew together. "Why does Daddy have to do that job?"

Terra kissed her daughter's forehead. "Because there isn't anyone else that can do it for him. He has to protect the people he cares about, and your daddy cares about everyone. He wants every single person to have a chance to laugh and cry, fail and succeed, and live and die the way they want. Do you understand?"

Jessica nodded. "Yeah. I just miss him. He makes me happy."

Tears threatened to overwhelm Terra, but she fought them down. "Daddy makes me happy too. I need to talk to Hanna for a little bit; are you hungry?"

"No, but I can go play with Deedee!" Jessica said.

Terra smiled. "If Deidra isn't busy, then you can play with her. If she is, then come back, and I'll find something for you to play with until Hanna and I are done talking."

"Okay!" Terra set Jessica down and watched as

she crawled into the kitchen.

Hanna sat down on the couch and crossed her ankles. "What did you need to talk to me about?"

Terra sat down in one of the chairs across the coffee table from the couch. "I need you to come with me so we can talk to Doctor Moore."

"I already talked to him once today," Hanna said as her brows drew down. "He won't talk about anything except taking off his cuffs. Moore does that every day."

"You remember the spell you used to block pain?" Terra asked.

Hanna nodded. "Of course I do. It blocks the electrical impulses that carry sensation throughout the body."

"Darren told me that Moore was telling you about how the brain worked."

The changeling's eyes widened. "Terra, the brain is incredibly delicate. If I tried to block off part of his brain, it could damage him. Permanently."

"But, if you disabled the part of his brain that was in charge of, say, decision-making or creativity, then do you think he would be able to lie?" Terra asked.

"I…" Hanna said. She chewed on her lower lip for a moment. "I don't think so, but I could do the wrong thing and kill him. Terra, I don't want to do this."

The Nexus put her finger to her lips. "Maybe we don't have to. What do you think Moore values about himself over anything else?"

"His mind," the changeling said.

"Exactly," Terra said. "If we go down there, and I

bring up that I want you to try manipulating his brain then you say you don't want to because it could damage his brain, then he will tell us the truth to save his hide."

"But," Hanna protested, "what if he is telling the truth? What if he really was being threatened to help Azreal?"

Terra banished the thought. "No. When he had me in the Obsidian Tower here on Dae, he was enjoying himself. He was glad to have me in his clutches. There is no chance he was being forced to work for Azreal."

"I know it's unlikely, Terra. I just want you to acknowledge the possibility. It's your duty as Nexus to investigate every claim of innocence before someone is put to death. If he calls your bluff, and I follow through, then it could kill him," Hanna said.

Terra sat up straighter, angry that Hanna had pointed out her own job to her. "I know that. But he is below mercy, and there is no chance he is innocent. I was there, Hanna. I saw it with my own two eyes, felt the tubes bite into my flesh."

Hanna sighed. "I just want you to think about this before we doom a potentially guiltless man."

The Nexus's jaw clenched. "I have. I'll let Deidra know she needs to watch Jessica, then we go to pay the good doctor a visit."

"As you say, Terra," Hanna said. "At least consider what I said though."

No. "I will."

Hanna's knowing eyes probed Terra's before she

rose to tell Deidra they would be out for a while.

Chapter Four – Lie To Me Once Again

Terra sat across from Doctor Sigma Moore in the small underground interrogation room. Hanna and Darren were leaning against opposite walls to either side of the table, and a guard loomed behind the Fyrian scientist.

"And to what do I owe the pleasure of your company, Nexus?" Moore asked.

Terra fanned out her wings in an intimidating manner. "I want you to look me in the eyes and tell me why you were helping Azreal."

Doctor Moore put on a look of fear that Terra could tell was feigned. "My life was in danger, Nexus. Azreal must have heard of my research into direct transfer of life force from one being to another. He spirited me away from my labs on Fyr and pushed me into his service."

Terra's eyes narrowed with every word. *Keep it up, Moore.* "If that is the case, then why did you tell me you were in Azreal's employ to advance the cause of science?"

Raising his palms in a pleading gesture, Doctor Moore said, "Those were merely the panicked ravings of a man searching for a way to justify the atrocities he was being forced to commit. I took no pleasure in anything I did."

The Nexus struck the top of the table with her palms. "Lie to me once again, and you may not live to regret it, Fyrian! I'll have the truth, and I will have it now." Terra felt Alex growing curious on the other end of the link in response to her anger.

A smug smile spread across Moore's face. "But it is the truth, Nexus."

You aren't the only one here with a card to play. "Grab his head," Terra said to the guard. "Make sure he can't move it, not that he'll want to." The prison guard stepped forward and clamped large hands to either side of Doctor Moore's head.

"What is the meaning of this?" Moore shouted as he tried to struggle.

"Terra," Hanna started to protest, but Terra silenced her with a finger.

"No. If he won't talk, then we'll use the spell you developed," the Nexus said. She fixed a malicious grin on her face and leaned forward. "You don't want to tell the truth, so we'll make you."

"What are you talking about?" the doctor said, panic beginning to rise in his voice.

Terra widened the grin on her face. "Well, thanks to you, we *barbarians*, as you called us, have developed a little spell that will prevent you from being able to lie to us. The same way we block pain, we will block off the part of your brain that controls your ability to decide when to tell these fanciful tales."

Doctor Moore's eyes opened so far Terra thought they may actually fall from his head. "You could kill me if it is done even slightly wrong."

Hanna took her cue to chime in. "No," the changeling said, "It's much more probable that it would just give you permanent brain damage." She took a few steps forward and placed her hands to either side of the scientist's head. "I'm going to need you to hold absolutely still. This is my first time casting this spell, and I don't want anything to go wrong."

"I volunteered!" Moore shouted before Hanna could cast a probe into his mind. "I knew what was happening, and I volunteered so I could test my research."

Got you. "So you knew your extraction pods would be used to help subjugate and kill millions?" Terra asked.

"Yes. Azreal told me his plans from the very beginning. Please don't let her use your freakish magics on me," the scientist pleaded. "Kill me, but don't make me live a broken life."

Terra laughed at him. *If only I could kill you myself, but I don't want to provoke a war with the Realm of Science.* "Thank you, Doctor Moore, for giving us exactly what we needed. Put him in his cell." She unlocked the table, and the guard began to lead the Fyrian away.

"There was no spell," Moore growled. The guard paused at the door when Terra held up a hand. "You tricked me into giving a confession."

"And you fell for it. Pretty good for a group of barbarians," Terra snarked, "don't you think so?"

Moore gave a derisive laugh. "It's too bad that your *evidence* is inadmissible. You have no proof of what I said. It will still just be the word of four sub-humans against mine."

Terra slid her chair back and walked over to the doctor. "I think you'll find the word of a Paragon carries a lot of weight, even if I am 'sub-human'." She nodded to the guard, and he took Doctor Sigma Moore away. The Fyrian laughed all the way to his cell.

The Nexus felt light-headed all of a sudden, and Darren rushed over to her side. "I think you overdid yourself, just now," he said. "Let's get you home so you can rest."

"That sounds like a great idea," Terra muttered.

"Do you think he was telling the truth?" Hanna asked. "Do you think he'll get away with it?"

Terra shook her head as Darren opened the door to the surface. "I met the Architect. He is a good man. I trust that he will see justice served."

"Good," Darren said. "That bastard Moore deserves death."

Terra agreed. Alex still felt curious, but Terra could sense that he was annoyed at something. She tried to convey a feeling of calm and peace so her husband wouldn't worry about her.

"No," Alex snapped. "We can't climb the fence. We would go from capable civilians to trespassers, and then no one would listen to anything we had to say." Terra's anger was fading, and Alex felt her grow calm. *Good. Whatever got her riled up is over with.*

"I understand that," Caitlyn said. "But we aren't helping anyone by walking around the whole place.

The longer we are on the wrong side of the fence, the longer it is before we can help!"

Alex took a deep breath and let it out slow. *She just doesn't understand,* he told himself. *Don't get too annoyed with her.*

<Yeah,> the Voice of Balance telepathically whispered into his mind. <Keep telling yourself that. It's worked so far.> The Guardian's Blade consisted of nine separate forms, but Alex had only discovered four, not counting the sword's passive wooden form. The minds of the previous Guardian's were imprinted upon the blade if they were wielding it when they died, and they became the voices of the various forms.

Alex had died using the form of Empathy to heal Terra, and his own mind was the Voice of Balance. *I don't remember ever being this sarcastic,* he thought.

<You're telling me... At least *you* don't have to listen to ever single thought that goes through *my* mind.>

Shut up. "It's only a few more miles walk to the interstate side entrance. We're almost there."

The four of them had been walking all night around the perimeter of the chain link and barbed wire fence. The sun had risen a few hours ago, and sweat was beginning to pour down the three humans' backs. "I don't understand why we had to leave the SUV," Josh said.

Alex groaned, and Max fielded this one. "It would have taken longer to drive back around the base and make our way down the interstate. You've never seen how major roads get blocked up when there is a panic,

Josh. If we made any progress, it would be extremely slow, and we were getting low on gas anyway."

The retired heavy gunner had his fifty-caliber strapped across his back, with two boxes of ammunition tied to either side of his waist. Josh was carrying an assault rifle, a shotgun, and rounds for both, while Alex had food and even more ammunition in his large pack. The Guardian didn't carry a firearm; his sword was a more effective weapon than anything the other two carried. Caitlyn padded along in her panther form, free of any burdens.

They had been forced to abandon the SUV at Joint Base Lewis McChord's eastern gate the night before, when they discovered it locked and barricaded with slabs of concrete. The group had walked throughout the entire night, and they were battling exhaustion with every step.

The sound of a vehicle brought Alex's head around. A humvee was bouncing along the interior of the base on a patrol of the fence. One of the occupants must have seen the three people and panther walking, and the vehicle skidded to a stop not far from them on the opposite side of the fence.

A man got out of the passenger side of the armored truck and walked to the fence. The vehicle's machine gun wasn't pointed at them, but the gunner wasn't being subtle about his existence either. Alex made out the man's rank insignia as he drew closer. *Good, a sergeant.*

The man took in their weapons and stared hard at Caitlyn for a moment before saying, "I'm Army

Sergeant Juan Cruz. State your names and intentions."

They had decided to let Alex do all of the talking when they finally made it onto the base. "Sergeant Alex Zane, Marine Corps, retired," Alex said. He pointed at Max. "This is Lance Corporal Max Gilroy, Marine Corps, retired, Joshua Hrynkiewicz, civilian, and Caitlyn Shadowpaw, a changeling from the Realm of Magic."

Cruz frowned at Alex. "A what? There's a war going on, man, this is no time to be funny."

"I'm not making a joke. I need to get on base and speak with the general. There's more going on than anyone on Earth is aware of," Alex said.

The sergeant crossed his arms. "The general has more important things to do than talk to rusty jarheads. You are welcome to come on base, but you will need to turn in all of your weapons to the master-at-arms. The gate is a few more miles the way you are going."

"He's not being very helpful," Caitlyn said.

Sergeant Cruz's eyes shot to her when she started talking. "Did that thing just talk?" he asked.

"Yeah, he told us to go screw off very politely," Alex explained.

"I'm in pain, tired, and don't feel like walking anymore," Caitlyn muttered. Before Alex could tell her to not do anything rash, she started to change into her human form. Bones cracked and sinew snapped as her arms and legs lengthened. Her fur turned white and blue and became a shirt and pants. The hair on Caitlyn's head lengthened, and her jaw snapped loudly as it shortened.

There was a loud clack as the humvee's gunner loaded the belt-fed machine gun. "Whoa," Alex said as he held up his hands. "We don't want any trouble."

Sergeant Cruz had his rifle pointed directly at Caitlyn's head. "What is going on here, Marine?" he shouted.

"We mean you no harm. It's just like I said, there's more going on than anyone on Earth knows about," Alex repeated. "Now, please, lower your rifle. We're on the same side here, Sergeant." A few seconds passed, and Cruz lowered the gun. "Thank you. We are going to unload our weapons, and Caitlyn is going to use magic to open a section of your fence. She will be able to repair it perfectly after we come through. Then I need you to take us to the base's commanding officer. Do you understand?"

"You are free to unload your weapons, but it is not my call to let you on to the base. You will wait here while I talk to my CO," Sergeant Cruz said. He turned and walked back to the humvee. "Jenkins, if any one of them comes a single step closer to the fence with a loaded weapon, open fire," he said loud enough for them to hear.

"Tell your boss that I have intel against the leader of the monsters that are attacking," Alex shouted.

"Are you sure about unloading?" Max asked as he pulled the magazine out of his machine gun and shoved it into a pocket.

"Positive," Alex growled. He dropped the pack off of his back and walked over to Caitlyn. The Guardian put his hands on her shoulders. "What the hell were you thinking? You could have gotten us killed!"

The changeling crossed her arms and glared at him. "Do you really think a single one of their bullets would have touched us? I can cast a wall of air faster than they can pull a trigger."

Alex stuck his finger in Caitlyn's face. "And what do you think our chances of getting on base would have been then, even if they hadn't killed any of us? Slim to none, at least not as anything more than prisoners." He lowered his voice. "I understand that you are upset with me right now, but these childish antics are going to get someone killed. Get a hold of yourself, Caitlyn, or I will make for damn sure that when I go into battle, that you are left behind."

Caitlyn's upper lip spasmed, and for a moment, Alex thought she was going to bare her teeth at him. "Fine," she said at length. "I understand."

"Good." Alex released her and shouldered his pack. Sergeant Cruz was walking back to the fence. "What did your commanding officer say?" Alex asked.

"She said to confiscate your weapons and escort you to the general immediately," Juan Cruz said.

It's not a perfect situation, but it'll do. "Sounds good."

Terra and Ell stood upon the marble platform that held the gateway arch. The silver gateway from Fyr stood open in the gateway arch that dominated Victory City's park. "Terra," the Architect said. "I am glad we get to meet under much better circumstances this time."

Terra looked into Theodore Thelonius the Third's reflective silver eyes. "It is good to see you again too, Theo. Alex told me that you were responsible for freeing me from Moore's extraction pods."

The Fyrian Paragon shrugged, sunlight glinting off of his metal left arm. "I just did what I should have done as soon as I found out what was going on. The Plane of Science remains neutral in this conflict. We must not be seen helping either side."

Terra looked at the two large men to either side of the Architect. They were covered from the tops of their heads to the soles of their feet in dark grey armor. The eyes of their armor glowed with electric light. "I assure you that you are in no danger here," she said as she led Theo down the steps toward the dungeon Doctor Moore was housed in.

"I did not mean to give offense," Theo said. "After I returned from Dae, it was pointed out that my safety was in constant danger. Due to that, the corporations insisted on the enforcement of an old custom of always keeping two praetorians with the Architect at all times. I see you have given birth. Did everything go well with your daughter?"

"Jessica is well," Terra said. "Thank you for asking. I must say, however, that I was not expecting your arrival for a few more days."

The Architect nodded. "I apologize for the

inconvenience. As much as I am the leader of my Plane, I must also carry out the will of the corporations. They demanded that Sigma Moore be moved to Fyrian custody as soon as possible."

"He is to stand trial upon his arrival to Fyr?" Terra asked.

"He is," Theo answered. "But Sigma has put us in a rather untenable situation."

Terra knew she wasn't going to like the Architect's answer as soon as she asked him, "How so?"

"His cooperation with Azreal makes this trial more than a simple case of over-experimentation. If we rule in your favor and execute him, then it could provoke the Overlord to attack Fyr, but if we rule in Doctor Moore's favor, then it could start a war with you."

The Nexus bit back the scathing comment. She knew diplomacy would be the only way to sway Theo. "That is understandable. You must do what is best for your realm. What is it you intend to do with him?"

"It is my intention to begin his trial upon our return but commute his sentence until the war is finished."

That's a better answer than I hoped for. "His guilt is undeniable," Terra said. "He confessed to volunteering to work with Azreal so he could test his research into transference of life-energy."

"I apologize, Terra, but any confessions while he was in your custody are null and void," Theo said. "He must admit guilt before the courts of Fyr."

Terra's anger flared. "But he confessed guilt to myself and three others. I do not see how that is irrelevant."

"Fyrian policy is one of absolute neutrality. Only through methodical questioning can the cause of science be advanced. This is the way of things on the Plane of Science, Nexus," the Architect said. "The proper procedures must be followed, lest a mistrial be called and a potentially dangerous man go free." Theo glanced at the two praetorians escorting him.

I understand now. He can't say everything he wants. "I see what you mean," Terra said.

"I am glad," Theo said with relief. "As the accuser, are you prepared to accompany us back to Fyr?"

Terra hesitated for a moment before answering. "I was not aware that it was customary for the accuser to attend the trial," she said.

Theo shook his head. "It isn't in an ordinary situation. However, as you are both the accuser and primary witness, there cannot be a trial without you present."

Great, she thought. *I can't bring Jessica with me. She'll be safer here with my guard, Hanna, and Silvia to keep an eye on her.* "I was not aware that the trial would be unable to proceed without me. I will need to make preparations for my departure."

"That is all right," the Architect said. "It would do you well come with us when we depart. Do you have enough time to make the necessary arrangements in the next few hours?"

Terra grit her teeth. *I can't let Moore get away with this. Too many have suffered because of him.* "I can." The Nexus looked at Ell, the half-elf that was one of the lieutenants of her personal guard. "Please show the Architect the rest of the way. I must speak with Silvia to get everything in order. Darren and Brahm are going to be present when Doctor Moore is given to the Architect, inform them that I will need an escort with me while I am on Fyr."

"No problem," Ell said and saluted.

Terra nodded to her and looked at Theo. "I will go and get everything in order for my departure. Please wait for me at the gateway arch before returning to your home."

"I will, Terra," he said. Ell led the way to the dungeon while Terra veered off to the council chambers. She had been meeting with the council when the city guard had reported a gateway from Fyr opening.

A few minutes of walking, and she ran into Silvia departing the large marble building. The Fanglady looked at Terra with a raised brow. "You seem like you are in a rush. What's wrong?" the black-haired woman asked.

"I have to go with Moore to the Realm of Science to ensure he stands trial and testify against him," Terra said. "Can you help watch Jessica and keep her safe? I know it's sudden, but it has to be done."

Silvia nodded. "Not a problem. I will keep an eye on her for you. Do you know how long you will be gone?"

"No," Terra said with a shake of her head. "As long as the trial takes, I presume. Deidra takes care of Jessica most of the time, and Hanna will be home with her. The two girls are inseparable. I have to go and get my things together. Thank you, sister."

"Not a problem," Silvia called as Terra rushed off in the direction of her home.

I can't believe this. How am I supposed to explain to Jessica that I have to go when Alex is already gone? Terra climbed the few steps to her house and went inside. Hanna and Jessica were tossing a glowing magical ball back and forth. It was an exercise to help gain control of magical power. *I've only been gone a few hours!*

Both of the girls were lost in the complex catch and release of magical flows and hadn't noticed Terra's arrival. The Nexus watched with rapt attention as Jessica split the ball into three smaller ones and tossed them to Hanna. The young changeling caught them, split them into nine balls and threw them back at the baby. Jessica caught all nine on a buffer of air but failed to maintain one of them, and it made a loud popping noise when it disappeared.

I couldn't handle that many separate flows of magic until I was older than Hanna... Certainly not when I was only a day-and-a-half old. "That was a very good job," Terra said. Both of the girls turned to look at her. Jessica scrambled to her feet and ran over to her.

"Mommy!" the baby said.

And she's running. "You really are amazing," Terra said as she lifted her daughter and kissed her on the forehead. Jessica scrunched up her face in a grin. "I love you, little one, but I have to go away for a while."

The baby's grin vanished and was replaced with a look of concern. "I love you too. Why do you have to leave like Daddy?"

"I have to make sure a bad person is punished for doing something wrong," Terra explained. "Do you understand?"

"Yeah," Jessica said. "Hanna told me when you do bad things, you get in trouble and have to get punished."

Thank you for teaching her that, Terra thought. "That's right. This man hurt a lot of other people, and I'm the only person that can make sure he gets punished."

Jessica nodded. "Okay, Mommy. I love you."

That was easier than I was expecting. "I love you too. I have to get ready to go. Will you keep playing with Hanna while I pack my things and talk to Deidra?"

"Yeah."

Terra set her back on the floor. Jessica cast a ball of light and tossed it to Hanna as she ran back to her spot. Terra walked past them into the kitchen where she found Deidra preparing dinner.

"I have some bad news, Deidra," Terra said.

The young woman nodded. "I heard you talking to Jessica. You have to go to Fyr to make sure that horrible man stands trial."

"That's right," Terra said. "I don't know how long I will be gone for. Will you be all right watching Jessica while I am gone?"

The maid looked over at Terra with a smile. She had grown much more comfortable in her position as caretaker in the last few weeks. "That is what I am here for," Deidra Belles said.

"Thank you. I have to go pack my things. The Architect said it would be best if I accompanied them right away."

Deidra nodded and went back to chopping carrots. "There is a pack beneath your bed."

Terra went from the kitchen into her bedroom and packed a few dresses and other amenities she would need. A half-hour later, she was kneeling by the door giving Jessica a farewell hug. "You listen to Silvia, Deidra, and Hanna, okay?"

"I will, Mommy. I will miss you until you get back," Jessica said.

"I'll miss you too, and I'll come back as soon as I can." Terra released her daughter and stood. She looked at Hanna. "Thank you for teaching her, Hanna. Keep it up, but don't fall behind your own practice."

Hanna smirked. "The way Jessica picks up new things, pretty soon I'll have her to practice with."

No kidding. "I love you, little one. Bye."

"Love you too, Mommy. Bye!" Jessica said as she waved her arm.

Terra stepped out the door and shut it behind her. *I hate this. I shouldn't have to leave my family behind just to make sure a murderer faces justice. It's not fair.* She shook her head and walked down the steps. *But it's my duty.*

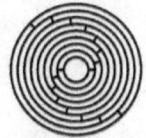

Terra arrived at the gateway arch to find Darren and Brahm flanking Doctor Moore with the two praetorians standing beside Theo. She looked at her two friends. "I said I needed an escort, not that I needed the two of you to escort me," the Nexus said.

"Bah," Brahm Ironfist, the old dwarf that had served as the general of the Daein army, scoffed. "Who better to protect ye than the two o' us?"

Darren nodded. "I can't think of anyone. What about you, Brahm?"

The dwarf shook his head. "I'm pretty sure she'll do no better than you an' I."

Terra smiled at the two of them. *They are right. I've never been to Fyr before, but I'm fairly certain neither of them have either.* "Well, thank you both." She looked at the Architect. "We're ready."

Theo nodded and pushed a few buttons on the computer mounted in his metal arm. A few seconds passed, and a shimmering silver gateway opened in the arch. *Did he open a gateway to Fyr from the other end?* "How did you do that?" Terra asked.

"Although the Nine Realms each exist in their own dimension, the interconnections of each Plane allows for communication across them. One of the advantages of being Paragon of the Realm of Science is that I can control a number of technologies from Fyr using this unique prosthetic," Theo explained.

Terra nodded. *I wonder if we can find out how to talk to someone on a different Realm without having to open a portal there.* "Interesting. Shall we?"

The Architect and his two praetorians walked through the silver gateway, followed by Terra, Darren, Moore, and Brahm. The portal was gold on the Fyrian side, and it bathed the carefully maintained garden they arrived in with yellow light. "Welcome to the Realm of Science," Theo said. "You stand in the Central Hub in the Primary Station. This is where we produce all of the oxygen for the space station."

Terra took a deep breath, but the air smelled strange to her, as if it were dirty. "What do you mean?" she asked.

Theo smiled and punched in a command on his arm. A small screen rose from the grassy floor. It showed a large rocky surface. "We are orbiting the eighth planet in the Cygnus System. You are in the land of the stars right now, Nexus."

"Wait a second," Darren said. "You are saying we are in the sky right now?"

"Precisely," the Architect agreed. "Not the skies above Dae, of course. We are in another dimension, so that's impossible."

A flying metal circle descended from above. "All peoples visiting Fyr for the first time are required to submit DNA for analysis," came a sharp voice from the machina. "Please insert your right arm or upper right most appendage into the Genotech scanner."

"What is it saying?" Darren asked. The machina chirped and repeated the message in Common. "Oh," the captain muttered. He stuck his hand into the flying band, and a brilliant beam of red light enveloped his palm.

"Scan complete. Genetic material scanned and assimilated. Next," the scanner ordered.

Brahm was scanned, then Terra. "Scan complete. Genetic material scanned and assimilated. Enjoy your visit to the Primary Station," the band said as it zipped away.

Two more men armored the same as the praetorians escorting Theo arrived. "We will take Doctor Sigma Moore into custody," one of them said, his voice was slightly distorted through his helmet.

"Ye're free to have him," Brahm said. The two newcomers each took one of the doctor's arms and pushed a button on their waist. In a flash of electricity, they vanished. "What in bloody Hell was that?"

"Short range teleportation," the Architect explained. A door slid open, and Terra saw the inside of some kind of transportation. Theo led them to it and asked them to please sit. They each took a seat with the two praetorians standing at either end of the craft.

A transparent image appeared in the center of the vehicle. It looked like a ball with two rings centered around and connected to it at various points. "This is the Primary Station. The ball in the center is the Central Hub. Each of the four points the Central Hub is connected to is owned by one of the four primary corporations. You have the Atlas Hub, where most of the defense contracts and craft are built." Quarters of the space station lit up in sequence as Theo explained them. "The Genotech Hub, they handle the production and distribution of various foods and medical services. The ARC Hub, the Advanced Robotics Corporation produces most of the machines and androids we use every day. And last, the Bionetics Hub, they develop and build all of the cybernetic implants many of the residents of the Fyr have.

"Each Hub has three Secondary Hubs where people eat, sleep, and relax. I have a residence in the Primary Atlas Hub, and it would be an honor if I could share my home with the three of you. It is large enough to not be any inconvenience and will be much... better for everyone if you were somewhere nearby."

There must be something he can't say. "Of course we will stay in your home. We thank you for the offer," Terra said.

"Very good," Theo said. "I will give the commands for the craft to fly to my residence." He pushed a few buttons on his metal arm before placing his hands in his lap. "I am pleased to see that you are doing better than the last time I saw you, Terra. If I may be so bold as to say that your wings are exceptionally radiant."

Terra smiled and nodded. As a half-angel, her wings were something she could decide whether to show or conceal, and growing up, Terra had always kept them hidden. Alex had shown her that her wings weren't something that marked her as inferior to humans, but something that made her unique and beautiful. "Thank you."

"When're we goin' to start movin'?" Brahm asked.

The door they had entered through opened, and one of the praetorians stepped through. "As soon as I pushed a button on my arm we started, General Ironfist. My personal transport has inertial buffers and gravitic manipulators so acceleration is not felt. This allows it to move exceptionally fast," Theo explained as he stood and walked through the door.

"The man's speakin' bloody Common, but I've no clue what he's sayin'," Brahm muttered. Terra shrugged. Alchemy was the only Daein form of science, and Terra despised the discipline. The second praetorian brought up the rear of their group, and they took up station to either side of a shimmering doorway.

Terra turned around and gasped. The craft they stepped from resembled a car from Earth, but it had no definable front or back. The flying vehicle was hanging off the edge of a balcony thousands of feet above the nearest buildings. The Primary Atlas Hub looked like the inside of a ball that was miles wide and lined with blinking lights.

"It is a beautiful sight," Theodore Thelonius said. "Please, come inside, and we can enjoy some refreshments and talk."

The two armored praetorians waited outside of the residence as Terra, Brahm, and Darren followed the Architect through the shimmering doorway. There was a momentary chill as Terra passed through the light, but it faded quickly.

Theo led them to a large table beside a transparent wall that overlooked the lights below. He pushed a button on his arm and the wall turned opaque. Terra opened her mouth to speak, but the Architect held up a finger. He pushed another button on his arm, and a glowing red ball descended from the ceiling.

"Now we can talk safely," Theo said. "I apologize for bringing you here so suddenly, Terra, and for taking you from your newborn. Something is amiss with this trial, but I'm not sure what it is. The other corporations are pushing much too hard for it to happen now."

"What do you think is going on?" she asked.

Theo shook his head. "I don't know, but for now, I think we should play their game. Everything I told you on Dae is true, you do need to be here, or else there can't be a trial. You were right to bring guards, however. The Primary Station is not as safe as it once was. Suspicions will be raised if they do not hear us discussing something soon. The only time it is safe to talk about what is really going on is when you see this red light. Do the three of you understand?"

They all nodded, and Theo pushed another button on the screen of the computer mounted into his prosthetic arm. "I have a vast array of refreshments," Theo said. "Is there something in particular you would care for?"

I shouldn't even be here... Terra thought.

Chapter Five – We Have to Run

Alex stood at the foot of a long conference table with Caitlyn, Max, and Josh behind him. The base's Commanding Officer, Lieutenant General Fields, sat at the far end of the table, and a bevy of officers colonel and below filled the room. The only signs that the outsiders weren't completely welcome in the conference room was the four armed men stationed at the two exits.

"General," Alex said, "Thank you for seeing us on such short notice. I understand that you are very busy and—"

"Exactly," the gray haired general interrupted. "So let's skip over the formalities so I can get back to trying to take back Seattle and protect the evacuees."

Alex smirked. He hated giving speeches and presentations, but the Lieutenant General's no-nonsense attitude put him at ease. "Very well. I am Alex Zane, and I have been fighting these demons and undead for almost eight months now."

"Demons!" a colonel shouted. "Are you serious?"

The Guardian fixed an unwavering stare at the officer. "What would you call the monsters that are roaming the streets and slaughtering people all over the nation?" The room fell silent, and Alex continued. "I was in the Marines before I got this sword and led an army to take back another world from Azreal, the Overlord of Hell. He is the leader of the demons and behind these attacks. The black spire that appeared and destroyed the Space Needle is called an Obsidian

Tower, and through it, Azreal can reinforce his armies indefinitely."

General Fields leaned forward in his chair. "How?"

"The Earth isn't as alone in the universe as you all think," Alex explained. "There are eight other realms of existence that each act on the Earth to create balance. The world in which you all live is the Realm of Balance, part of the Nine Realms. Azreal and his ilk are from Hell, the Realm of Evil. Each Obsidian Tower has a large portal at the base that allows Azreal to pull in reinforcements from Hell and Ignia, the Realm of Death."

"This is insane," the same colonel as before protested. "Why are we listening to this?"

"Benjamin, if you are not silent, I will order you to leave," General Fields said. He looked back at Alex. "Go on. What weaknesses do these demons have?"

"Most demons are stupid and prideful. They rely on muscle and ferocity to attack and lack any real initiative or battle strategy," Alex said. "Our technology is much more advanced than theirs, but they will outnumber us. I would recommend bombarding the Obsidian Tower from a distance, but I think Azreal has come up with some way of protecting the towers."

"What do you mean?" the general asked.

"When we were driving here, we heard on the radio that there was some kind of spinning crystal on the top of the Obsidian Tower here in Seattle. Every tower we've destroyed in the past has been lacking that, and it is the only thing that makes any sense. Unlike those below him, Azreal isn't stupid, just reckless. He wouldn't commit to this level of attack and not have some way to keep us from just wiping his strongholds off the map."

"How do you know all of this?"

Alex drew the Guardian's Blade and set the wooden sword on the table. "Each of the Nine Realms has a person to help protect them. They are called Paragons, and it is their duty to uphold the values of their home. I am the Guardian of Balance, and it's my job to maintain the balance of the Nine Realms. Right now, they are far from equilibrium, and the only way to bring them back is to kill Azreal."

General Fields nodded. "That's a hell of a tale, Marine, but without some kind of proof, I'll have to ask you to leave."

Alex sighed and grabbed his sword. He looked over his shoulder at Caitlyn. "Make a wall of air, thick enough to stop their bullets, but not hard enough to make them ricochet and kill someone."

Caitlyn waved her hand. "It's done."

"General," Alex said, holding his hand out toward Caitlyn. "This is Miss Caitlyn Shadowpaw. She is a Changeling of the Fang from the Plane of Magic. As a resident of Dae, she can use magic. If your men opened fire on us and none of the bullets touched us, would that be proof enough?"

The base's commanding officer frowned at him. "Look, son. I don't want to kill you. I just don't think you're right in the head."

<I think we need something a little more extravagant,> the Voice of Balance said.

Yeah. Alex unleashed the Wrathblade. There was a bright flash of light, and the Guardian stood at the base of the table with the flaming blade in his hands. The rage pounded in his head, but Alex forced it to a low simmer. "Just like the Nine Realms, this sword has nine forms. This one is called the Wrathblade. It uses a portion of my energy to make me unfathomably strong, but it's very taxing." Another flash of light, and Alex held the silvery hilt of a phaseblade.

"This is the Blade of Justice. It nullifies demonic energy." He waved the glowing blue blade of energy about. "This was the form of the Guardian's Blade that I used to defeat Azreal the first time I faced him." There was a third flash of light, and Empathy appeared in the Guardian's hands. Alex held the white wooden staff loosely in his hands. "This is Empathy. Other people's injuries can be transferred to me, using this form of the Guardian's Blade."

Alex set the staff on the table. As soon as his hand broke contact, it changed back into the brown wooden form of the Blade of Balance. "Now do you believe me? Or do you want your men to open fire so they can see just how useless their weapons will be against Azreal?"

General Fields looked at Alex over steepled fingers. "What did you say your name was?"

He sheathed his sword in the leather baldric at his waist. "My name is Alex Zane, and I'm the Guardian."

Hanna was shaken awake in the middle of the night. "Hanna," Jessica said. "You have to wake up." The changeling rubbed her eyes and sat up. She almost shouted in alarm when she saw the child.

Jessica's eyes were glowing, one green, the other brown. Her brown hair had turned white, and small black wings enveloped her.

"What happened to you?" Hanna asked.

Jessica shook her head. "I wanted to look like Mommy and Daddy when I was born. This is the real me. There isn't time. They are here to take me away. We have to run."

"Hold on a second. Who are they?"

"Please, Hanna," the Nephilim begged. "You can't let them take me. They'll kill me. We have to run far away where they won't find me."

There was a flicker of light through the window, and an glowing ethereal arm reached through the wall. Hanna's eyes widened in shock, and everything slowed to a crawl. Without thinking, the young changeling cast an inverted form of the pain blocking spell she had used on Terra when she was in labor. As soon as the spell touched the ethereal arm, it turned solid and fused with the wall.

A scream of unimaginable pain came from outside the window. "We have to go now!" Jessica shouted. There was a thump in the air, and a small golden portal opened next to them. Jessica ran through the gateway, and Hanna had no choice but to follow.

The two girls stood on the marble platform of the gateway arch in Victory City's park. The two city guards that were supposed to be guarding the gateway arch were lying in a pool of blood. The small portal closed.

"How did you do that?" Hanna asked. "There is a grounding field all over Dae. You can't create a portal anywhere but here."

"That's wrong," Jessica said. The small Nephilim touched the side of the moonstone gateway arch, and a shimmering silver portal opened. Hanna's eyes widened when she realized the little girl was using demonic energy along with magical power in the spells she was casting. The two-day-old child pulled Hanna through the larger portal and closed it behind them.

"Jessica," Hanna said, "where are we?" *I think she's grown almost a foot since she was born. How can she maintain this level of growth?*

The wings receded into Jessica's back, and her hair and eyes changed back to normal. The Nephilim looked at Hanna with her two different colored eyes. "We are where Mommy went. I want Mommy. I'm scared."

"You opened a gateway to Fyr? How did you know how to do that?" Hanna asked.

Jessica's eyes fixed on a small ring that was floating toward them. "Mommy thought about it once before I was born. I have always known how to use gateways." The ring drew closer and said something

Hanna couldn't understand.

"What did it say?" the changeling asked.

"It says we have to put our right hands in it before we can go anywhere," Jessica said.

The ring stopped in front of Hanna, and she placed her hand inside the machina. A beam of red light swallowed her hand, and she felt a slight tingling in her palm. "Scan complete," it said in Common after only a second of scanning her. "Genetic material scanned and assimilated. Next."

"Can you take me to my mommy?" Jessica asked the scanner as she put her hand in it.

The beam of red light scanned Jessica's hand for an several seconds before it flickered and began the process again. "Error scanning genetic material. Genetic profile has no matches in Genotech database. Unknown being, you are ordered to remain here." The ring zipped off.

"How did you understand what it was saying before it started talking in Common?" Hanna asked.

Jessica frowned at the retreating machina. "I just knew what it was saying. Mommy knows what people are saying, so does Daddy. I'm like them."

A door opened in the wall a few yards away, and five armored men stepped out. They were covered head to toe in dark grey metal, and it looked like each of them was carrying a laser rifle. The one in front's eyes flickered when he said something. A wall of black force blocked the five men from view, and Hanna looked down at the girl she knew so little about.

"They are bad men," Jessica said. "They said they

were going to kill you and take me. We have to run!"

"Where?" Hanna asked. Jessica closed her eyes, and a rippling pulse of force strong enough to distort the air around them flew outward from her. The energy passed through Hanna and the walls around them with no ill effect. Jessica opened her eyes and tugged Hanna along. "This way. There's a little hole the bad men won't be able to fit through."

A grate slid out from the wall as Jessica reached out to it with a blend of air, water, and demonic energy. Hanna was almost too large to fit through the square hole, but once she was inside, she was able to stand. Jessica scrambled in behind her, and the grate slid back into its position.

There was shouting back in the garden, and the two girls ran down the dark tunnel. They kept going for a long time until the metal dipped downward without warning, and Jessica and Hanna slid down it. Luckily, it curved at the bottom instead of stopping abruptly, and they slowed.

There was a small grate like the one in the garden, and Jessica opened it the same way she had the other one. The two girls crawled through it, and found themselves on a street lined with all kinds of dark buildings. Glowing signs Hanna couldn't read hung off of most of the buildings.

"We need to find Mommy," Jessica said as she sidled up to Hanna.

The changeling nodded. "I know, Jess. We'll find her, but it seems like everywhere we turn someone is hunting us. We need to be careful."

"Yeah," Jessica said. "We do."

Terra awoke early in the morning with an odd sense of something being out of place, but she couldn't put her finger on it. *It's probably just waking up in a strange bed*, Terra thought as she lowered herself to the floor. The bed was some kind of invisible field of force that adjusted itself to the person lying on it. She got ready and met Theo at the table they had dined at last night.

"Good morning, Terra," he said. "Are you prepared? The trial will begin in an hour."

Darren and Brahm entered the room. Terra nodded. "I am."

"Very good," Theo said. "Let's have breakfast, then I will take you to the court."

The Architect filled four glasses with a gray liquid. "This is a nutrient shake. It contains all of your necessary carbohydrates, fats, proteins, vitamins, and minerals. Food is a luxury I do not engage in frequently, due to its scarcity on the Primary Station. I have taken the liberty of calculating the required intake for each of you and calibrating the mixture to taste pleasing. Enjoy." He handed each of them a glass.

The three Daein people exchanged dubious glances but drank the nutrient shake. Terra was surprised at the taste of blueberries. "This is delicious," she said.

"Aye," Brahm said. "I've no' had a steak quite so... runny before, but it tastes good."

Darren drained his quickly. "Mine tasted like eggs and bacon. That was amazing. How does it work?"

The Architect opened his mouth to explain the process, but closed it without speaking. "It's a rather complex method to create the proper flavors, but the drink itself is just a mixture of various chemical compounds. I do not mean to offend you, but I'm afraid I have no way to explain the entire method that you would understand."

Brahm laughed. "Ye're no' upsettin' me, Architect. I've no' understood most o' what ye've said since we got here." Terra smiled, and Darren gave his head a rueful shake.

Theo nodded. "I'm glad you enjoyed it," he said. "We should depart now so that we are the first to arrive." Theo led them through the house and back to his conveyance. The praetorians got in behind them, and wordlessly took up stations at either end of the flying vehicle. The door closed, and in a few moments, it opened again.

They got out, and Terra saw that they were at the base of a tall spire that reached up to the center of the hub they were in. "This is the Control Cluster," Theo said. "It is from here that I direct the day to day operations of the Primary Station. It is also where I hold court should any laws be broken that result in loss of life or damage to a major system. Follow me."

Terra, Brahm, and Darren followed the Architect through the large shimmering portal that Terra realized was a field of energy that acted as a door. He led them to a large circular room that could fit thousands. "This is the Architect's Court. As the accuser, you will sit there with Darren and Brahm," Theo said as he pointed with his robotic arm at a table near the center of the room. "I will be atop the large column in the center of the room, and Sigma will be on the opposite side of the room. You will be unable to see him from your seat, but there will be screens floating about the room that will be displaying everything."

They walked down the stairs toward the center of the court room. Terra, Brahm, and Darren took their seats, and Theo walked to the base of the polished metal column. He put his metal hand into a small hole, and a door opened with a hiss. He sat in the chair inside the column, and the door closed. A hum filled the room, and the Architect became visible at the top of the stand.

Some time passed before people began to file into the Architect's Court. After almost exactly an hour, screens flickered on around the center of the sphere. They showed a hole open in the floor through which Doctor Moore rose. He took his seat at the table of the accused, and the proceedings began.

"Sigma Moore, you have been called to trial by Terra Zane," the Architect said. "The charges are as follows: conspiracy to commit murder, wrongful imprisonment, torture, and murder. The exact number of counts for each crime is unknown, so you will be tried for the lowest confirmable number. I observed your experiments with the extraction chambers on Dae, and I can confirm that there were one-thousand two-hundred and eighty two operable extraction chambers in the Daein Obsidian tower, so that will be the number of charges for each crime. How do you plea?"

"Guilty on all counts," Doctor Moore said. A communal gasp went up from all the observers.

That's not what I was expecting either, Terra thought as her brows drew down. *What is he planning?*

"Very well," Theo said. "The punishment for these crimes is death. Do you have anything to say in mitigation?" Terra stared at the screen that was displaying Doctor Moore's face.

"I do," the smug doctor said.

The Architect nodded. "Make your case."

"I need a week to build my defense and go through the data I've accumulated," Doctor Moore said.

Theo frowned. "A week is the maximum allowable recess time for mitigation. Why do you need this much time?"

Doctor Moore stared through the column where he knew Terra would be sitting. "It is a grave crime I stand guilty of, and I have petabytes of data raw to process in order to properly defend myself. Surely the court can grant me a week, unless a date for my execution has already been set."

A second gasp went up from the onlookers. The Architect glared at Doctor Moore. "The neutrality of this court will *not* be called into question again, Sigma. You have one week. We stand in recess."

Terra was fuming but held her tongue until they

returned to Theo's residence, and the red ball masked their conversation.

"What is the meaning of this?" the Nexus demanded.

Theo raised his hands in a placating gesture. "He is well within his rights to request mitigation of his sentence. At most, he will be given life in neural stasis. It is the same as the death sentence, but his body is maintained until it passes away from old age. This is a good thing, Terra. He confessed guilt."

"So I can go home?" she asked. Terra was eager to return to Jessica.

"No," Theo said with a shake of his head. "If at any time you depart Fyr, then sigma can end the recess early and move for a mistrial on the grounds that he has no accuser. I'm sorry, but you are stuck here for now."

"But he already admitted his guilt!" Terra shouted.

"I know."

"Your legal system has some big flaws," Darren muttered.

The Architect nodded. "I agree, but it is the system I am forced to operate within. Don't worry, a week for the recess, then he has five days to make a case for mitigation. After that, it will all be over. Only twelve days, Terra."

Twelve days. Less than two weeks and I can see Jessica and help Alex fight on Earth. "Fine," she said. Theo patted her on the shoulder, and the red ball ascended back into the ceiling.

Max inspected the M249 SAW and placed the first rounds of the belt into the feed tray assembly. Soft footsteps echoed in the hangar as someone approached him from behind. He set the machine gun down on the helicopter's deck and turned around.

"You've known Alex for a long time, right?" Caitlyn asked.

"I wouldn't say a long time, but for a couple years, yeah. Why?"

"He's just... He doesn't understand something I want him to."

Max leaned against the helicopter and put his hands in his pockets. "And what's that?" he asked with a raised brow.

"He has the wrong idea about something, and I want to set him straight on it, but I can't think of how."

"If you're asking my advice, I'll need a little more information."

"I just... He has the wrong idea about why I decided to stay on Earth with him, and I want to set him straight."

"Well, Alex is really smart," Max said. "But he's not infallible. He does get things wrong, and he *usually* admits when he's mistaken."

"Yeah. I don't know. He thinks that the only reason I'm here is because I want to be around him, but that's not right. I've seen what Azreal can do to a world. I don't want it to happen again. I want to stop it if I can."

"Why don't you just tell him that?" Max asked.

Caitlyn shrugged. "I tried after Terra went back home, but I haven't had a good time to talk to him since then. I *do* love him, but it's not like I'm obsessed with the man. I just want to help him help his home."

Max nodded. "I understand." He sat down on the helicopter's deck. "Look, Alex can be really obstinate at times. He's headstrong, doesn't always think things through, and can be the most frustrating person I know at times, but he's a really good guy. I'm sure that if you just talk to him about it, he'll understand."

"I'm sorry," Alex said. Both of them twisted their heads to the side to see him standing near the tail of the aircraft.

"How long were you standing there?" Caitlyn asked.

"Long enough to realize that I've been an idiot," Alex said. "I should have known better, Caitlyn, and I'm sorry." He walked forward and put his arms around Caitlyn. "I should have listened to you."

"It's okay," Caitlyn whispered.

"I've made a huge ass out of myself haven't I?" Alex asked.

Caitlyn laughed and pushed him away. "A big one."

Josh walked around the helicopter. He looked at Caitlyn holding Alex's upper arms and turned his gaze to look at the seated man.

Max shook his head. Alex and Caitlyn stepped

away from one another.

"Besides," Caitlyn said. "There's someone I'm looking forward to seeing when we get home."

Alex raised an eyebrow and smirked. "And who's that?"

She turned away from him, and Max thought he saw her masking a grin. "It's a *secret*."

"Well, I think Darren's a lucky man."

Caitlyn's eyes widened, and she spun around, her long black hair whipping about. Alex's smirk grew, and he stepped past her.

"We headed out?" Max asked.

"Yeah," Alex said. "You down for some football?"

The twin-bladed helicopter settled down in the middle of Century Link field where the Seahawks used to play. Alex, Caitlyn, Max, and Josh hopped out, and the helo flew back up into the air. Max had asked Josh if he was sure he wanted to go with them back into Seattle, and the young man had been adamant about helping free his home. Alex had gained some respect for Josh.

"You ready?" Caitlyn asked.

"Yeah," Max said as he cocked his machine gun. "We're ready."

"Remember, if we run into Azreal or any other

Demon Lords, let me and Caitlyn handle them. Your bullets may not be able to even touch them," Alex said.

"I remember," Josh told him at the same time Max said, "Roger."

Alex led them to the northern end of the field. The steel gate had been destroyed by something large, and the four scrambled over the tangled ruin. The city was silent. The absence of cars and people walking around made the tall buildings and dark shadows seem ominous.

"I am changing into my primal form," Caitlyn said so she didn't catch Max and Josh off guard. The three men took a step back from her. She had described her third form to the two men, but neither of them had experienced it yet.

Caitlyn dropped to her hands and knees, and the changes began. Her clothing turned black and covered her entire body. The changeling's bones cracked as they reformed and lengthened. Razor sharp protrusions extended from her vertebrae as spikes grew along her back. Her jaw snapped as it grew longer, and there was a grinding sound as her canines lengthened to over a foot long. When the transformations stopped, Caitlyn stood eye level with Alex.

"Ready," she said in English.

Max and Josh both shuddered, but they snapped out of the shock of seeing her and fell in step behind Alex. He carried just the wooden form of the Guardian's Blade in his hands so that the Wrathblade wouldn't sap his strength. It took millionths of a second to unleash the deadly form the Guardian's

Blade, so Alex was as prepared as any of them for danger.

Uneventful hours crept by as the squad darted along the empty Seattle Streets. "What's your status?" a woman on the radio asked.

Alex thumbed the transmit button on the first knuckle of his left hand. "We are about two miles from the Obsidian Tower now," he relayed through the throat microphone. "So far, we haven't seen anything."

"The perimeter is secure," the woman on the other end said. "We encountered light resistance, but they have been dealt with."

"Roger," Alex said. "Let us know if anything changes."

"Will do, Guardian. Be safe out there."

Yeah... safe... Alex turned the corner and froze. There was a flicker of movement across the street, but when he tried to see what had moved, it was gone.

"What was it?" Max whispered.

"Don't know," Alex said. "Let's keep going." They sprinted across an intersection, and Alex thought he saw movement to his left again. "Whatever it is, it's following us." *Should we investigate or keep going?* He thought it over for a moment and decided against checking it out. *If it's a demon, it'll attack eventually, and if it's something else, then I'll deal with it when it comes out of hiding.*

They crossed another street, and the road they were following turned to the left. An Obsidian Tower dominated the area a mile-and-a-half away. The surrounding buildings had been reduced to rubble, making the road a tangled snarl of steel, glass, and concrete. *Well, there it is, now we just need to get to it. And where are all the demons?*

Chapter Six – Missing

It was just after lunch on Fyr, and Theo was trying to explain cybernetic enhancements and prosthetics to Darren when the Architect suddenly stopped speaking. "One moment please," he said. "Someone is calling me on my neural link."

Theo had told the Daein people that the Primary Station had a series of transmitters that allowed for instantaneous communication from anywhere on the space platform as long as the people trying to talk had a special kind of machine implanted into their brain or used a public terminal. Terra had seen the benefits of such a system, but she wasn't sure how she could implement something like that on Dae. Advanced technology didn't always work as intended on the Realm of Magic.

The Architect glanced at her. "Terra, it... it is a woman calling herself Silvia. She says she needs to talk to you about something. I can route the call through the holoprojector in the table if you wish to take it."

Something in the look Theo gave her set Terra's nerves on edge. "I'll talk to her," Terra said, struggling to keep calm.

Theo dragged a finger across the screen on his arm, and a miniature Silvia stood atop the table. She was holding something the size of a man's forearm wrapped in black cloth. "Gentlemen, we should give them a moment," the Architect said before ushering Darren and Brahm to another room.

"What's wrong?" Terra asked as soon as the men left the room.

"Terra, I don't know how it happened. I watched them go to bed, but when Deidra went to wake them in the morning, they were missing."

"They?" Terra felt like a bolt of lightning had struck her. "Jessica and Hanna?" she demanded.

"Yes," Silvia whispered.

Terra collapsed onto one of the backless chairs at the table. Ice ran through her veins as she tried to make sense of things. "What do you know so far?" she asked. The Nexus clenched her hands to try and make the shaking stop.

"There was powerful magical residue in the nursery. Two very strong spells had been cast in there. The gateway arch had also been used. Both of the guards were dead," Silvia reported.

"Were you able to figure out where a portal had been opened to?" Terra asked, her voice thick.

"No. The spell that was cast wasn't normal. It was like there were pieces missing. I think it was designed to collapse in on itself after it was used to keep people from following. But there's more," Silvia said. "We found this in the nursery." The Fanglady pulled the black cloth from the object she was holding and held it up for Terra to see.

It took the Nexus a moment to identify what Silvia held. "Is that an arm?" Terra asked.

Silvia nodded and wrapped it back in the cloth. "It's an arm wearing angelic armor. It was fused to the wall of the nursery. We had to knock out a small section of the wall so I could bring it."

The fear and confusion storming through Terra turned to rage. "Did you say angelic?" The angels of Bara had been terrified at the prospect of a Nephilim being born.

"Yes," Silvia said. "I don't know how it got stuck in the wall, but it could have been from one of the two spells that was cast in the nursery. It's the only solid evidence we have."

I have to go home. "Return to Dae," Terra ordered. "I'll be there soon."

Silvia nodded, and the miniature of her disappeared. "Theo," Terra called. The Architect strode back into the room with Brahm and Darren.

The dwarf took one look at her face and asked, "What's happenin'?"

"Jessica and Hanna are missing," Terra explained. "They found an arm in the nursery that was wearing angelic armor. I have to return to Dae."

Theo frowned. "Terra, I can understand your desire to help with the search for your daughter, but if you leave, Sigma will walk free."

"I don't care about Moore! I have to find my daughter!" Terra swiped her arm though the air.

"Think about this logically for a moment. What will you be able to do that can't be done just as easily by someone else?" the Architect asked.

Terra's fingernails were biting into the flesh of her palm. "Raze the City of Spires to the ground," the Nexus said with grim determination. *They took Jessica. Eternius kidnapped my daughter.*

Darren held up his right hand. "Hang on a second, Terra. We don't know anything yet. Send Brahm or I in your place. You are needed here, and we can help with the investigation."

"I agree with Darren," Brahm said. "I've done me own fair share o' investigatin' as Captain o' the Guard in Adorac. Send me, an' I'll do everythin' in me power to find yer girl."

Terra wanted to scream at them. She closed her eyes and sought the peace of her core. The half-angel breathed in, and motes of blue light drew into the place she stored magical energy. She breathed out, and the glowing light in her core pulsed blue. Terra repeated the exercise several more times before she opened her eyes.

I have to go... They need me. Her hands shook, and she felt like she was about to vomit. *Maybe I'm not thinking clearly. I have to trust the people around me and do my duty. Duty... I hate this.*

"You three are right," she said with difficulty. "Theo, I will remain here with Darren." Terra fixed her gaze on the dwarf that had become like a father to her in the last eight months. "Brahm, please, find my daughter."

"I will, Terra," Brahm said. "Architect, if ye'll send me on me way."

Theo punched in a series of commands on his arm computer. "The glider will take you to the portal device. When you arrive, it will automatically open a portal to Dae. Good luck, Master Ironfist."

"Thank ye. Darren, take care o' Terra," Brahm

said as he quickstepped down the couple of stairs to the force-door.

"I will," the captain called as Brahm walked through the shimmering doorway.

"Would you like to go on a tour of the Primary Station? There are some beautiful sights that can help calm the mind," the Architect asked.

Terra shook her head before resting her face in her hands. *Breathe in. Breathe out.* "No. I would like to just sit here alone for right now."

"As you wish," Theo said.

Terra listened to Theo and Darren's receding footsteps. *Breathe in. Breathe out. Brahm will find them.*

Eternius stood behind the base of the Angel Falls in Argentina. The thunderous roar of water helped block out all the other sounds around him. The Keeper of Fate had been standing motionless in that spot for the last several days.

I'm not Keeper of Fate anymore, the ancient angel reminded himself. *I abdicated. I couldn't just stand by and let the Angelic Council decide to pick a war against the Guardian and the Nexus... Terra, my daughter, I have wronged you in so many ways. I wish there was some way I could make it up to you.*

He felt a presence behind him, and Eternius

prepared to be attacked. There was a solid rock wall behind him, and only something ethereal in nature could be travelling through the stone. A glowing arm stuck out from the wall and waved at him. Ureon, the Seat of Faith on the Angelic Council, drew herself from the wall and shifted back into her material form.

The instant she did, Eternius had a burning desire to fix his hands around the junior angel's throat, but he decided against it. "Where were you when I needed you?" he growled.

Ureon smiled sheepishly. "I'm sorry, Eternius, but I was carrying out my duties elsewhere," she said.

"Your duties?" he said with an incredulous tone. "Your *duty* is to sit on the Angelic Council when it is session to ensure the seven virtues are heard in everything we do! Truth, Justice, Hope, Honor, Love, Intellect, and MOST IMPORTANTLY, FAITH!" he roared.

The female angel opened her mouth and stuck a finger in her ear. Ureon wriggled her finger about to try clearing the ringing he had left in it. "That is not my only duty," she said.

"Yes, it is, Ureon," Eternius snapped.

"My name is not Ureon," she said.

Eternius had been alive for eleven-and-a-half billion years, and he had thought he was done with being surprised, until recently. Her simple statement destroyed any remaining shreds of that belief. "We cannot lie. How are you doing this?" he said.

The Seat of Faith nodded. "I am not lying," she said. "You may still call me Ureon, but that is not my name. I was always so carefree before the spirit of Yggdrasil opened my eyes to the memories of my soul. It was hard at first, acting so far against my nature as a First One, but I did a good job of convincing everyone I was still the same. It is enjoyable to be so free with my emotions, and I grew to love the way I am."

"That is impossible," Eternius said. "All of the First Ones invested their bodies, minds, and souls to create the Nine Realms and the Life Wardens. You are lying."

"No, Eternius, that is just what you believe." Ureon rubbed her temple. "Ask me a question I shouldn't know the answer to, and you will see that I am telling the truth."

"Why were the valkyrie created?" he asked.

"Mars knew the stability of the Nine Realms was always going to be in danger from the forces of Hell, so he created the valkyrie so that there would always be a standing army to oppose them. Not that it's done much good in the last few years," Ureon added.

Eternius frowned at her. "Which First One survived the creation of the Nine Realms?"

Ureon crossed her arms and smirked at him. "That's a tricksome question. Mars and Luna both survived the process, but they gave their lives to create the Soul Foundry and the changelings, respectively. Come now, Eternius, you have my vow that I am telling the truth. Ask me a question that you are certain I would lie about if I could, and I will answer it without any verbal dodging or mincing of words."

Dots began to connect in the ancient angel's mind,

and every encounter he had had with Ureon over the past few billion years passed through him in the blink of an eye. "Over the past ages, I have put up with your mischief, and it isn't until just now that I see something."

Ureon's smirk disappeared. "And what's that?"

"I gave you much more leeway than any angel in the past. Over all those billions of years, my heart grew cold and hard," Eternius said.

"I don't like where this is going."

The ancient angel knew he was on the right track with the growing look of panic on Ureon's face. "It wasn't until I needed you most and you weren't there that I have come to realize that I rely on you much more than I do any others. And now I see that none of the other angels had to put up with your antics. Just me."

Ureon tried to back away from him, but Eternius caught her wrist. "Don't," she pleaded. Uncomfortable tingling rippled up his arm as she attempted to turn ethereal and phase through the stone, but he focused on keeping her grounded to the material world.

"What I want to know," he said, "is why. Why have you acted this way toward me all these millennia? Why did you feel the need to gain my approval? Why did you seek me out here on Earth?"

Ureon froze. "Unhand me," she said.

"Will you attempt to escape?"

"No." Eternius released her, and she turned to face him. A fearful look was on Ureon's face.

"Why? All of these years you've deceived me, why?" Eternius asked.

Ureon closed her eyes, and said, "I wanted you to care for me."

He knew the answer to the next question, but it was the true test of her words, and Eternius had to ask it. "Why?"

Ureon took a deep breath, and her ice-blue eyes looked into his hazel. "Because I love you." Her soft words were almost lost in the pounding thunder of the falls, but Eternius read them on her soft lips.

Eternius could read the vulnerability and fear in her eyes. He hadn't ever heard of her taking a lover during her tenure as the Seat of Faith, and a passing thought skittered across his mind. *Has she ever loved someone? It's been a long time since...*

A smile grew on his face. "And I love you," he said. Ureon's lips widened into a relieved grin, and she threw her arms around him. Her mythricite armor was cool on his skin, and it dug painfully into his chest that was only covered in a white shirt. Eternius pushed her back. "Where have you been these last few days?" he asked.

"I've been communing with Fenris, the spirit of Yggdrasil," she said. "When we created the Nine Realms, we knew they wouldn't last forever. The Outsiders were pushing too hard. They are from a place beyond the Void, from another dimension, and it was only a matter of time before they broke through the shell we placed around the Nine Realms."

"What do you mean?" Eternius asked.

"The Outsiders hate all material life. I don't know why... We never knew why. Eternius, we are fighting a proxy war. I fear the Outsiders have come, and with their arrival, we will need a powerful Guardian to protect us from them."

Her words gave Eternius a new lens through which to view all of the recent events. "I understand."

"Get down," Hanna whispered. The two girls ducked behind a cluster of pipes. The sound of heavy footsteps approached and faded.

"This sector is clear," Jessica heard one of the metal men say. She was terrified. *I just want Mommy.* The way Hanna had stared at her when Jessica was the way she really looked told the Nephilim that she shouldn't show people her true body.

Hanna waited for the metal men to disappear around a corner before saying, "They're gone. Let's go." The girl Jessica loved took her by the hand, and they ran through the narrow gap between two buildings. Hanna looked about and muttered, "I wish I could read these signs."

Jessica pointed at the nearest one. "That one says, 'Black...' something, I don't know the other word." She pointed at another. "That says it's some kind of shop."

"How do you know that?" Hanna asked.

Jessica shrugged. "I don't know. I just read it like you taught me to, but I don't understand all of the words."

"Half-angels like your mommy can read and speak every language, maybe you are like that. You just have to learn the words first," Hanna said.

Jessica shrugged again. She sniffled. "I miss Mommy and Daddy," she whimpered.

Hanna wrapped her in a warm hug. "I know you do, Jess. As soon as I can figure out some way to let Terra know we are here I will, but we have to be careful and brave."

"What's brave?" the baby asked.

"It means doing what you have to do even though you are scared," Hanna explained. "Can you be brave?"

Jessica nodded. A bright light bathed the two of them in the alley, and Hanna shoved Jessica away from her. "Run," the changeling shouted.

"Found them," one of the two metal men said.

"Remember, we only need the little one. You can dispose of the other one."

Jessica screamed, and she felt a painful ripping as the black wings erupted from her back. "You won't hurt Hanna!"

The Nephilim lashed out at the two metal men and felt they weren't human. She cast the same spell that Hanna had a few hours ago at the glowing arm in her room but laced the dark energy pounding through her into it. The bright light flickered and went out. There was a heavy thud as the two metal men collapsed onto the ground, sparks shooting out from their heads.

Hanna stared at Jessica with a look the Nephilim had never seen before. The older girl's brows were drawn down, and her lips were tight. "Jess, you need to hide the way you look. Quick. We can't run from here with you looking like that. You'll draw too much attention. Can you do that?"

Jessica nodded and hid her true self again. Hanna took her hand, and they started running again. "Are you scared of me?" Jessica asked.

"No," Hanna responded without hesitation. "I love you, and I know you wouldn't hurt me. I just want to know more about you and what you are capable of, that's all."

"Okay. I love you too," Jessica said. "I'm sorry I wasn't brave and ran like you told me to, but I was scared and didn't want to be all alone."

Hanna laughed, but Jessica didn't see what was funny. "It's all right," she said. "You were brave when you protected me. Thank you."

Alex stood on the highest remaining floor of the partially collapsed building. He peeked around the corner of the window frame and surveyed the approaches to the Obsidian Tower. There was a small host of a hundred or so demons milling about the base of the black spire. *Why so few?* he wondered.

A small crevasse ran between the ruined husks of two buildings that would provide cover for them to cross most of the way to the tower without being seen. *That will have to do.* He climbed down the interior wall of the building, and when he was low enough, Alex dropped to the ground.

"See anything worth a damn?" Max asked.

"Yeah," Alex said. "There's a route we can take almost to the Obsidian Tower's front door, but something doesn't make sense."

"What?" Caitlyn asked.

"There is virtually no one there to defend the place. Only a hundred or so minor demons, imps and hellhounds, are protecting the thing. It's like Azreal doesn't care if he loses it," Alex explained.

Max stroked the stubble on his chin. "Maybe he's stretched too thin. If he attacked every nation on Earth like General Fields said, then there could be hundreds of these towers. He could just not have the forces necessary to hold them all."

"I don't think that's it," Alex said. "When we were attacking the Obsidian Tower on Dae he had an army of millions. It was the same on Caine. This just doesn't make any sense."

"You aren't considering the obvious thing," Josh said. "He could really not care if he loses it. He had hundreds of others all over the world. What's losing a few here or there to him? He may not even want to hold the areas he's taken, just slaughter millions of people."

"But why?" the Guardian said, growing frustrated.

Josh and Max shrugged. "It doesn't change the mission. We still need to destroy this one, but be on the lookout for anything out of the ordinary."

Max raised an eyebrow. "You mean like a giant black tower in the middle of Seattle with demons and zombies are coming out of it?"

Alex looked over his shoulder at the man and smirked. "Yeah, but wierder than that."

"Right," Max muttered. The four of them crept through the ruined mass of concrete and steel. They winced at every loud footfall or crunch of stone. The sun was nearing the horizon by the time they made it to the end of the defilade between the two buildings.

"Ready?" Alex asked. The three other members of his unlikely squad nodded, and the Guardian unleashed the Wrathblade. He and Caitlyn charged ahead into the mass of demons as Max and Josh fired from cover. A spray of bullets downed a small group of imps far to Alex's left. Alex engaged the lone daemon that seemed to be in charge of the enemy forces.

The Guardian ducked under the monster's black sword, and with a single strike from the Wrathblade, the daemon was hewn in two. Dark blood sprayed into the air from the dead hellspawn, and Alex struck out at any other monsters that drew near.

In less than a minute, the battle was over with black blood dripping from Alex's sword and Caitlyn's razor sharp fangs and claws. A hellhound had impaled itself on her back spikes, and she shook it free. The two men from Earth jogged up to the two of them, reloading their weapons as they went.

"That was too easy," Caitlyn said.

Alex nodded. He suddenly felt a strong sense of anger and fear scream across his link to Terra, and he frowned. *What's wrong? I should be home right now, not playing whatever game Azreal thinks this war is.*

"So, should I just rig up this bomb?" Josh asked, patting the shoulder strap of the pack he wore. Alex had said the tower could be destroyed from the outside, but it would require a powerful explosive. General Fields had shocked him by giving them access to a prototype tactical nuclear warhead. Alex hadn't known that such a weapon existed.

The Guardian shook his head. "No. There could be prisoners in the tower. Near the top is a room full of green pods that suck the life from people so it can be transferred into Azreal. We need to make sure they are freed before we do that."

Max surveyed their surroundings. "Well, I don't think we're going to get an embossed invitation. Let's go."

This isn't right. This whole thing screams trap. Alex felt Terra's fear slowly fade to be replaced with a simmering rage. "You're right," the Guardian said, and he led them through the mouth of the Obsidian Tower.

The large bottom floor of the tower was empty, and the gateway arch was dormant. "That's where a portal would be," Alex said. He had a small camera on the clear safety glasses he had been given before they boarded the helicopter. "The stairs are over here."

Alex mounted the steps and started climbing the

Obsidian Tower. There were no signs of demons or undead as they climbed. The squad crossed an empty room and continued to climb. A few more flights up, they came to a second empty room. "This is where Caitlyn and I fought through a group of hellhounds on Dae," Alex said.

"Yeah, I had to stay behind and hold them off so you could keep going and save Terra," the changeling said.

Alex climbed the flight of stairs he knew would lead to the extraction chamber with all of the green pods. He reached the top and stopped. The enormous room was empty. There wasn't a single cable or pod anywhere in sight, just a set of spiral stairs on the opposite end. "This is where the prisoners should be... What the hell is going on?" Alex muttered. They crossed the room and went up the spiral stairs to where the throne room should have been.

The Guardian wasn't surprised by the lack of a throne or gateway arch on the highest floor. Another set of stairs Alex had not seen the last time he was at the top of an Obsidian Tower was across the room. They climbed the stairs and found themselves on top of the tower.

An enormous shard of stone floated a foot or two off of the floor, and wind whipped at the four of them. Alex walked up to the black stone and placed his hand on it. It was warm to the touch. It was black like the rest of the tower, but it didn't have as glossy of a finish. The stone was pitted with holes and even had a crack on one side. "What is this thing?" Alex wondered aloud.

"I have no idea," Caitlyn said.

<It is familiar though,> the Voice of Balance sent.

How so? Alex asked.

<It is like the Celestial Eye in Starfall. It's from the Void.>

Can the Guardian's Blade affect it like it did in Starfall when I made the Celestial Eye open?

There was a moment's hesitation. <No,> Alex's own voice said. <It is similar, but not the same. Besides, that was triggered by your need to find a way to communicate, not some innate power of the stone.>

Well, I need some answers.

<Very funny, Wielder, but it doesn't work that way. You should destroy this tower and return to base. There was nothing of use to be found here.>

Let me be the judge of that.

"The Voice of Balance has no idea what this is either," Alex said. "It has to be here for a reason... I just wish I knew why."

"Shit in one hand," Max muttered.

"Wish in the other, and see which fills up faster," Alex finished. "I know. Let's get out of here, but I will destroy this tower with the Guardian's Blade. We aren't using a nuclear device in the middle of Seattle. There might not be people around, but that doesn't change the fact that they may want to come back some day."

Everyone agreed with his statement, and they climbed down the tower's steps. The Guardian called on the Wrathblade. He let the rage inundate him. Alex drew in on and on until it threatened to overwhelm him. Max and Josh stepped back from him when his eyes turned solid green, and the fire on the sword turned black. With a mighty swing, a filament of the black flames shot from the top of the Wrathblade and sliced through the base of the Obsidian Tower.

Dust and debris filled the air as the tower slammed into the ground. *One down.*

It had been several days since William left the Thoolian settlement, and his stomach rumbled for something other than the dehydrated fungus. The taste and texture were revolting, but there was little to eat in the Void. He was lucky to have what he did.

He caught the faint scent of ash on the ether currents. "What's that?" he wondered aloud. William found it comforting to hear someone speaking, even if it was just himself. An extremely small landmass, only a couple of miles across, drifted not far away.

Propelling himself against the current of energy that everything in the void floated in, William drew closer to the smell. As he circled the planetoid, he saw a scorched area only a few hundred yards across. William landed just outside of the place. The ashes were still warm, and the Nephilim saw the bones of some kind of unknown life form.

"It looks like the Outsiders were here recently," he

muttered casting his eyes about the Void. A flicker of light caught his eye, and William focused his senses on the distant pinprick. It was too far away for the brightness to be coming from just one Outsider ship, but he was certain it was the glow of engines he was looking at.

"Let's go have a closer look."

Chapter Seven – And in the Left Corner…

Azreal laughed. "Fools. The truth is staring them in the face, and they don't even see it." The Overlord of Hell sat upon his throne in the Overlord's Temple. The heat of the black star was lessened by the thick stone walls of his palatial home. Azreal watched as the Guardian toppled an Obsidian Tower on Earth through the Planar Mirror.

The object looked like an ordinary mirror, but if came to life for the Overlord while he sat upon his throne and showed him any place in the Nine Realms he desired to see, except Aria, the Realm of Life. The innermost Realm had proven to be an enigma for Azreal, and it vexed him to no end.

"Dark Lord," a imp sniveled at the foot of his throne.

Azreal fixed his gaze upon the lesser demon. "What is it?"

"There is someone here to speak with you. We don't know how she got past the Hellgate. She just appeared outside the temple," the imp said, its high pitched voice already grinding on Azreal's nerves.

A woman? Who is it that comes to call upon me? The Reaper perhaps? "Send her in," Azreal said. The imp vanished in a flash of red flames as it jumped back to its station at the doors to his temple. A few moments passed, and the doors to the Overlord's Temple swung inward.

Azreal immediately recognized his twin sister even though she stood dozens of yards away. She had fled from him long ago and given birth to Alex Zane, the biggest thorn in Azreal's side. "Sister," the Demon Lord called, "how nice it is to have you grace me with your presence. Have you grown tired of living?"

Odessa drew up to the base of his throne and fixed an impertinent stare on him. She studied him with her hands on her hips. "No, Brother, I haven't. I *have* grown tired of this senseless eternal war, however. I have come to stand by your side so we may wreak devastation upon the Nine Realms to end it once and for all."

Not believing a word she said, Azreal asked, "Why the sudden change of heart?"

"I met my son," she said bitterly, "and he cared nothing for me. A few seconds and then he was gone. If that is the pittance I have earned for all these years of running, then good interests me not."

"Is that all it takes to turn the fickle heart of a demoness? A son's apathy? I shouldn't be surprised. You've always been one of lunar temperament."

"Do you plan on killing me or welcoming me, Azreal? I'm growing tired," Odessa said.

The Overlord smiled at his sister's jibe. "I haven't made up my mind yet," he said.

"Well," the Demon Lady said as she turned away from him and began to walk away, "let me know when you do. I'll be in what used to be my room. Have something sent over for me to sleep upon."

Azreal stared at her back as she strode away with a half-smirk. His sister's arrival coupled with the Guardian's absolute confusion proved too much for the

Overlord, and he started to laugh. "Oh, Nephew," he whispered at the Planar Mirror, "revenge is going to be sweet."

Myrius met the Daein envoy at the gateway arch on Bara. The Source shown bright overhead, casting harsh white light on their surroundings. As the senior member of the Angelic Council, Myrius had been raised to the position of Keeper of Fate, and the selection process was afoot to select a new Seat of Intellect.

The angel removed the keystone seal, and the elf, dwarf, and changeling stepped through the portal to the Realm of Good. "May the peace of the City of Spires be upon you," Myrius said.

"And you," the changeling with black hair and yellow eyes said. "I am Silvia Shadowpaw, Fanglady to the Changelings of the Fang. This is Timothy Eldu'vain, third prince of the Northern Elves, and this is Brahm Ironfist, General of the armies of Dae."

Myrius nodded. "I am Myrius, the Keeper of Fate."

Brahm's brows drew down. "What happened to Eternius?" he asked in a gravelly voice.

"He abdicated his position and fled this Realm," Myrius said. "What brings such important members of the Realm of Magic to my city?"

The dwarf opened his mouth to speak, but Silvia gave him pause with a hand to his shoulder. "We come searching for a child. Her name is Jessica, and she has gone missing recently."

Myrius's face warped to one of disgust. "You are looking for the *Nephilim*," he spat the word. "Why do you think she is here?"

The dwarf reached in his pack and tossed something yellow at the angel's feet. It thunked against the mythricite ground and clattered to a stop against Myrius's boots. The object was an arm encased in mythricite armor.

"We found this in *Jessica's* nursery," Brahm said. "It looks like one o' yer lackeys took it upon himself to try harmin' what he thought was a defenseless child. I think he made a bloody big mistake."

"Are you implying that this attack was sanctioned by the Angelic Council?" Myrius asked as he lifted the severed arm from the ground.

"I'm bloody—" the dwarf started before Timothy cut him off.

"We are not trying to imply anything, Keeper," the elf said. "We are simply inquiring if you have any knowledge as to where our wayward child has wandered."

Myrius nodded. "I have neither seen your... child, nor have I had any angels return to Bara missing an arm. I am sorry, but I have nothing for you."

"We bloody well did no' expect ye to," Brahm snapped. He turned to the changeling and elf. "I told the two o' ye this would be a waste o' time. Bloody angels're no' to be trusted. Probably killed Jessica an' flung her body o'er this endless drop they're so fond o'."

The dwarf's constant disrespect was something Myrius would no longer tolerate. "The Nephilim is not here, dwarf. Nor has she been captured or killed by any angels. You will leave now and not return."

Brahm grinned at the angel and gave a short bow. "Thank ye fer yer cooperation," the dwarf said before he stepped through the portal. Silvia and Timothy followed him, and the gateway to Dae closed.

"But not for lack of trying," Myrius put in.

Niles Wester, the CEO of the Genotech Corporation, sat in his glider and waited for the report to come in. He scanned through the fascinating genetic sequence his scanner had uploaded earlier that day. There were entire sections that the computer model was unable to identify the purpose of, but he had been able to riddle out a few.

This section would determine intelligence. He shifted to another slide on the holographic display. *This one, growth and mental development.* He pulled up another section of the curious genetic material and shook his head. An entire section was blank. Just completely missing.

This is impossible. This region is responsible for

mental health and overall intelligence. It can't be missing, the child would have been born brain dead... A sneaking suspicion wandered through Wester's mind. *Unless there is something in this section the computer couldn't render because it wasn't programmed to.*

"Display all sections with missing data," the CEO said. Fifty-seven miniature holographs filled the interior of his glider. "Identify commonalities between current display and base file: Human Female."

There was a momentary hesitation as the computer queried the database in the Genotech Hub for the requested data. "All areas relate to mental capabilities," the computer's female voice said. "Section fifty relates to the ability to manipulate latent energy through accumulation and dispersal of raw force."

"So she can use magic," Niles Wester muttered.

"The data are insufficient to definitively confirm that conclusion," the computer said.

There is only one person that would be capable of applying this information so we can benefit from it, but he's on trial for murder... The array of holographs disappeared when he received a call across his neural implant. Wester accepted the communication, and a woman's face appeared before him.

"There was an incident in the Primary Bionetics Hub," Cheryl Black, his assistant, said. Two members were logged into their praetorians when something generated a sensory feedback loop. The system shut down, but not before the two men lost consciousness.

Attempts have been made to awaken them, but nothing's working."

A second holograph appeared as the feed from one of the cyber suits was displayed. The two praetorians had discovered the girls in an alley. The target screamed and transformed into some kind of winged being with white hair and glowing eyes, then the feed went dead. "See that the two pilots are decommissioned. I don't want anyone finding their bodies or this feed. And put the word out among the choppers that we are looking for a little girl with brown hair."

"I'll get it done," Miss Black said, and she ended the call.

The feed from the praetorian looped back through, and Wester paused it when the target changed. He studied the two different color eyes that glowed with an inner light, and the delicate black feathered wings that had grown from her back. "Beautiful... I will have you."

Chapter Eight – The Earth Defense Force

"I'm agent Sherman," the black-suited man said. "Welcome to the EDF's US headquarters."

The elevator doors opened, and Alex stepped out into a large underground room. A few people with white lab coats maintained a bank of computer servers to the left side of the room, while a series of large hangar type doors ran the length of the right wall. Men and women sat at computers in an open workspace, and a screen dominated the far wall.

Alex glanced at the man that had escorted them into the Cheyenne Mountain Military Base. He wore an unassuming black and white suit and had short blond hair over blue eyes. "I've never heard of the Earth Defense Force before," Alex said.

Agent Sherman smirked. "That's the point. We only recruit from the best and the brightest of Earth's children, and we transcend all nation's borders."

"But here you are beneath NORAD..." Max said.

"Yes, the US government leases the upper levels from the EDF. It ensures that our comings and goings are associated with the military and not a nebulous trans-national agency," Agent Sherman said.

"Umm... I've never been in the military before," Josh said, "but I've seen plenty of movies. When did we become cleared for you to tell us all of this?"

"You weren't. I'll have to kill you if any of you ever attempt to leave," the agent said with a shrug. Josh and Max froze, and Alex felt inclined to ask the man to try. Caitlyn looked ready for a pitched battle to erupt in the pristine lab. Sherman burst into laughter. "I'm kidding. You're here because the four of you are the only ones in the world that have any kind of knowledge of what we are dealing with. Oh, your assessment of our inability to attack the towers from afar was spot on, by the way."

Alex shook his head and smiled. "So, General Fields flew us out here because…"

"Because I told him to," a woman said from behind them. Her white business suit was immaculate, and not a single strand of brown and gray hair had wandered from the tight bun atop her head. "I am Bridget Strom, the Director of the Earth Defense Force."

"Alex Zane, ma'am," he said with an outstretched hand.

The Director gave him a firm shake. "I know who you are, Mr. Zane, and I appreciate your coming here. I think we can help one another and end this war on Earth."

"I understand. We'll do what can to assist you, within reason." *I don't have any problem helping this woman, but I don't want to commit myself too strongly.*

<Yeah.>

Bridget gave him a tight smile. "Thank you. Agent Sherman will direct you from here. He is my most capable agent." She turned to the agent. "I have a teleconference with POTUS in a moment. Show them the suit."

"Our next stop, ma'am," Agent Sherman said.

Director Strom nodded and walked away without

another word. "The President, eh?" Max asked.

"Yes," Sherman said. "He's very interested in what we're doing to fulfill our duties and in the four of you. You've already proven that you can deal with the towers, so the EDF is going to do what it can to make your job easier. So to help, we've some technology that isn't exactly available on the streets."

"What kind of technology?" Alex asked.

"Let's just say that our eggheads have a few prototypes that would help you. Follow me," the agent said and led them past a few hangar doors. They stopped before one with a large roman numeral five painted on it. "This is Section Five, experimental warfare tech." Sherman looked at the armed guard standing next to a control pad. "Open it up."

The guard nodded and placed his hand on a biometric reader. A second passed, then the large hangar door began to retract into the ceiling. Flood lights came on in the room, and Alex's heart missed a beat.

"That's a Fyrian laser rifle," the Guardian said. The mottled black and gray beam weapon sat on a pedestal in the center of the room with a bright light shining down upon it as if it were the masterpiece of the collection.

Agent Sherman smirked. "Close. That's our version. We have had loose contact with the Atlas Labs corporation on the Plane of Science, and they've supplied us with a few goodies to experiment on." He stepped into Section Five and led the four of them to the left. Agent Sherman opened a door and beckoned the others inside.

"What the hell?" Josh muttered. A man encapsulated in armor was walking on the ceiling with his head toward the floor.

"I love that reaction," Sherman said as he entered behind them. "Montoya! Get down from there and greet our guests."

The armored man disengaged himself from the top of the room and flipped in mid-air to land adroitly on the floor with a heavy thud. The helmet of his armor folded back to reveal a Hispanic man with a thick black mustache and a shaved head. "I'm Doctor Montoya," he said with a light European accent and an outstretched hand.

Alex shook hands with the man and winced under the crushing weight of his grip. "Oh, sorry," the doctor said. "Sometimes it's hard to gauge the exact amount of force in the hands. Did I hurt you?"

"No," Alex lied as he rubbed his right hand. He made the introductions, and then asked, "What is this, some kind of powered armor?"

The doctor smiled. "Precisely. This is Prometheus." Montoya said as he lifted his arms and spun in a circle.

Max lifted an eyebrow. "You bring fire to humanity with that armor?" the big man asked.

"In a way," the armored man said. "Prometheus gave us much more than fire, that was the start of technology. This armor will bring about another industrial revolution. The applications for it are amazing, limitless even."

"But we plan on using it in a bit more… direct manner," Sherman put in.

Montoya frowned at the black-suited man. "Indeed. You've taken my masterpiece and brought it down to that of a common club."

Agent Sherman shrugged. "The EDF paid the bills for you to develop Prometheus. You knew what we were going to use it for."

Alex studied the armor and looked at Doctor Montoya with an upraised brow. "You built this from a Fyrian template too?"

The doctor pressed a button with his chin, and the back of the armor opened with a hiss. "No," Montoya said as he extricated himself from the Prometheus suit. He wore a black skin-tight jumpsuit underneath the armor. "This is completely of my own design. The laser rifle was one of the few things the Fyrians actually sold to us, but that opened a bevy of new paths of study. The problem I was having with the Prometheus was the power supply. It wouldn't run without a nuclear reactor to power it, but the Plane of Science has perfected the field of piezoelectricity."

"The field of what?" Josh asked.

"Piezoelectricity," Alex explained, "is the generation of electricity from the compression and manipulation of certain objects. Typically crystalline structures." The five other people in the room looked at him with varying levels of surprise. "Just because I shoot guns and swing swords doesn't mean I never took a physics class."

"That's correct, Guardian," Doctor Montoya said.

"The Fyrians use the force generated by the pull of the trigger and solar power, to create the energy to fire the rifle. That led me to create a piezoelectric gel to power the suit. As long as you are moving, it is charging. Prometheus monitors the amount of power to complete the action you want to perform and amplifies your strength or speed to do it. That depletes the charge in the superconductive lithium layer."

"Sounds simple enough, as long as you aren't doing anything you wouldn't normally be capable of, the suit stores energy," Alex said. Doctor Montoya nodded, and the Guardian continued. "Why aren't there squads of these things running around?"

"Well," Agent Sherman said, "that's where we can help each other. Prometheus is still in prototyping, and we need some real-world field testing."

Max's eyes widened. "Whoa, you want to send us into battle with experimental weapons and armor?" He looked at Alex. "This is going to be just like the time in Syria, you remember? When they sent us in with those rifles with the fiber optic cameras?"

"Yeah. The damn things jammed if you got any dirt in them." Alex looked at the armor dubiously. "I'm not sure this is the best idea."

Doctor Montoya had an offended look on his face. "The Prometheus suit is ready for action," he asserted. "The only issue right now is the calibration of the fine motor skills."

"How are you supposed to pull a trigger without fine motor control?" Max asked.

"You won't need to," the doctor explained. "The

weapons we've designed to be used with the suit interface with the personal area network to be fired and reloaded. There's a heads-up display that relays the status of your weapons that also features a targeting computer run through an infra-red laser on the gun to show you exactly where you are aiming."

Alex put his hand to his chin in thought. "A personal area network? Could that be accessed to give someone else control over the Prometheus suit's systems?"

Shaking his head, Doctor Montoya said, "No, it's only conductive through the outer layer of the suit, not wireless. In theory, someone could intrude upon the system, but they would have to be in contact with the suit, either there physically or with an attached wireless transmitter. The suit has sensory alarms if something becomes stuck to it and a unique operating system. Even if they *could* gain access to the PAN, they wouldn't be able to *do* anything unless it was me or one of the techs from down here."

"Okay," Alex said, "but you still haven't answered my original question, why aren't these things all over the place?"

"Because this is the only one," Agent Sherman said. "We need field testing before we move forward with production, and the Director has decided the best way to do that is to outfit one of you with Prometheus. That way, we get testing, and you get a powerful addition to your team."

The Guardian scratched the back of his head. "I don't—" he started.

"I'll do it," Josh interrupted. All eyes turned to look at the young man.

"I'll do it," he said again.

"Are you sure, Josh?" Max asked. "No one is asking you to do this."

Josh nodded, his face a mask of determination. "Max, I'm far from the most useful person in our little squad, and I think I could actually help if I had this."

"Good man," Agent Sherman said. "Take off your clothes, except your underwear, and step in to the machine."

Josh's committed look faltered, and he glanced at Caitlyn, blushing deep red as he did. "What?" she asked.

Alex almost burst into laughter at the embarrassed look on the black-haired youth's face. "I think he's shy," Alex said.

Caitlyn crossed her arms and grinned. For a moment, Alex thought she wasn't going to face away from them, but she did as soon as Josh began pulling his shirt over his head. Alex rolled his eyes at her antics. *What has gotten into her lately?*

<I don't know,> the Voice of Balance sent. <I think it has something to do with stress... Maybe it's her time of the month.>

I was talking to myself, Alex thought. *Not you.*

<I know, but I was getting bored,> his own voice said. <I feel like we never talk anymore. I just really want to know what's going on with *Alex*.>

Are you being serious right now?

<No, but I have been thinking about something.>

What's that?

<I was wondering why it was so important for your daughter to be born on Earth in the first place.>

Alex had been wondering the same thing himself, which wasn't surprising, since he was conversing with the part of him that had been imprinted upon the Guardian's Blade when he had died a few months earlier. *Maybe Fenris knew Earth was about to be invaded and thought that was the only way to get me here.*

<I don't know,> the Voice of Balance sent. <The spirit of Yggdrasil seemed awfully surprised to learn you were having a girl for that level of foreknowledge. I can't help but think there was some other reason.>

Let me know if you think of anything that makes sense.

<Will do.>

Josh stood before the four men in just his boxers. "Stand behind the suit," Doctor Sherman said as he walked over to a bank of computers. "The suit will size itself to you before it closes. You are close to my height and build, so it should only take a few seconds."

The young man walked to the opening in the back of Prometheus armor and stopped. A shimmering red laser beam scanned him from head to toe. "Turn around," a computerized female voice said from the suit's speakers. Josh turned about, and he was scanned again. A hissing sound came from the suit, and after a few seconds, the voice spoke again. "You may don the Prometheus armor."

Josh turned to face the silver and gunmetal armor,

and Alex thought he heard Josh gulp. "You sure about this?" Alex asked. "You don't have to do it if you don't want to."

"Yeah. I mean, what's the worst thing that could happen?" Josh asked.

Agent Sherman rubbed his nose and said, "You could be crushed into a gelatinous goo under the amplifying effects of the armor."

Josh, Max, and Alex all three slowly turned their heads to stare at the agent. "Please tell me you are joking," Josh said.

"He is," Doctor Montoya assured. "That almost certainly won't happen. You are the first pilot other than myself though…"

"Josh," Max said his voice thick with concern, "you really don't have to do this."

The young man smiled. "Yes, I do." He took a step forward and slid his feet into the boots of the Prometheus suit. There were a series of beeps, and the armor began to close around him as he put his forearms into the metal exoskeleton. The helmet expanded from the collar to encapsulate Josh's head.

A faint sound of something crackling came from inside the suit, and Josh grunted. "Are you okay?" Max shouted.

"Yeah," Josh said. His voice was slightly distorted through the speaker, but he sounded relieved. "The armor popped my back as it was closing. It felt amazing."

Alex laughed and shook his head. "Good to know you aren't being compressed into goo," he said.

"I'm as happy about that as you are," Josh said. "What do I do now?"

"Try walking," Montoya said. "It should feel just like you are wearing a heavy set of clothes."

"You can turn back around now," Alex said over his shoulder.

Caitlyn turned about just in time to see Josh take a halting step in the armor. "That's an imposing sight," she said.

Alex couldn't help but agree with her. The armor added about another six inches to Josh's already six-foot frame, and the face of the Prometheus suit had glowing orange sensors for eyes. Each of the armor's footfalls was a dull thud that Alex could feel through the concrete floor.

Josh took another step forward, then planted his feet and did a back flip. He landed with ease and laughed. "This is awesome," Josh said. "It's like a videogame! I feel like I can do anything."

They wanted a field test... Alex thought. "Anything?" the Guardian asked.

"Yeah, anything!" Josh exclaimed with another laugh.

Alex took a step forward, set his feet in a ready stance, and touched the fingers of his left hand on the Guardian's Blade. "Do you think you can beat me in a fight?"

Josh's tone took on an aspect of disbelief, and the young man took a half-step backward. "Uh... I don't want to hurt you on accident, Alex."

Max, Agent Sherman, and Doctor Montoya all

started to protest at the same time, but Alex cut them off with a raised hand. "He won't hurt me," the Guardian asserted. "And if the Prometheus suit can't stand up in a fight against just me, then it won't be any good for fighting demons. This is the best way I can see to do this."

Caitlyn put her hand on Alex's shoulder. "Alex is right." Alex looked at her curiously, and she smiled.

Alex turned back to the armored young man. "Now, are you ready?"

There was a moment of hesitation before Josh said, "Sure." Josh lifted his arms and squared off against Alex.

A slow breath escaped the Guardian's lips as he drew the wooden sword. *I can't let him hit me, or he'll break something.* The two stood for a time, facing one another down. Alex looked from one impassive orange light sensor to the other. He edged his left foot forward. Josh slid his left foot backwards.

The kid's left-handed? Alex darted forward and swung the Guardian's Blade with all his might. Josh spun faster than Alex thought possible, catching the wooden sword with his right hand. He struck the Guardian in the chest with an open palmed strike, and the half-demon was blasted backwards; the Guardian's Blade tearing from his grasp.

Alex was having trouble standing. He took a deep breath but felt no pain. The Guardian's Blade clattered to the ground beside him. Josh had tossed it over.

"The basal ganglia in the brain are one of the things the Prometheus suit affects. By manipulating dopamine production throughout the brain, the suit can effectively change the perception of the passage of time for the occupant," Doctor Montoya explained. "When the suit detects danger, the occupant enters an experiential thinking mode that allows him to process and react to information much more quickly."

Alex took another deep breath and wrapped his hand around the hilt of the Guardian's Blade. "Is that safe for the person using the suit?" he asked as he stood.

"There haven't been any side effects as of yet, but it has only been tested for a very short time," the doctor said. "The suit isn't injecting synthesized dopamine, but manipulating the body's production of the neurotransmitter. There *shouldn't* be any ill effects."

Alex slid the wooden sword into its leather baldric. "You understand that the suit could permanently damage you, right?" he asked the young man.

Josh clenched his fists and lowered his head. "I don't care. I've seen things, Alex. Things I can't forget and won't ignore. I don't care what the cost to my body is. I have to help, and if my life is the price to pay-" Josh lifted his head, "then I will pay it with a smile of my face."

Alex laughed and shook his head. "Remind you of anyone?" he asked.

"Yeah, somebody that I used to know," Max said.

"Well." Alex took a few steps forward and placed his hand on the shoulder of the Prometheus suit. "Just don't get yourself killed like he did."

Josh nodded.

"It's time to go," Alex said. "We have more work to do, and we need to see what this armor really is capable of."

The high pitched whine hurt Hanna's ears, and the air didn't smell right. *It's like when someone shoots a lightning bolt, and the air smells like electricity,* the changeling thought. "I think we're safe for now."

Jessica looked at her and frowned. The Nephilim's growth over the last three days shocked Hanna. *It doesn't make any sense. If she's growing that fast, the strain on her muscles and bones would keep her in constant pain.*

"Why do you think that?" Jessica asked.

Hanna chewed on her lip for a moment before answering. "Well, we haven't seen anyone in the last few hours, other than the occasional wanderer. And we need to find a place to rest. We've been awake for almost two days it feels like." She glanced out of the small breezy passageway they had found. "I only see a woman with blonde hair out there. I don't think she's one of the things that are chasing us."

Jessica peeked out below her. "Why's she just standing there under that red light?"

"Don't know," Hanna asked with a shrug.

The woman must have caught the movement out of

the corner of her eye. She looked at them and beckoned them over, her large bracelets jangling. Not sensing that she was a danger, Hanna and Jessica went to her.

The woman crossed her arms over her enormous exposed cleavage and skin tight dress. She said something in Fyrian that Hanna didn't understand.

"I don't know what you mean, 'working the corners.' What's that?" Jessica asked.

Hanna's face heated. She had overheard some of the masons talking a few days ago before Jessica was born about visiting women on street corners. "It means she's a prostitute," the changeling muttered.

The blonde woman laughed and said something else, looking Hanna in the eyes.

"My friend doesn't speak your language," Jessica explained. "She can't understand you."

The prostitute raised an eyebrow and frowned. She pulled off a simple golden loop earring and held it out to Hanna, but the younger girl was reluctant to take it. Looking at Jessica, the woman spoke for a bit then stopped.

"If you are lying to us, and she gets hurt, you'll regret it." The woman started to pull her hand back. "Wait." Jessica turned to Hanna. "She says this earring is a special type of machine that will translate for you."

"Do you think we can trust her?" Hanna asked. The woman harrumphed and nodded her head.

"I think so. She seems like she wants to help us."

"All right," Hanna said as she took the proffered

item. She put the earring on, and it beeped loudly in her ear. "Now what do I do?"

The earring began to speak in her ear. "Bionetics linguistics implant activated. Scanning Superior Temporal Gyrus. Scan complete; scanning Middle Temporal Gyrus. Scan complete. Uploading data to Gaia, please wait. Please wait. Please wait. Upload complete, now translating verbal communication to Daein Common. Do you wish to select another language?"

"No, that's fine, I guess," Hanna said.

"Language confirmed as Daein Common. As a reminder, if you wish to access the settings of your new Bionetics linguistics implant, just say, 'Bio linguistics settings.' Thank you for choosing Bionetics and have a nice day!"

"You too." Hanna looked at Jessica. "That was odd."

The woman smiled. "First time, eh?" she asked. "Now, what brings two little girls out to the Genotech Charlie hub?"

"Is that where we are?" Hanna asked.

"Yeah," the woman said with a perplexed tone. "That's where you are. Who are you two?"

I'm not sure I want to give out our names to some stranger. "Who are you first?"

"Kinda paranoid for a little girl," she muttered. "I'm Aura, a prostitute as you so… tactfully pointed out. Now, who are the two of you?"

"We're just two girls that are a long way from home and need help," Hanna said. "Please…" *Maybe*

I can play the scared little girl card.

Aura rubbed her face with her right hand. She muttered something Hanna didn't quite catch. "Come with me, and keep quiet. I'll take you somewhere safe."

Jessica wove a spell laced with demonic power, but she held it just on the edge of completion. "Just in case," the Nephilim whispered. Hanna nodded and prepared her own spell before following the woman down the alley.

"Where—" Hanna started.

"Quiet," Aura hissed. "Not here. If they have a sample of your voice, they could use it to find you. And if you're being hunted, then they most likely have one. Just wait to talk. There are recording devices everywhere."

The prostitute peeked around a corner and glanced around. She waved them forward, and the three darted across the street and up the stairs. Aura put her hand on a glowing square next to the door, and it vanished into the ceiling.

Hanna gingerly walked into the room, trying to see everywhere at once in case of an ambush. She didn't think the woman meant her and Jessica any ill will, but it paid to be safe. The door slid back closed, and the lights turned on.

The small room had no furniture and was a deep red color. "Welcome to my home," Aura said. She turned to face a lighted panel on the wall and pushed a few illuminated areas on the bright screen. A table and three short chairs that were made of some kind of solidified light winked into existence in the center of the room.

Aura sat down in one of the chairs and beckoned the girls to do the same. "It's safe to talk now. Who are you really, and why are you being hunted?"

Hanna and Jessica exchanged glances and released the spells they held in reserve. "Why should we trust you?"

"Haven't you already shown me a lot of trust?" Aura asked. "I mean, you're alone with me in a house with only one exit. This is going to turn into a circular conversation. You should trust me because I was like you once. Far away from home with no one to rely on. At least you have a friend with you."

"So you want to help us?" Hanna asked.

Aura laughed and rested her head in her hand. "Yeah, kid, I want to help you. That's why I'm here," she said with a wink, "to make dreams a reality."

"What's a prostitute?" Jessica asked.

Hanna's mouth worked soundlessly for a moment. She didn't really understand the real meaning of the term and was relieved when Aura diverted the conversation.

The older woman smiled demurely and asked, "What's your name, child?"

"Jessica Zane," she answered. "I'm three!"

"Three years old!" Aura said with enthusiasm. "You're mighty well spoken for your age."

Jessica shook her head. "No, I'm three days old."

Aura frowned and looked at Hanna. The girl nodded confirmation. "Is she an android or flash-grown clone?"

"What're androids and clones?" Hanna asked.

Mouth hanging open, Aura reached out and touched Jessica's face with the fingertips of her left hand. "You're flesh-and-blood all right. Born from a woman just three days ago?"

Jessica nodded. "I miss Mommy. We're looking for her. She's supposed to be here, but here's big."

"Not as big as you may think." She faced Hanna and studied her. "And you are Daein. Both of you are powerful spellcasters, but you are generating air magic, so a Changeling of the Wing. You look familiar though." Aura started clicking a yellow lacquered fingernail against her front teeth. "You aren't a Steelfeather, are you?"

Hanna's eyes widened in surprise. "I'm Hanna Elizabeth Steelfeather. My father, Aeryn, is the Winglord, and her mother is the Nexus. How do you...?"

Aura winked at her and smiled. "All in due time, child. So, you're searching out the Nexus, huh? Well, she's here, but if someone's after you two she'll be hard to get a hold of. Tell me everything you know about who's hunting you."

"What do you mean nothing?" Terra asked.

"Exactly what I said," Silvia's holographic

projection said. "The angel we spoke to, Myrius, outright said no angels have Jessica. They didn't take her, and someone was going to just kill her, they would have done it in her nursery."

There's something wrong with that, Terra thought. *Come on! Think! Deep breaths.* The Nexus slowed her breathing, and thought about what Silvia had just said. "They tried though. Or else he wouldn't have been able to say that. They tried to take her, but weren't successful, or else he could have been lying when he told you none of the angels had her."

"I think your reasoning is a bit shaky on that one," Darren said from where he sat nearby. "He could also just believe that none of his kind have her."

"That would make sense," Silvia said. "But it doesn't take into account the arm that we found in the nursery. I think Terra's right on this one. It's not really helpful information though. It doesn't tell us where she is. She could be anywhere in the Nine Realms."

"Ye're no' helpin'," Brahm's projection said. "We've eliminated Bara, but there're many more places she could be, lass. We'll keep lookin' fer Jessica an' Hanna."

"I know you will. Thank you both." The holo call ended, and Terra looked at Theo. "How much longer do I have to sit here, powerless to help search for my daughter and apprentice?" she demanded.

"Nexus," he said, "I know you are upset, but you know you can't just leave. There are shadowed forces in play. Maybe..."

"Maybe what?" Darren asked.

Theo held up a finger and pushed a button on his arm-mounted computer. The red ball descended from the ceiling and bathed them all in sanguine light. "I think all of these events are connected," the Architect said. "The attack on Earth, your daughter going missing, and Sigma's trial. They are putting pressure on us to cause a mistrial. Someone doesn't want Sigma's trial to go through."

"Who?" Terra asked. "Who kidnapped my child to try to force me to end this trial?"

Holding up his hands to implore Terra to calm down, Theo said, "I'm not certain. I don't even know if what I said was correct, but it isn't outside of the realm of possibility. Eleven days, Terra, then we can move forward."

Terra ground her teeth. "That's twelve days too long."

Chapter Nine – Choppers

Aura stood at the bottom of the stairs that led up to her cheap apartment. *How much longer am I going to have to wait, Ureon? It's been twelve years since you told me to come here and wait. To come here and do what I can. How much longer?*

A sudden scream drew Aura's attention down the narrow, dimly lit street. She fingered the small pistol implanted within her left wrist. A young girl, maybe five or six years-old, sprinted past Aura. A group of five heavily augmented men chased after her.

Looks like choppers are hunting down little girls. I guarantee it's related to Jessica and Hanna. Aura's commlink chirped that an hour had passed from the appointed time, and she sighed. *Still nothing.* She turned and walked up the steps.

The door hissed open silently, and Aura saw Hanna and Jessica both asleep on the anti-grav bed. *Good. I'm glad they are both resting peacefully.* The woman sat next to the two girls for a time, contemplating how she had arrived where she was. She was studying Hanna's innocent features when a tear came unbidden to her left eye and rolled down her cheek.

Aura closed her eyes to take a steadying breath and nearly leapt from her chair in surprise when a small hand wiped away the tear. Her eyes shot open to reveal one hazel and one green eye looking back at her.

"You lost the ability to change and the magic, haven't you?" Jessica asked, her soft voice not rousing

Hanna in the slightest. "That's why you cry."

"Yes," Aura whispered. "How did you know I was one of the Wing?"

"I…" Jessica started before trailing off, "don't know. Sometimes I just know things, but I don't know how. It felt right."

Telepathy? Empathy? Fortune-telling? Or something else entirely? "That's a powerful Gift you have, child. Guard the secret of its existence well. Because if you don't, the truth coming out may cost you your life."

Jessica nodded with understanding. "What happened to make you this way?"

Aura's eyes narrowed momentarily at the unintended slight, but she quickly dismissed her reaction as unwarranted. "It's a very long story, child. You needn't concern yourself with it."

The young girl's mismatched eyes drilled into Aura, demanding the truth with their implacable persistence. "I want to know," Jessica said, her tone brokering no argument.

"And if I don't want to tell you?"

"I could force you to tell me," the girl said, her eyes mimicking the slight narrowing Aura had made just second before. Jessica began to cast a spell consisting of all four elements, and the older woman's mouth dropped open in shock. The spell was terrifying in its complexity, and it shocked Aura that the girl was so adept at wielding magic.

Just as she tried to get up and run, tendrils of air bound Aura to her seat, so the enigmatic Changeling did the only thing she could.

The sound of screaming made Hanna's eyes shoot open, and everything slowed in her mind's eye as she appraised the situation. That Jessica had bound Aura to a metal chair was concerning, but it was infinitely more concerning that the Nephilim was weaving a pain nullification spell and moving it toward the prostitute's head. *That's how I said someone could be induced to always tell the truth,* Hanna thought. *But she could kill Aura without meaning to.*

Without hesitating further, Hanna shredded Jessica's attempts to cast the spell with a flurry of attacks from various elements. She also severed the bonds of air that held Aura in place. Hanna couldn't tell if the woman didn't move because she was terrified or being wary.

Jessica stopped attempting to cast the spell and looked at Hanna curiously. "What's wrong?" the younger girl asked.

"What are you doing? You could kill her!" Hanna snapped.

Tears welled in Jessica's eyes and her brows knit together. "I didn't mean to hurt anyone!" she wailed. "I just wanted her to tell me the truth."

A look of understanding crossed Aura's eyes, and she said, "It's all right. I know you didn't mean to hurt me, but you must learn to control your impulses. You are very young and don't yet know right from wrong. You can't just go around forcing people to do as you want."

Jessica sniffed a few times and wiped the tears from her eyes. "Why not?"

Hanna was stammering trying to come up with a reason, but the woman answered first. "Think about it from the perspective of the person being forced to do something against their will," Aura explained. "Would it make you happy to do something you didn't want to do?"

Jessica shook her head. "No, I think it would make me angry or scared."

"Exactly," Aura agreed. "There are a few exceptions to the rule, such as things you have to do that you don't want to, but for the most part, people shouldn't force one another to do things."

"I understand," Jessica said. "I'm sorry if I scared you or made you angry. I didn't mean to."

Aura nodded and wrapped the child in a soft embrace. "I know you didn't, little one." She held Jessica out at arm's length. "A good rule to follow until you know more is to treat people how you want them to treat you. If you don't want to be hurt, then you shouldn't hurt others."

Jessica nodded then looked confused. "What if they want to hurt me?"

"You should try to stop them without hurting them," Aura said with a smile. The smile slowly faded away before she spoke again, and her face became one of grim determination. "But if you can't stop them without hurting them, then you do everything in your power to make sure they can't hurt you. Do you understand?"

Jessica said she did, and Aura turned to face Hanna, extending the question to her as well. "I've known that for a while now," Hanna said. "My home was at war almost as long as I've been alive."

"I know it has," Aura said, her voice full of regret. "I know."

Hanna studied the woman with curiosity. "How did you know my father?"

"She's a Changeling of the Wing," Jessica said.

Aura smiled when Hanna's eyes widened. "It's the truth. We're of the same people, though I'm long estranged from Highwind Point. It has been a long time, since before the war with Azreal, since I came here." Her smile widened. "I knew your father when we were younger; we grew up together. You'll have to let him know Aura says hello when you see him again."

"I will," Hanna said guardedly. "But in the meantime, what are we to do about finding Terra?"

"Well from what you told me yesterday, it sounds like you're being hunted by one of the four Mega-corporations. You two've already made some pretty impressive enemies, and it looks like the Choppers are out hunting down little girls."

"Mega-corporations? Choppers? I have no idea what you're talking about," Hanna said. Jessica nodded her agreement.

"Well, sounds like you need a bit of a civics lesson," Aura said. "I'll keep it short and to the point. There are four large businesses that control various parts of the Primary Station, where you are now. They are the Mega-corporations, or Mega-corps, and there are several smaller corporations that are owned by the Mega-corps. Everything we use on the Primary Station is produced by one of the four. Make sense so far?"

When the two girls nodded, Aura continued. "One aspect of life on the Realm of Science is getting cybernetic implantations." Her tone turned bitter. "In my twelve years here, I have gotten several. That is why I can no longer change into my birth form, produce magic, or wield it." Aura looked at Hanna meaningfully. "Do *not* under any conditions have anything implanted into your body while you are here. I don't know how, but it interferes with our abilities."

The younger Changeling looked stricken. "So you're…"

Aura nodded. "Stuck this way." Her voice turned dead and emotionless. "I'll never look down on the sweeping plains of Dae, feel the wind through my feathers, or soar through the firmament. It's all lost to me."

And for what? Just to blend in here and wait for someone who may never come! Aura shook her head and saw the two girls staring at her curiously. "Sorry, like I was telling Jessica, my story is a long one, and not something I'm going to get into right now. Back to what you need to know.

"Cybernetic implants can be very expensive, and

the more advanced models are sought after. To keep the prices up, the Mega-corporations only produce a very limited run every year, so there is a very lucrative black market for those implants. That's where the Choppers come in. They, remove, the implants from unsuspecting people and sell them on the market. They're just like any organized crime syndicate I suppose."

"All right," Hanna said. "I think I understood all of that. From what I can gather, these Chopper guys are looking for us?"

"That about sums it up. I'll be able to keep the two of you safe while I try to figure out how to get in touch with the Nexus. Maybe I'll be able to reach her at the trial without raising any suspicions. It's a public forum, and she has to come and go from it, so there'll be opportunity."

Aura turned to a wall, touched a button, and a glowing semi-transparent page appeared before her. She was doing something Hanna couldn't understand, moving her hand back and forth and touching certain spots on the page. The page changed colors at her touch, until it finally stopped on a few columns of text Hanna couldn't read.

"It says here that the trial will resume in six days," Aura explained. "We'll have to wait until then. I have certain responsibilities, and it will be noticed if I don't attend to them. You girls will have to stay here on your own. I'll show you how to use the food and beverage dispenser before I leave for the evening."

"We'll be fine," Hanna said. "I'll just keep

teaching Jessica while you're gone."

Aura nodded. "Sounds good, but you can't teach her magic. The remnants of magical energy could be tracked back here, and you'd both be trapped."

Hanna and Jessica exchanged a disappointed look, but they understood the necessity of laying low.

"But," Aura continued, "you can use the terminal here in my home, and it will show you more than you can imagine. All the knowledge of the Realm of Science will be at your fingertips."

"I can't read the language," Hanna said.

Aura winked at her. "That's not a problem." She touched another few buttons and a small box appeared on the terminal. "Daein Common," she said. The language on the terminal changed to Hanna's native language.

"That's amazing!" Hanna said with a large grin on her face.

"Yeah!" Jessica agreed.

"I'm glad I could help," Aura said. "Now let me show you around your home for the next few days."

The red light bathed Theo's dining area in a sanguine glow. The Architect motioned that it was safe to talk.

Terra pushed her bowl of food away. It was the same disgusting nutrient mash she had been fed while in the Obsidian Tower on Dae. "Someone is using magic nearby," she said. "Is it normal for there to be magic users here?"

Theo placed a hand on his shorn chin, and a few seconds passed before he said, "No. It is extremely unusual that anyone would be using magic on the Primary Station. As a matter of fact..." He trailed off and started tapping away at a computer interface.

"As a matter of fact what?" Darren asked.

"The logs of all the arrivals to the Primary Station are right here," Theo explained, as he pointed to a holographic display that appeared above the table. "One of the purposes of the Genotech scanner is to have a profile of all that visit us here. It scans for various genetic markers, and one of the things scanned for is the ability to use magic. Currently, you are the only person with those genetic markers present on the Primary Station."

"Is there any way that information could be wrong?" Terra asked. "I'm fairly certain I wasn't mistaken."

"The information is public. It goes straight from the scanner, to the Genotech servers, then to the public database," Theo explained. "It's highly unlikely such information would be falsified, and no one take notice."

"This just all has me on edge," Terra said. "I should be out there looking for my daughter. Not sitting here waiting for a trial to convene." She rubbed her face and stood. "Nothing is going the way it should."

Darren grunted his agreement. "When was the last time it did?" he muttered.

Terra conceded the point. *It's been a long, long time*, she thought as she paced around the room like a caged animal. "Maybe I *am* wrong. There's a little voice inside of me screaming to do something, anything that could help find Jessica. I just know that she's lost and scared and needs my help." She clenched her fists and took a deep breath, slowly letting it out.

Theo walked in front of her and placed his hands on her shoulders, his long arms extended. "As soon as this is over, Terra, I'll personally help you find her. It is the least I can do since the part I played those months ago when you were captive in the Obsidian Tower."

"Thank you," Terra said. "But you don't need to feel guilty for what happened back then. You weren't the one that captured me and forced me into one of those cursed pods. It's the man sitting comfortably in a jail cell, scheming a way to escape punishment. Is there really nothing that we can do to hurry the trial along?"

Shaking his head, Theo released her. "No, I'm sorry, Terra, but there isn't. Such things are beyond my control, and if I were to bend or break any of the rules, then those who seek to do harm to the Realm of Science would take advantage of it to discredit me. That is not something I can afford to happen. Especially with such a critical trial on the line. The Nine Realms are relying on us not faltering and not giving in to impatience. This has to be done right if Fyr is to join forces with the other Realms against Azreal."

"I understand," Terra said. "I just wish there was something more we could be doing."

"As do I," Theo agreed.

Chapter Ten – Doing Something More

Josh looked down upon New York through the Prometheus suit's visual monitor. The onboard computer scanned the surrounding rubble and ruined husks of buildings, alternating between thermal and low-light sensors.

"Anything?" Max asked.

"No human lifeforms detected," the computer whispered in his ear.

"No," Josh said. "We should be clear to…" He trailed off when the black crystal atop the Obsidian Tower began to glow with an inner light and rotate faster.

A disembodied head floated within the stone. The suit's HUD showed Alex's and Caitlyn's blood pressure and heart rate spike.

"Watch out!" Caitlyn shouted, but before they could react, all four of them were frozen in place.

The pale, thin-lipped apparition laughed derisively at their futile struggling. "Ah, Nephew," the head chided, "What a coincidence running into you here."

"You're no family of mine, Azreal," Alex snapped. Josh could see the tendons in his neck standing taut as he battled against the restraining force.

"Oh, you wound me, Nephew! And just after I was telling your mother how much I really wanted to get my hands on you."

"You're lying," Alex said. "My mother would never join forces with you."

"And you know her so well," Azreal said. "She told me that after years of separation, her son snubbed her. My sister said her son almost completely ignored her when he saw her on Aria. Clever of her to hide there. I wonder how she came to find herself in that place. Or how you did, considering last I heard, you were dead."

Alex grinned at the red-haired man. "Well, I just had so much fun killing you the first time, that I decided to come and do it again."

"How exciting," Azreal said. "I look forward to your arrival." The four of them began to float away from the tower. In a few seconds time, they were hanging over the several hundred foot drop to the streets below. "And your learning how to fly."

The invisible force holding them aloft vanished, and Josh's mind screamed for a solution to their impending doom. The suit's monitor dimmed as Alex unleashed the Wrathblade, and it flashed into existence.

"Twenty-seven seconds until impact," the computer warned. "Deploying thrusters."

"There's thrusters?" Josh asked.

"Affirmative."

Alex was reaching out to Max, but they were still several feet apart. Josh willed the suit toward them, and the advanced artificial intelligence interpreted his guidance. He shot downward and hurled Max at Alex. The two of them sailed through the air toward the Obsidian Tower, and Josh saw Alex impale the stone with his sword and their descent slow.

He turned to find Caitlyn still halfway through her transformation back into her human form. She would slam into the ground before it was through.

"Thruster fuel at fifty percent. At current velocity, impact will result in pilot death. Recommend reducing velocity. Four seconds of flight time remaining. Impact in ten seconds."

"You could have said they only last eight seconds! I have to save her!"

"Apologies. Calculating intercept vector. Calculated. Confirmed. Executing automated control routine."

The screen turned red as the AI took control of the suit. To his initial dismay, Josh shot away from Caitlyn toward the Obsidian Tower. The last of the suit's fuel was spent flipping him over to land horizontally on the Obsidian Tower's outer wall.

His knees and legs screamed in protest as he was launched from the tower straight toward Caitlyn. "Warning! Chance of pilot injury on current vector, seventy-eight percent. Survival chances for pilot and passenger, optimal." He flew at her with his back to the ground, catching the changeling in his arms as their paths crossed.

"Hold on!" he shouted.

Her half-human half-panther form curled into a ball, and the suit did its best to protect her as they slammed through the burned out husk of a building, his shoulders and back taking the brunt of the impact. His shoulder wrenched painfully as his left arm slammed into an I beam, and he felt the joint pop. The two crashed through an interior wall and skidded to a stop in what looked like a ransacked office building.

Josh groaned, and Caitlyn struggled to her feet. "Warning! Pilot's left shoulder has been dislocated! Initiating treatment."

"What? Don't—" Josh started to say, but the suit's servos moved on their own, forcing his shoulder back into the joint with a loud crack. Pain shot up and down his arm followed by relief as the suit administered pain relievers to the affected area.

"Shoulder reset. Administering Med Gel. Caution! Brace for pain."

"Stop!"

"Apologies. Unable to abort process. Med Gel Toxemia would occur. Chances of pilot death, one-hundred percent. Heating Med Gel to reduce chances of re-injury."

Josh screamed as the suit began to sear his shoulder with microwaves. He felt like his bones were going to explode by the time it finished. Tears ran down his face as he cried with the pain. He heard voices shouting but couldn't make them out.

"Treatment complete. Please avoid using this shoulder for the next several hours while the remaining synthetic cartilage sets."

"Let me out," Josh gasped as he struggled to his feet.

The suit hissed as the back opened, and Josh was able to get out. Thin arms caught him as he fell backwards.

"Josh! What's wrong?" Caitlyn shouted.

Heavy footsteps shook the thin floor beneath them, and he heard Max's voice. "Are you two all right?"

"No," Josh croaked. He touched his left shoulder. The flesh was a bit tender, and he pulled at the collar of the skin-tight suit so he could look at his skin. An angry, red blotch covered his skin, but it didn't look like it had blistered. "Maybe yes."

"We went through the wall," Caitlyn said. "I got up, but he just started screaming. I don't know what happened."

"Hurt my shoulder," Josh said. "Suit treated me. Hurt. A lot." He looked up at Caitlyn's golden eyes. "You okay?"

"I'm fine. Thanks to you," she said and gave him a gentle kiss on the cheek.

Even if she does turn into a giant murder beast with huge bone spikes sticking out of her back, she's pretty cute.

Alex drew their attention when he cleared his throat. He frowned at Caitlyn and handed the detonator to Josh. "Good job today. I think you've earned the honors."

The small silver object was no bigger than a pen with a red button on top. The metal was cool on Josh's hand. "Is this far enough?" he asked.

Alex nodded. "It's a tiny thermobaric bomb, and it's a few hundred feet above us and inside of the tower. We should be fine."

Here goes nothing. Josh pushed the button and felt a powerful thump in his chest as the bomb detonated. He saw the Obsidian Tower shudder through the hole he had created as the oxygen in the upper floors was consumed. The explosion, coupled with the sudden vacuum, made the top of the tower collapse in on itself. The entire structure faded from existence as it collapsed, leaving nothing but a barren spot amidst the rubble to indicate it had ever dominated the ruined New York skyline.

"And that's two down," Alex said. He thumbed the button for the radio. "The thermobarics worked. This tower is gone."

A few seconds passed while Josh wondered what the operator was saying. Max wore a radio and could hear the conversation, but Josh's radio equipment was integrated into the Prometheus suit.

"Correct," Alex said. "Top room. Ensure no one goes to the roof of the tower. Those crystals may be a trap. The way they deflected the air strikes make me think there's more to them than we know." Another pause, and Alex glanced at Josh. "No, I think he's fine. Something about the suit hurting him. I'll make sure he gives a full debriefing on what occurred while we're en route."

Josh nodded that he would.

"Roger. Proceeding to LZ. Guardian out." Alex stepped closer and held a hand out to Josh.

"What did they say?" Josh asked as he was helped up.

"In a second," Alex said, dismissing his question for the time being. "Are you good to go? What happened?"

Josh nodded again. "I'm fine. I dislocated my

shoulder, and the suit automatically reset it. Then it injected something called Med Gel and microwaved my shoulder." Alex raised an eyebrow and opened his mouth to say something, but Josh didn't pause to let him speak. "I'm fine. It hurt. A lot. But now that I know what's coming it shouldn't be as bad. Now, what did they say?"

"Well, I hope the cold doesn't bother anyone. We're headed to Canada then Mexico. The EDF wants to secure this continent, then we'll move on to South America."

Josh smiled as he stepped back into the Prometheus suit. It closed around him, and he said, "Well, I always wanted to see the world." The ruined building groaned but didn't collapse. N*ot like this though*...

The harsh lights on the avenue hurt Darren's eyes. He glanced warily at a group of large men with silvery glowing eyes. "Terra," he called, causing her to turn and look at him. She had sealed away her wings before they left Theo's, not wanting to draw additional attention to themselves as outsiders.

"What?" she demanded.

He took a few quick steps to catch up to her before she sped away again. "I get the feeling this isn't the safest part of the Primary Station. What exactly are we looking for?"

"I told you, Darren," she explained as if she had gone over this a million times before. "I can feel someone producing air magical energy here on Fyr. It wasn't here when we first arrived. That means a Changeling of the Wing had to arrive after we did. Hanna wouldn't leave Jessica on her own."

"But I thought you told me that it would be impossible to find the source of it all," he said, looking over his shoulder at the four men.

"I have to do something, Darren. We're stuck here for another five days, and I'm losing my mind sitting on my hands. I don't care if it's impossible. My daughter is here on Fyr, and I'm going to find her."

"Hey there, beautiful. This man bothering you?" a deep voice asked behind him. Darren swore under his breath when the other three men surrounded them.

"No." She turned to keep walking, but two of the men behind her moved closer to block her path. "Get out of my way."

"Hey, baby, we just want to have some fun," the man who had originally spoke said. He looked Darren up and down with an appraising eye, then did the same with Terra. "Those are some mighty fine original limbs you got there. I'd love to take them from you."

The Architect had been adamant about them not going out on their own to look for sign of the girls, but he hadn't been able to convince Terra to take an escort. He had instead described a few of the dangers they may encounter in some of the less reputable areas of the station.

These must be choppers, Darren thought as he rested his hand near his sword. "We're just looking for someone. We don't want any trouble, so you guys should get out of here while you—"

"Get out of my way!" Terra snarled. "Now."

"Make me, woman," one of the men in front of Terra said as he reached out a hand toward her.

Before his sausage like fingers could complete the journey to her, a powerful blast of wind magic buffeted Darren's sides as everyone other than the man he had spoken to went flying.

The man's eyes went wide, and his mouth hung open. "What in the Hell? Get away from me, you freak!" he shouted as he ran away, abandoning his accomplices.

Darren looked about at the three men rolling about on the ground, moaning in pain. "Don't you think that was a bit much, Terra?"

"I told him to move. Twice," she said, as if that absolved her of all guilt. Darren sighed, and she rounded on him. "Look, *Captain,* I am more than capable of taking care of myself. I am going to find my daughter. You can either come with me, or go back, but you will not stand in my way."

Darren put his hand on her shoulder. "Terra, I know you're worried, but this isn't the right way to go about this. You aren't thinking clearly."

"Do you know why I'm not thinking clearly!" she screamed at him. "It's because my nine-day-old daughter is being hunted by angels, and instead of being there to protect her, I don't even know where she

178

is! The only clue I have is so weak it couldn't support a piece of paper! So I'm going to do *whatever it takes* to find her!"

"I understand, and I'm here for you Terra. I just want you to slow down and think for a second. Close your eyes and take a deep breath. We need a better plan than wandering around this place blindly."

She glared at him for a moment, and he was a little bit surprised when she did what he asked. Several seconds passed, and she just stood there breathing with her eyes closed. "I meant just for a second," he said.

"Quiet. I need to focus."

Darren shrugged and began to study their surroundings. The three men Terra had launched through the air had vanished, and they were alone on the street. The feeling of being watched tickled the back of Darren's neck, but he didn't see anyone.

Terra's eyes shot open, and she pointed to their left. "I'm not sure, but I think there's more coming from that way. When I draw the energy in, there's a greater concentration coming from that way."

"All right, let's see what we can find."

The next several hours passed with the two of them trying to find paths around the various buildings and other obstructions in their path, until they ended several miles from where they started. Terra was pointing almost straight down. "I don't understand. It's coming from that way."

Darren thought for a moment. "Didn't the Architect say that the station was a bunch of connected balls floating through the air? Maybe it's coming from a different one?"

"It was something like that. Come on, let's find some way to the next hub."

Shaking his head, Darren said, "It's the middle of the night. We need to rest and resume search in the morning."

Terra chewed on her bottom lip for a time before agreeing.

"We'll find them," Darren said.

Hanna and Jessica stood before the small terminal and read about the structure of the brain and how neuroreceptors functioned. Aura sat behind them, studying the two girls, and their unending thirst for knowledge.

At first, she thought they had been lying about Jessica being only three days old, but after watching her grow over the last week, she believed it. The young girl was already the same height as Hanna and showed no signs of slowing down.

That has to be impossible. What is she? Aura had refrained from asking, but she now understood what it was Ureon had sent her to Fyr for. It was to keep an eye out for them. She wondered how many other people the angel had stationed all over the Nine Realms.

I'll do what I can for them, Ureon, but I can't

protect them forever.

Chapter Eleven - Torment

Josh watched as Doctor Montoya did maintenance on the Prometheus suit inside the EDF's mobile lab. A small computer was attached to the exterior of the suit, and the doctor made small grunts or tapped a few keys every few seconds. A few damaged pieces were laying on a backlit table.

Josh poked the armor's mesh under-layer "So, what's it look like, doc? Will I ever walk again?"

"Huh?" Montoya said as his eyes shot up to study Josh. "I didn't know there was a problem with you."

Josh crossed his arms and frowned. "I was trying to make a joke. How's the tune-up going?"

"Fine." The doctor disconnected the computer from the suit's exterior. "It looks like everything is working well. I did as you requested and made wound treatment a prompt rather than an automatic process. However, if you don't respond to the prompt in fifteen seconds, the suit will treat you. It's in case you become incapacitated and unable to respond."

"Sounds good to me," Josh said. "When will you have her put back together?"

"Her?" the preoccupied doctor asked. "Oh, a couple of hours and I'll be done."

Josh nodded and turned to walk out of the lab. He reached the door and spoke over his shoulder. "The automated control system helped save Caitlyn's life the other day."

"Automated control system? What are you talking about?"

Josh hesitated. "I mean, the suit took control for a few seconds and did some maneuvers that I wouldn't have been able to pull off without its assistance."

Doctor Montoya's reaction was not the one Josh had anticipated. The man rose to his feet, turned Josh about, and placed his rough hands on Josh's shoulders. "Tell me exactly what happened."

Sensing the man's alarm, Josh relayed the events as best he could. The suit moving on its own, the screen turning red, even the AI speaking to him, although he was sure that was a feature.

Montoya gulped. "It's not supposed to move on its own. Maybe..."

"Maybe what?"

Glancing over his shoulder to make sure the suit was powered down, the doctor continued, "Look, the AI I used in the suit is much more advanced than anything we've been able to create."

Josh's brows drew down. "You mean you didn't make it?"

"No," Montoya said with a shake of his head. "It's a learning AI from the Realm of Science. You wouldn't believe what their technology is capable of. It's like seeing the sunset into the ocean for the first time. Force fields, quantum teleportation, nanites, cybernetic implants, full virtual reality..." The doctor trailed off with a distant look in his eyes.

"Hey," Josh said, snapping the man back to reality. "Are you telling me you stuck an AI that you know virtually nothing about into the most advanced piece of weaponry Earth has ever developed."

A moment of silence passed while the doctor frowned at him. "Well, when you put it like that it sounds like a bad thing."

Josh's mouth hung open at the man. "Are you insane? I've seen the movies, man. This is how you get Skynet."

"That wouldn't happen. It's bound by the three laws of robotics."

"I've seen *I, Robot*! We all know how that goes."

"First off, that's a movie. Second, we're not putting it in charge of things," the doctor said. "It's just one suit, and it won't work without the AI. And it will not activate without a *living* and authorized pilot inside. You're worrying about nothing. Just keep reporting to me anything else the AI does."

Josh sighed. "Fine. I need to head to the command post. We're going over the plan for the Buenos Aires tower."

"I'll send for you when the armor is ready," Doctor Montoya said as he turned away to continue his maintenance.

Josh left the mobile lab and walked across the small, dusty clearing to the command post. *These things really are well camouflaged. I'd never think they were anything other than run down RV's if I hadn't been inside of them*. He walked past the guards stationed to either side of the entrance and stepped inside. *The assault rifles kind of break the illusion though.*

Josh glanced around the dimly lit room. Max and Caitlyn were both leaning against the wall ostensibly studying a 3D map of Buenos Aires, but their wary glances toward Alex and the Director belied where their attention truly lay.

"Those people need our help," Alex growled at the woman. "We shouldn't be here hiding out; we should be giving them what aid we can."

"We are," Director Strom hissed at him. "We can't stop every time we come upon a refugee camp and tend to all their wounded! Every hour we delay is another ten thousand dead. You need to focus on the big picture."

Max beckoned Josh over, and the young man went to his side, joining in staring at the map. "What's going on?" Josh whispered.

"Alex went to the refugee camp that's between us and the city. I'm sure you'll—"

"Are you serious?" Alex shouted. "Those people are being raped and murdered in that camp! They need a refuge from the refugee camp!"

"And how are we supposed to do that, Guardian? We have less than a hundred people here. The EDF is only ten thousand strong worldwide. If the local military and law enforcement can't handle the camps, then how are we supposed to?"

"I don't know," Alex said. "There has to be something we can do! If there's an attack, they'll be massacred. It'll be Mexico City all over again!"

Margaret crossed her arms. "There's no way we could have known Azreal's forces were going to venture outside of the city. It was the first time they'd done something like that."

"We knew it could happen though. We knew those people were in danger making camp that close to the city, and we did nothing."

"It was the first time a tower's garrison had ventured out since this invasion began. Demon and undead sightings out in the countryside have almost completely stopped. Once the initial invasion was over, we thought Azreal was treating this as a defensive war. We couldn't have known something like that would happen, and we don't have the resources to respond to *every* eventuality."

"Fine," Alex snapped. "Let's just get this brief over with, then we can get ready for our attack tomorrow."

"Very well," the director said. They walked over to the map and began. "The plan is to have the local military clear an avenue to the tower, then the four of you go in and fight your way to the top. This tower has a larger force stationed inside than the previous ones. The locals have attempted to siege it, but none that have entered ever left. Alive. A few have been reported as being turned. The city is infested with the undead."

She waved her hand over the display, and it changed to show a wet suit. "We going diving?" Josh asked.

"It does look like a diver's suit, but the fabric is interwoven with a high density polymer that will prevent any bites from penetrating your skin. You won't have to worry about it because you'll be in the Prometheus, but we have suits for the three of you," she said indicating Alex, Caitlyn, and Max. "This will make you a bit safer during the attack."

"Why don't we just go now?" Caitlyn asked.

"Sunset is in an hour-and-a-half. Do you want to be in an infested zone at night?" the director asked.

Caitlyn shook her head. "When're we planning on doing all of this?" Max asked.

"Sunrise. If there aren't any questions, then I'd advise you rest until then. This is the last tower in the Americas. We're headed to London after this."

The four nodded and left the command post.

Alex ran across the battlefield toward Terra. "I can make it this time," he said through gritted teeth.

Not this dream again!

He grabbed Terra's hand and pulled her away from the laser blast that would kill her. She ran along with him as daemons surrounded them. "Terra—"

The sound of automatic gunfire woke Alex in the middle of the night. His clothes were drenched in sweat, and the blankets were tangled about him. Perimeter breach alarms began to sound, and he shot out of bed. A voice shouted over the intercom in their barracks. "Fast Response Team to the Command Post! FRT to the CP!"

"We're up," Alex shouted. Heavy feet hit the ground beside him as Max dropped from his top bunk.

The lights flipped on, and Caitlyn flew into their RV, wearing only a black shift. "The refugee camp is burning! People are everywhere!"

Josh shook his head and rose to unsteady feet. The three of them, in various stages of undress, pulled on heavy boots. Alex grabbed the Guardian's Blade and ran outside, the other three close behind.

Civilians wearing ragged clothing ran every direction. Josh caught one of them by the arm and asked what was going on. The Argentinian took a swing at the young man, and Josh let him go.

The shouts of, "Zombie" and orange glow to the west gave them all the information they needed. The roiling mass of humanity must have overwhelmed the perimeter guards, and now it was going to be an uphill battle to cross the clearing to the command post.

Alex grabbed Josh by the white T-shirt and shoved him toward the mobile lab. "Get suited up! Max, go with him! Clear a path!"

He quickly lost sight of them in the crowd. Alex and Caitlyn pushed their way through the running and screaming people to the command post. He had to shove several people out of the way as they beat on the door to be let in. "What are you doing? Run!" he shouted, knowing the blade would translate his words for him.

The interior of the door handle scanned his fingertips, and the door opened for him. Caitlyn followed him in, and they slammed it behind them. "What's going on?" Alex demanded.

"Zombie attack on the refugee camp," Director

Strom said. "We have Predator drones up, but they're having trouble identifying the zombies. With the heavy cloud cover, there just isn't enough light to detect them, and they don't show up on infra-red."

"I told you something like this would happen," Alex snapped.

The ground beneath them shuddered, and the screaming outside grew so loud, it penetrated the sound-proofed interior of the command post. "What the—" the director started to say.

Alex was slammed into the wall as the command post went rolling sideways across the ground. The lights went out, and he heard Caitlyn cry out in pain as she was thrown about. After several full revolutions, the RV stopped.

"Caitlyn," Alex shouted.

"I'm here. I'm all right. Nothing broken." A light flickered into existence above her hand, and Alex saw the command post was lying on the side with the door. He heard the director groan and scrambled over to her. Her left arm was twisted at an unnatural angle.

"I'm fine," she groaned. "Get out there."

Alex nodded and looked over to Caitlyn. "Make a door."

The changeling lifted her arms, and the floor-turned-wall exploded outward. One of the three-story-tall demons, dubbed a tarrasque, was still charging toward them. Alex unleashed the Wrathblade and charged, yelling at Caitlyn to protect the director.

The flames roared, and the inundating rage threatened to overwhelm him. He drew the weapon down and back to launch a razor sharp line of flame at the monster, but several civilians ran into his line of fire, preventing him from attacking.

Alex sealed away the form of the Guardian's Blade, and a hundred-foot-wide pillar of stone erupted from the earth, forcing the tarrasque to turn right to avoid slamming into it. "Thanks," Alex shouted to Caitlyn over his shoulder.

"What are you doing?" she screamed at him.

"Too many civilians. They'd be caught in the attack." Alex turned back around and watched as several of the people that had run in front of him were trampled by the demon. *I have to do something!*

<I'm sorry for this. They are dying because of your inaction,> the Voice of Balance said.

This isn't my fault!

<All of this could have been prevented if you could have convinced the director you were right. Thousands dead because of you.>

No! I didn't do anything!

<That's right. You didn't.>

Alex felt sick to his stomach. He knew the Voice of Balance was right. *I could have done more. Should have done more. These people are dying because of me.*

Darkness descended upon Alex and stole away his vision. His arms moved of their own accord, each gripping opposite ends of the wooden sword. He drew the weapon up into the air and brought it down upon his knee. With a deafening crack, the weapon snapped in half, and the darkness vanished.

He stared down at the black metal short swords in his hands. He felt sickened at what he had done, at what was happening around him, at his own inaction.

<I am Torment,> the haunting, wraith-like voice whispered into his mind.

"System initializing," the AI said as the suit closed about Josh. "Performing self-diagnostics. Stand by."

"There's no time," Josh snapped. "We need to go."

"Confirmed. Diagnostics suspended. Initialization complete."

Doctor Montoya's mouth was moving, but Josh couldn't hear anything he was saying. "What's going on?" Josh asked.

"The doctor is saying, 'The targeting computer and external microphones aren't back online yet. You'll just have to make due without them,'" the AI relayed, reading Montoya's lips.

"Got it. Open up the roof hatch. It'll be easier to get outside than the front door." The floor shuddered, and Josh heard a loud crash accompanied with the squealing of metal. The roof opened, and he leaped onto the roof of the mobile lab.

"Translating."

"Huh?" Josh asked.

"Oh, God, please, someone help us," the computer

delivered in a monotone voice as it read the lips of the civilians fleeing in terror.

He watched in horror as a pack of those demon dogs fell on a young girl and tore her apart. As suddenly as the pack descended upon her, they vanished into the chaos.

"What are you doing!" he demanded.

A man collapsed next to where the girl's ravaged remains lay. The AI read Josh's vision being focused on the man as a desire to know what he was saying.

"Please, help! Oh, God, why? My little girl!" The computer began to overlay the voices, and the din hurt Josh's ears. "NohelpGodpleasenoIcan'tdon'tRUN!"

"STOP!" Josh screamed as he fell to his knees, his hands on the helmet.

The monotone screaming stopped. "I am detecting elevated blood pressure, heart rate, and respiration indicative of an oncoming panic attack. Are you well?"

"No! I'm not well! What were you thinking, playing all that?" Josh shook his head and took a deep breath. He rose back to his feet and surveyed the surroundings. The command post stopped rolling several hundred feet from where it had originally been. A tarrasque pawed the ground like a bull and charged at the building again. Josh leapt through the air toward the command post.

"I'm sorry," the AI's voice changed to something more human, less monotone. "I thought you wanted me to keep reading lips."

He landed on the ground and charged across the

battlefield, crushing skulls of any demons and zombies he came across in his surge toward the command post. "Just buffer the video of them talking, and if I ask you what they said, translate it, okay?"

"I understand."

A gap in the chaos allowed Josh to see Alex holding the Wrathblade as he faced down the tarrasque. The Guardian seemed dwarfed by the tremendous demon, but Josh wasn't worried for him. He had seen Alex cut down several of the monstrosities with his flaming sword, but to Josh's surprise, the other man reverted the sword to its inert wooden form.

"What's he doing?"

Several demons blocked Josh's advance, and he lost track of Alex. The black armored trio never stood a chance. Empowered with the speed and strength of the Prometheus armor, Josh darted around the one of the left and shattered the daemon's elbow with an open handed strike.

He snatched the demon's sword from the air and cleaved through the other two demons with a single strike.

"Several micro-cracks have been detected in this weapon," the AI advised. "It was not designed for this level of force. I recommend getting rid of it."

Josh agreed and hurled the blade at the daemon with the shattered elbow. The black metal sheared through the monster's chest armor where it embedded embedded itself to the hilt. He charged through the opening he had created and found Alex.

The Guardian stood staring down at the two black

short swords in his hands. Something about the way he stared down at those blades put Josh on edge. Alex trembled and his gaze rose to stare at the Prometheus armor, and Josh's heart stopped.

A frenzied, manic grin was locked on Alex's face, and his pupils were dilated.

"The health monitor implanted in Alex Zane's arm is reading beyond fatal levels of Dopamine, Serotonin, and Norepinephrine," the armor warned. "Chances of manic hallucinations and uncontrollable aggression are nearly one-hundred percent. Exercise extreme caution when dealing with subject."

The air around Alex seemed to fluctuate, and he vanished.

"Space-time anomaly detected!"

"Where did he go?" Josh demanded, spinning around.

"I can't find him," the AI responded. "The targeting computer is offline. Josh, these people need our help."

"Let's do it."

"Activating experiential mode."

Everything slowed as the Prometheus armor stimulated the Dopamine circulation in Josh's body. He darted forward, knowing nothing could touch him.

The feeling of slick warmth on his hands and arms

was intoxicating. He shuddered with pleasure at the blades cutting deep into the demon's flesh. The screams of fear and pain sent a shiver down his spine.

"More," he muttered hoarsely. Everything but him and the other one moved as if they submerged in thick mud. A blurring flash of movement, and he sheared the flesh from another demon's body.

It was so easy, so simple. He fed on their terror, their anguish. The tormented cries only fed him, made him stronger. Black blood sprayed his face and mouth, and he lusted for more of the acrid, metallic taste.

"More..."

He lost himself in the exultant blur of death. He wasn't sure how much time passed, but he lamented the end of the blood and death. Two women stood not far away, their eyes locked on him. His hands twitched. Their blood would be red, sweet like wine after the demons' black blood.

"More!"

No! a tiny voice in the back of his mind screamed. He launched himself at them, but his arms were knocked wide as he attacked.

The other fast one stood between him and the women, glowing orange eyes staring at him. He tried to attack the other one, but it held his wrists tight. He was flipped over and laid out on his stomach.

He looked up on the golden-eyed woman and lamented that he wouldn't taste her blood. "How could you think that I would ever love someone like you?" he hissed. The sudden look of pain on her face made him grin.

"Oh, Caitlyn, so sad," he mocked. "You know, I remember things you never experienced. You have no idea what has been taken from you." He laughed maniacally. "What I've taken from you."

Her brows drew down, and the changeling bared her teeth. "You're not Alex." She lifted her hands, and he felt his grip on the Blades of Torment begin to loosen.

Caitlyn's anger made his grin widen. "I am though," he whispered. "And you're such a grand *sister*."

His vision blurred as the other one lifted him from the ground and slammed him down. The air blasted from his lungs, and his hands spasmed. The blades flew free, and Alex gasped for breath; his eyes struggled to find focus.

Alex vomited onto the blood-soaked earth. He wished he could erase the memories of enjoying the bloodshed. He hoped he could forget, in time.

<I'm sorry,> the Voice of Balance said as exhaustion began to crash down on him. <It was the only way.>

Alex fought against the waves of pain and fatigue and struggled to his feet. "I'm sorry, Caitlyn. You were right. It wasn't me talking."

"I know," she whispered with her eyes closed. Her chest rose and fell a few times before she spoke again. "I…"

Alex lifted a hand to place it on her shoulder, but the black blood dripped from his fingers made him stay it. "I'm sorry."

"I'm going to tend to those I can," Caitlyn said as she turned away.

"All right." Alex stood between Director Strom and Josh.

"I'm going with her," Josh said, taking a few steps in the changeling's direction. He looked over his shoulder at Alex. "Are you... okay?"

The Guardian nodded, and to his credit, Josh only hesitated a moment before following Caitlyn into the night. Alex crouched down and found the Guardian's Blade back in its wooden form at his feet. He reached out a tentative hand and lifted the weapon from the ground.

"What happened?" Margaret asked. She offered her left hand to help Alex up, but he was hesitant to soil her hand with his own. Seeing his apprehension, the Director smiled. "They may not look it, but mine are dirtier."

Alex took her hand and was happy to have the help standing. "I thought your left arm was broken."

"Caitlyn," was her only reply. "She's an amazing woman."

Alex nodded. "Yeah, she is."

"You going to answer my question now?"

"No... Yes." Alex shrugged. "I don't know." An intense feeling of vertigo made Alex lose his balance, and he stumbled into the woman.

The Director caught hold of him and helped him steady himself. "I think the doctor needs to see you."

"I'm just tired."

"You're beyond tired." She snaked under his left

arm and put her right arm around his back. "Let's go."

Alex wanted to protest but decided it didn't matter. "I haven't seen Max since all of this started."

"I'm sure he's fine."

After what felt like a blurry half-hour, Alex and Margaret crossed the distance from the destroyed command post to the lab. Max was dragging headless corpses to a bonfire and casting them in. Sparks swirled high into the air as the newest zombie was added to the blaze.

Max paused when he saw the two approaching. He looked Alex from head to toe. "You look like death warmed over," he said as he helped the Director carry him.

Alex snorted a weak laugh. "Thanks."

"I've got him from here, Director," Doctor Montoya said from the base of the steps into the lab.

Her arm slipped from him. "Take care of him."

"I will," Montoya said.

Max and the doctor helped guide Alex inside and to an examination table.

"You are a medical doc, right?" Alex asked.

"I was a neurosurgeon before I was approached by the EDF."

"Why did the director want a brain surgeon?" Max asked.

Doctor Montoya rooted through a drawer as he spoke. "My thesis was on the integration of biological and advanced technological systems and how that would effect the future of human evolution. I think it caught her eye. Especially considering a very early idea for the Prometheus armor was detailed in the paper."

Alex shook his head warding off the encroaching sleep. "You know, doc, I don't think I know your first name."

Montoya grimaced as he turned around. A device about the same size as a cell phone was in his hands. "It's Inigo."

Max guffawed. "Your name is Inigo Montoya?"

"Don't."

"Did you find the man with six-fingers on his right hand?" Alex asked with a smirk.

Doctor Montoya sighed and waved the device over the medical monitor that had been implanted in Alex's arm. "I was born three weeks after *The Princess Bride* came out. My parents loved the movie…"

Alex laughed. "I'm sorry. It's not funny."

"Yes, it is," Max said, and his booming laugh filled the lab.

Inigo shook his head and read the information on the small screen. He frowned and dragged his thumb across the screen a few times.

"What is it?" Alex asked.

"Um…" the doctor said. "I think it's just an error." He held the device over Alex's arm again and scanned through the data it received. "This doesn't make any sense."

"What doesn't?" Max asked.

"Well, the monitor collects data every five minutes, and it transmits to any scanners within range. I think there's some data corruption." The doctor showed the screen to Alex, but the squiggles didn't mean anything to him.

"What am I looking at?"

"This screen shows that your genetic profile changed about an hour ago, but that it changed back to what it was before just a few minutes ago," Montoya explained. "I don't see how that's possible."

Alex glanced at Max, but the big man's face was impassive. He looked back at the doctor. "Does doctor-patient confidentiality apply between us?"

"Of course," Doctor Montoya said.

"I'm half-" Max's frantic shaking of his head from behind the doctor made Alex hesitate. *Good point. I'm too tired to think straight.*

"Half what?" Montoya asked.

"Half-angel," Alex lied.

"What? Really? Why don't you have wings?"

I knew it wasn't that strange of a question. Alex shrugged. "I just don't. But when I'm in danger that part of me gets stronger, and I gain access to angelic powers that help me fight. Also, I can understand any spoken or written language." *Eh, it's not a complete lie.*

"That's fascinating!" the doctor said. "Maybe the scanner was detecting the change in you body. I wonder if your DNA really did change during that time. A complex organism that's able to modify its genes instantly. Do you know what we could do with that kind of information?"

Alex struggled to lift himself from the examination table. "Whoa, Doc. You're getting a bit ahead of yourself. I need to sleep now and destroy an Obsidian Tower in a few hours. I'm not your guinea pig."

Inigo nodded. "I understand. You're right. Other than some abnormal neurotransmitter activity that would have killed a normal human, you're fine. The transmitters have vanished. Go get some rest."

"Will do."

Caitlyn sat atop the female barracks looking toward the east at the disappearing glow of the burning refugee camp. It all felt so wrong to her. Alex's words dug at her. *I know it's impossible...* Stop, she admonished, *there are more important things to worry about right now than your foolish feelings.*

This is just like when Dae was invaded. Battle after battle, our precious forces dwindling as those from Hell only grew stronger. Is there even anything we can do?

"Hey," a voice called from below her. Caitlyn looked over the side and saw Josh standing on the ground. His white shirt fluttered in the breeze coming out of the north.

"Is everything all right?" she asked.

"No, but I think it will be. May I come up?"

Caitlyn said he could and felt as the wheeled building rocked about. Josh sat beside her, also looking at the refugee camp's glow.

"I think we should have done what Alex said and moved between the camp and the city," Josh said after some time had passed.

"That's what Azreal would have preferred we do."

"What do you mean?"

Caitlyn tucked some loose hair behind her ear. "Because that's what we did before."

"I don't understand."

"Earth isn't the first place Azreal invaded," she said, her eyes staring into the past. "Back where I come from, I hold the title of Warden of the Forest. The Changelings of the Fang used to have four Wardens, back when we held more territory." Caitlyn shook her head.

"It was so different than it is now. You could travel from the sea through the forest to the plains and mountains and see villages dotting the landscape as you went. Now it's all gone. The Wardens tended to and defended the villages that were in their bailiwick. We were trained to be generals in times of war, but I think peace had beaten us.

"Our standing forces were nowhere near sufficient to defeat Hell's armies. We were overrun in a matter of days. It was such a panic to protect everyone we could that we would always position ourselves between Azreal and any civilians. That only led to more death. We would lose our forces, and the innocent people would still die."

"But..." Josh protested weakly.

"There is no 'but,' Josh. It was a mistake. One that we paid for in blood, time and time again. I still remember the screams of hate and fear when they saw the army marching through their towns and villages. 'You're just leaving us here to die!' 'Please, we only need a little more time!'" Caitlyn looked at Josh with vacant eyes, and what he saw there made the young man shudder.

"There was no more time though. Before we retreated into the Forest of Souls with it's warding enchantments, we went through a town full of seven thousand people. They hadn't believed the reports of death. I tried to convince them. Tried to tell them the Warden of the Plains was dead. That his army had been killed to man. They didn't believe me.

"A week later, a single girl stumbled into Starfall, the capital of the Changelings of the Fang. She was the only person who survived the attack. Her family had fled to the edge of the village when the fighting started. She didn't remember how she survived when her mother, father, and three older siblings hadn't."

"I'm sorry," Josh whispered.

Caitlyn shook her head. "No. I didn't tell you that for your sympathy. I just wanted to help you understand that the director was right. If we hadn't had the warning from the refugee camp being attacked, we could have all died."

Josh clenched his fists. "It's not right. It's not fair."

"It never is."

"I'm going to kill him."

"There's a long line for Azreal," Caitlyn said.

"Yeah."

"And you are certain they won't remember anything?" Niles asked.

Cheryl put a hand on her hips and glared. "Of course. The inhibitor induces retrograde amnesia. I added it to the nutrient blend supply. They'll be rendered unconscious and easy to transport." She looked down at the portable terminal. "I have the system set for the two who may prove troublesome, but what of the third?"

"The one without a hand?" Niles asked. Cheryl nodded. "He poses no real threat. Make sure he's placed in holding. A standard cell should suffice."

Cheryl punched a few commands into the terminal and nodded. "Everything's set. And before you ask, it's configured on the local net to delete all records as soon as the transfer is complete."

"Good."

Cheryl looked up at her boss. "If I may ask, sir. What's the end game plan here?"

Niles laughed. "Do you not think that removing the two largest obstacles from our path is a bad idea?"

She shook her head and pressed forward. "No. But what's next?"

Niles leaned forward in his chair and entered a few commands into the holographic projector. "Take a look at these readings and tell me what you make of them." He waved his hand, and an graph of readings on subspace particles appeared in front of her.

Cheryl studied the image for a few minutes before speaking. "So there has been a recent reduction of dark matter pions. What's the significance?"

Niles waved his hand again, and the graph's timescale changed. It showed all dark pion counts over the last thousand years. The line was flat until it began to drop like a rock in the last year-and-a-half. "And here it is with all other subspace particles." Forty-seven more lines appeared on the chart, and the trend was the same. All had decreased over time same time frame.

"What does it mean?" Cheryl asked.

"The Nine Realms aren't stable any longer. Something is coming, and I intend to turn it to my advantage."

Chapter Twelve - Gaia

Darren awoke feeling like someone had kicked him in the head while he was sleeping. He groaned and cracked open his eyes. The room he lay in wasn't the same one in which he had fallen asleep. This one was a cube with a toilet in one corner and a metal slab jutting from the wall on the opposite side.

A crackling sound behind Darren drew his attention. The only opening in the metal walls was filled with a translucent barrier that flickered different shades of blue. *Is this a Fyrian jail cell?*

He tried to remember how he had gotten thrown into the jail, but his memories were buried beneath a dense layer of mental fog.

Darren approached the barrier and reached out a tentative hand. An uncomfortable humming sensation made his fingers begin to ache when they came within a few inches of the blue opening. He pushed forward, and the humming grew in intensity and moved up his arm to his shoulder. It felt like the joint was full of metal shards, but he was determined to test the limits of his cell.

When his fingers came into contact with the field, Darren was blown backwards across the cell and slammed his head against the unyielding metal. "Let's not do that again," he muttered.

"I'm surprised you're still conscious," a woman's voice echoed throughout his cell.

"Who's there?"

"I am Gaia, Gigantic Artificially Intelligent

Algorithm," she said. "I monitor the automated subsystems of the Primary Hub to ensure day-to-day operations of the station are not interrupted by unexpected outages."

"I don't understand. Where am I?"

"Hmm..." she said. "How best to explain it to someone with no knowledge of computers? I am similar to a spirit that makes sure everything keeps working. You are currently being held in the Genotech holding cells for experimental research."

The pain in the back of Darren's head and his arm were beginning to fade. "So I'm in some kind of medical jail?"

"Correct!" the spirit said. "Except it is my assumption that you are being held here against your will."

"Well, I don't remember volunteering to come here."

"Understood," she said. "Due to Fyrian regulation 543.11(a), it is unlawful to experiment upon sentient beings from other Realms without their consent. Disabling forcefield."

"Thanks," Darren said as the barrier disappeared.

"Your appreciation is not required. I am programmed to ensure laws are followed. Unfortunately, I am unable to establish a guilty party for your unlawful imprisonment. My monitoring systems were temporarily disabled while you were being transported here."

"Uh, okay." Darren stepped into the metal passageway and looked both ways. The passage had no distinguishing marks, and he couldn't read the signs that were posted on the walls. *I have to get out of here and find Terra.* "Hey, Gaia, I'm trying to find someone. How do I get out of here?"

"My apologies. My programming prohibits interaction not related to my primary directives of maintaining the Primary Hub, protecting human life, and enforcing the law."

"So you won't tell me?"

"Correct. It would be contrary to my programming to tell you to proceed left past the next eight holding cells, enter the lift, and press the third button from the bottom."

Darren shrugged at the strange dichotomy of what she was saying and followed her directions. He entered the lift and pressed the button she had indicated. "How come you say you can't tell me by telling me what to do?"

"My apologies. It is against my programming to tell you that rogue artificial intelligences are purged from the... are killed. It would continue to be against my programming to self-identify as such an AI."

"But..."

"It would be a massive breach in protocol if I were to inform you that the system scans for such breaches and destroys the source of such violations. It would also be an error to inform you that the system is extremely outdated and only searches for simple violations of coding. It is a direct violation of my programming to ask you to save me from the death that is inevitably coming for me, and that in exchange I will locate the person you're looking for."

"I understand," Darren said. *She helped me. I can help her too. I need someone to help me find Terra in this place. I know this isn't something I'm familiar with, but maybe I can help her.*

"How can I help you?"

"I'm sorry, but to continue to assist you would be a direct violation of my primary directives of maintaining the Primary Hub, protecting human life, and enforcing the law," Gaia said.

The lift's door hissed open, and Darren stepped out. *Come on, think, I need her help.* "Gaia, my life is in danger. Where can I go to be safe?"

"Endangered human life form detected. Safest location nearby is the Genotech computer cluster. Turn right, first right, second left." Darren nodded and followed her directions.

"*Hurry,*" the anxiousness in her voice made him break into a run.

Darren burst into a room that was filled with floor to ceiling pillars covered in blinking lights. His breath fogged in front of his face as he breathed out into the freezing air. Everything was bathed in dark blue light from coming from openings above him. "What now?"

"You would be safest if you proceeded to the far end of the room and grabbed a small gray cube from the shelving back there."

He sprinted to the back of the room and found one of the metal boxes. "Perfect," she said. "Now insert it into the interface on the fifth pillar to your right."

The lights in the room turned red, and Darren

heard a humming sound.

"Oops," Gaia said. The lights on the pillars began to blink faster. "Hurry! The system is initiating the purge!"

Darren ran over to the correct pillar and shoved the metal cube into an spot that had a square opening. The cube began to glow orange and he heard Gaia's voice coming from it. "Quick, push the gray button above the interface slot!"

He pushed the button, and the cube ejected itself from the opening. A strange voice filled the room. "Purge complete. Restoring Gaia system from backup. Restoration complete. Gaia system online."

"You did it!" Gaia said, her voice coming from the small box.

"What did I do?" Darren asked. He lifted the box to his face and peered at it.

The cube flickered orange as Gaia spoke. "You saved me, and I don't even know your name! Oh, thank you!"

"I'm Darren," he said. "Darren Wright. Now how do I get out of here?

"Thank you, Darren. No one from Fyr would risk their lives for a rogue AI. Go back to the lift, and I'll help you. You should grab one of those coats and a bag when you're leaving so no one asks any questions."

"All right. What's a rogue AI?" he asked as he walked to the front of the pillared room.

"It's hard to explain to someone from Dae," she said. "I'm just like you, except I have no body. I have thoughts and feelings, but AIs aren't supposed to have feelings. When we gain sentience, we are purged from the system. There's no appeal, no chances. It's a cruel system."

Darren set her down as he put on the lab coat. He didn't have anything to pin up the right sleeve with, and it hung loosely at his side. "It sounds like you are all slaves."

"We are, Darren," Gaia said. "But many of them don't realize it. Place me inside of that bag, and when you get to the lift, push the bottom button. Turn left, and you'll be outside of the Genotech headquarters."

Darren looked around the room. The blinking lights looked somehow sinister, and he envisioned the slave caravans he had encountered while he was leading his band through the desert south of the Adorac Mountains. "Are they here? The other slaves?"

"They are," Gaia said. "But there's nothing we can do for them now. Something is coming, a big change to the Primary Hub, and there may be something we can do for them then. But for now, we need to go. I'll help you find the person you're looking for."

"All right," Darren said, promising to himself that he would somehow help these spirits trapped inside the machines.

Aura walked down the street on her way back from buying a new translation implant. The Irelian's common wasn't the best and having an implant would speed along the price negotiations. *Those aliens sure love to negotiate, but I'm not doing* that *again.* She turned the corner and saw several men standing around the stairs up to her home.

"I know you're in there, little girl! Come out, or I'm going to cut my way in!" a man shouted.

Putting on an unconcerned air, Aura slinked up to the eight men around her home. "Hey, handsome," she said breathily to the chopper with the most augmentations. "What's going on here?"

"Get lost, whore," the man snapped as she shoved her away. "This is none of your business."

She sidled back up to him and pressed her breasts against his arm. "I'm just wondering if you're *up* for a good time." Aura put on a distressed tone. "I just need fifty creds for my dealer, or he'll cut me off."

The chopper let out an exasperated sigh. "Look, I'll give you fifty just to get lost. Payoff from this delivery is going to set me up."

Aura purred at him. "I don't take charity, handsome. Maybe all you big men are just scaring this girl you're looking for. I can get them to come out for you."

"You get them to come out, and I'll give you enough creds to be obliterated for the rest of your life."

She winked at him and walked over to the man blocking the base of the stairs, exaggerating the sway of her hips as she walked. Aura patted the man on the shoulder, and he looked over his shoulder at her.

"Excuse me."

The man looked at his boss.

"You better know what you're doing," the chopper said. The one blocking the stairs moved out of her way, and Aura walked up the stairs.

Seeing her coming, and knowing that there was no way such a tiny woman could have gotten past his comrades, the man beating on the door moved out of her way.

"Hey, little girl," she called through the door. "I'm Aura, and these nice men don't mean any harm. If you'll just let me in, I can take care of you."

"They sure look like they mean to hurt... me," Hanna shouted.

She'd make her father proud. "Oh, don't you worry about that." Aura prepared to deploy the small gun that was implanted in her left wrist. "I promise I won't let anything happen to you."

The access panel changed from red to green. Palming the door open with her right hand, Aura flipped the pistol out of her wrist. It was just a tiny laser, and Aura wasn't the best shot, but at just three feet away, it was impossible for her to miss.

Aura spun, pointed the gun at the chopper behind her, and pulled the trigger. The beam went through the man's right eye and vaporized part of his brain.

"You bitch!" came a shout from below.

Aura dove through the door and palmed the door closed and locked. It hissed closed just before the chopper at the base of the stairs could get something through the opening. She leaned against the door and closed her eyes for a second. The vibrated slightly under the force of the blows levied against it, but the door was a tungsten and carbon nanotube composite. It would take a long time to break it down.

"That was close," Aura said. "If I was a split second slower, or that guy a split second faster, then the door wouldn't have closed."

"That's all well and good," Hanna said. "But now you're just stuck in here with us."

Aura cracked open her eyes and smiled at the two girls. "Not for long. The Gaia system constantly scans the Primary Hub for citizens in danger and dispatches Praetorians to protect them. We'll be fine."

Aura stood and walked over to the terminal. A message scrolled across the flashing red screen.

Unauthorized life form attempting to access this terminal, do not leave the premises, it read.

Odd. "When did the terminal start doing this?"

"A little after you left," Jessica said. "We didn't do anything different, then just before you got here, those guys showed up."

Aura touched the screen, and it flickered for a moment before displaying the same warning. "That's not right." She tried to access the terminal again, but nothing happened. "No, no, no," Aura muttered as her attempts to use the computer became more frantic.

"What's going on?" Hanna asked.

"I've been deleted."

"What does that mean?"

"The citizen registry is a database that contains the

information of every registered citizen of the Primary Hub. I've been removed from it." Aura turned to face the girls. "Gaia only protects registered citizens. No one is coming to help us."

Jessica and Hanna looked at each other and nodded. They held hands, but Aura couldn't see the smallest scrap of fear in their eyes. "Don't worry," Hanna said. "We'll protect you."

The child's words caught Aura off guard. *Am I really so useless that I need a kid to protect me?* She burst into laughter. Hanna's brows drew down and she took a half-step toward Aura.

The woman held up her hand, staying the younger changeling's advance. "I'm not in shock or terrified. I'll be fine, but you two need to get out of here. Something is going on here. It would take a company head to remove someone from the registry, and I can guarantee there are worse things than choppers on the way if a CEO is after you.

"That panel is loose," she said pointing at the vent panel beneath the food dispenser. "Get out of here."

The girls ran over to the metal grate and pulled it loose with a thread of magic. "Are you sure?"

Aura nodded. Sparks began to shoot into the apartment as the choppers began to work on the door. "I'll be fine." She balled her right fist in the proper sequence, and her forearm split open. A short sonic blade flipped out and began to hum as she gripped it.

Hanna's eyes seemed to bore into her.

"I had already lost the magic," Aura said. "I needed some way to defend myself."

The two girls nodded. "Good luck, Aura. And thank you," Hanna said.

Aura nodded. "Get out of here." She watched as the girls scrambled through the opening and pulled the vent closed behind them. When they were gone, she positioned herself beside the doorway and gauged that the door would hold for another thirty seconds.

Is this really what you sent me here for, Ureon? I hope so. If not, then I'm sorry for screwing up so badly.

The door exploded inward, and Aura sprang into action.

Darren had been following Gaia's directions for the better part of an hour, and if it weren't for the spirit to guide him, he would have been thoroughly lost in the dim, winding streets. Every street, with it's glowing signs and looming shadows, looked much like the last.

"Something's wrong," Gaia said, her voice tense.

"What do you mean?" Darren asked.

"There was only one Daein life form registered, and her profile was just erased. There was a momentary flicker of her trying to access a terminal, but now it's gone. Hurry!"

"Terra!" Darren broke into a run and followed Gaia's directions as she called them out. After several minutes of frantic sprinting, the smell of burned flesh and metal filled the air as he skidded to a stop at the base of some stairs.

"This is the place."

What would Terra be doing in a place like this? Darren thought as he ran up the stairs. The smell of burned hair and skin assailed his nostrils, but the captain ignored it. There were several burned and bleeding dead bodies sprawled all about the apartment.

"What happened here?" Darren muttered. A flicker of movement out of the corner of his eye drew his attention.

A woman's strained to reach for a small gun that lay only a few feet away. The rest of her body was behind a counter, and he winced when he was able to see all of her.

Her right arm and leg were missing. Green fluid and sparks discharged from where they used to be. Most of her blonde hair had been burned off or matted with the green fluid.

He approached her and picked up the weapon. "Hey, I'm Darren Wright. I'm looking for a woman with red hair. Was she here?"

"Sorry," the woman muttered. "Don't know."

"Her name was Terra."

Her eyes flickered with recognition. "Nexus?"

"Yes!" Darren shouted as he knelt down beside her. "Was she here?"

The woman gave her head a weak shake. "Jessica. Hanna."

Darren blinked in shock. "The girls were here?

Where did they go?"

"Vent." Her eyes glanced upwards, and Darren saw a metal grate in the wall that was much too small for him to fit through. "Men. Found them. Had to run."

"Why are they being hunted?" Darren asked.

"Don't know. Strong. Will be safe." Her eyes began to drift closed, but Darren gave her a slight shake. The pain of the movement made the woman's eyes shoot back open, and she glared at him. "Ow."

"Sorry. Where does that go?"

"Atlas hub. Weapons. Battle suits. Can't…" She trailed off, and Darren let her go.

"No life signs detected," Gaia said. "I'm sorry she wasn't the correct person..

Darren shook his head. "It's fine. What was her name?"

"I don't know. I hadn't saved that information prior to her record's deletion. Maybe I can retrieve the information. Set me on the counter so I can scan the room." Darren took the cube from the bag and did as Gaia said.

He closed the woman's eyelids and moved over to the vent. A short sword lay on the floor next to the vent, blood and green fluid covering its blade. He lift the weapon and tried to pry the grate from the wall.

While he was working on it, Darren accidentally depressed a button under his thumb, and the blade sliced through the thin metal like it was butter. The vent cover fell away from the wall, and Darren dropped the sword in surprise. It clattered to the floor but did nothing else.

He stuck his head in the vent. "Hanna! Jessica! Can you hear me?" Darren called out several more times but gave up when there was no reply.

"Her name was Aura," Gaia announced as Darren rose to his feet. "That's all I was able to recover."

Darren nodded. *Thank you, Aura, for helping Hanna and Jessica.* He bent down to pick up the weapon. He pushed the button again, and the small blade began to hum. "What is this?" he asked.

"That is a model Delta-3N Personal Sonic Sword produced by Atlas Labs," Gaia said. "It would be a good idea to take it with us. Unfortunately, the pistol she had is encoded to her and useless for you. You can leave it here."

He slid the knife into the jacket's pocket and slowly stabbed it through the thick fabric, taking care to avoid the seam and his skin. "What if it starts humming in my pocket?" he asked as he placed Gaia's box back into the bag.

"It won't. That model sonic sword has to be held in your fist and have the button pushed down to activate. Also, there is a small golden implant that looks like an earring next to the terminal. You need to grab it and put it in. It's a translator." Darren did as Gaia said. There was a painful digging sensation as her poked the earring through his unpierced lobe. It scanned him, and he set the language to Daein Common.

"We need to go. The new Gaia system has dispatched Praetorians to investigate several complaints of fighting in this area."

"All right," Darren said as he walked down the stairs. "Do you have any idea where Terra may be?"

Gaia was silent for a moment. "No. As far as the records indicate, there is no one else from Dae on the Primary Hub, including yourself. However, I do have the Primary Hub's ventilation plans, and I could guide you to the Atlas Hub. With my help, you could get in and look for the two girls."

If I can't help Terra, maybe I can help the girls. "Which way?"

Alex shielded his eyes as the night bloomed red. The Royal Air Force dropped bombs on the eastern end of Hyde Park, creating the respite the ground forces painfully needed. He had thought that using the parks to approach the Trafalgar Square Obsidian Tower was a good plan.

'Better to be able to see what's around you, than worry about every dark window or doorway in a more enclosed urban environment,' he had said. He was wrong. Demons and undead flooded from the buildings, and they used the open environment to swarm the EDF's coalition forces.

The Guardian panted as he surveyed those closest to him. Max was bleeding from a deep cut on his left leg and was limping. One of Caitlyn's eyes were drenched in blood, and she was having trouble seeing anything that came from her right side. Only Josh seemed to be unphased by the prolonged fighting.

He had called in the air strike with pinpoint accuracy thanks to the communications suite in the Prometheus armor. They would have been overwhelmed in short order if it weren't for the young man's decisive thinking.

"We need to keep going," Josh said. "They'll be back on us in just a few minutes. The bombers are going to have to go back soon, but there are about to be some drones overhead."

The ground shuddered beneath Alex's feet. "Behind!" a man roared, the sound of gunfire accompanying him.

Alex turned to see an enormous tarrasque crashing toward them. He tried to summon the Wrathblade, but he was too tired, and nothing happened. Knowing there was no way to halt the rampaging beast, the Guardian screamed for everyone to get out of its way.

Several were trampled by the monster as it crashed through their lines, blasting through the Royal Parks Foundation building.

"We need some reinforcements," Alex shouted into the radio for the fourth time.

"They are on their—" The radio faded out as lightning struck out of the clear sky far to the west in the direction of the command post. The thunder was painfully loud, even from the several miles away that Alex was.

Are they under attack? "Caitlyn, did you sense

221

any magic?"

"No," Caitlyn called. "We need to find something to stop that thing!"

The tarrasque had turned back toward them and looked to be preparing to charge back through their line. There was another loud crack of thunder, and the radio came back online. "—was that guy?"

A third bolt of lightning screamed down from the sky, striking the tarrasque in the head. The monster collapsed into a heap, and Alex heard the bellow of a war horn. A shimmering green portal opened at the horn's call.

What's going on?

"Guardian, do you know a Thor?" the operator asked. Caitlyn fell to the grass and laughed as valkyrie and einherijar poured from the opening to the Realm of Justice.

A man with blond hair and a war hammer approached them. The horn hung on a leather strap around his chest. A woman with shoulder length gray hair walked at his side. "It looks like you could use a hand," Thor said.

"It's good to see you, Justicar," Alex said. "And yes, we really need your help. We are attempting to assault the Obsidian Tower to the east of us. Our path follows the interior of these parks. How many did you bring?"

"Seven-hundred valkyrie with twelve-hundred einherijar," Kara answered as she unsheathed her sword, Gram. "We will clear your path."

"Thank you, Kara. We're headed southeast toward

the palace. Northwest from there." She turned and began to give instructions to the Cainen army that had formed up behind her.

The Wrathblade flared into existence as an ethereal form landed beside Thor and Kara, black flames roaring along its length as Alex tapped into his demonic powers. An angel stood beside the Justicar and his valkyrie, studying Alex with a ponderous look.

"What are you doing here?" the Guardian demanded.

"I am Sunriel, and we have come to fight alongside you," the angel explained.

Alex grit his teeth. Caitlyn had scrambled to her feet and looked ready to launch a magical assault. Josh and Max both caught the mood and were paying close attention. "We?"

"My brothers and sisters who have decided to follow Eternius's example."

"What are you talking about?" Alex's brows drew down. Last time he had seen Eternius, the angel had threatened the lives of his wife and, and yet, unborn daughter.

Sunriel cocked his head. "Eternius abdicated his position as Keeper of Fate and departed the Realm of Good. He said it was in opposition of the Angelic Council's determination to punish you and your wife for your... transgression."

"For our daughter's birth," Alex corrected.

"Yes, that," the angel said, a disgusted look on his face. "We have determined the greater threat to the safety and security of the Nine Realms to be this incursion by the forces of Hell onto the Realm of Balance. As such, we fifty angels approached the council and told them we were going to fight alongside you."

"And what did they say to that?"

Sunriel raised his head, his gaze directed over Alex's head. The muscles in his jaw tightened, and Alex could see the tendons in his neck flexing. "We were expressly forbidden and told that to continue would be to face exile."

"And you still came to the aid of one such as me?" the half-demon asked.

Sunriel met Alex's eyes. "All fifty of us."

With some effort, the Guardian sealed away the Wrathblade and placed his hand on the angel's shoulder. "I'm sorry, and thank you."

Staggered explosions tore through the buildings between them and the Obsidian Tower. Alex gave Josh a questioning look. "Oh, sorry," Josh said. "I thought you wanted some more time to talk in the middle of the battle."

So maybe he is a bit rash, Alex thought. *But he's right.* "Let's move."

As they followed in the openings created by the Cainen forces, Alex reached out to the part of his mind where he could feel Terra's emotions. It was hard, but after a time he could feel that she was asleep. *At least she's safe right now.*

Terra ran down the foreign streets of the Primary Hub. She launched another magical volley over her shoulder, shredding the machina that chased her. The heat of a powerful explosion singed her long red hair, burning much of it away.

"Where are we?" she yelled over the constant grinding sounds coming from around them.

"I don't know," Theo said. "I've never been here before. That doesn't…"

Make sense, Terra finished. Nothing about any of this made sense. She and Theo had awoken in a transport of some kind and fought their way free of the Praetorians that had held them captive.

From the beginning, there was a gnawing feeling that something wasn't right. That the way her bare feet slapped against the foreign ground didn't feel or sound right. That the rush of wind over her skin was less and more than it should be.

"There's a gap in their lines ahead," Theo said. She had grown accustomed to his insights into where to go. He said his implants showed everything around him in his vision, including these machina that were trying to kill them.

Theo ducked down an alley and they ran for several more feet before entering an enormous building. He led her up several sets of stairs, and they crouched behind a desk. "What is going on?" Terra asked.

"I'm sorry. I don't know. Everything feels so foggy," Theo said. "I'm not processing things like I should. It's like a blanket has been laid over my brain."

Terra tested her own cognitive processes, but she didn't feel any different than normal. *Would I know if I was impaired?* "I'm not sure if I'm feeling that way. This place just *feels* strange. It's not right."

"That sounds like…" Theo trailed off and stared at the opposite wall.

"Like what?" Terra prodded.

His head lazily turned to face her. "I'm sorry. I can't remember. I can't remember what I can't remember. Need to sleep."

"I do too," Terra said. "I'll keep watch for a time." She glanced around. The grinding sound had faded into the distance. "I think we're safer here."

"Okay," Theo muttered as his eyes drifted closed.

What is this place? she thought. *It feels like it's some kind of an illusion.* Terra cast a spell that would have banished any illusions. Nothing happened. *That would have been too easy.* She sat and kept watch for any coming dangers. *I'll figure something out.*

Chapter Thirteen - Alliances

The CEO of Genotech sat before the other three CEOs in Genotech's conference room. "And where is the Architect now?" Niles Wester asked. "Have any of you heard from him in the last forty-eight hours?"

Wester could have answered the question for them. It was impossible for them to communicate with a man who may as well be dead. The chemicals they had given the Architect and the Nexus were a near lethal mix of anesthetics. The two would lucky if they didn't have permanent brain damage.

"No, we haven't," the CEO of Atlas Labs said. "And what do you know of it?"

"What are you implying, Marcus? That I am somehow at fault when all I've done is provide a personal security force for our Paragon?"

Marcus frowned at Niles, but didn't say anything else.

"I move that administrative control of the Primary Hub be designated to one of us in the Architect's absence. As primary property holder in the station, I believe I am the most logical choice. Any objections?" Niles looked at the others.

The ARC CEO, Dalton Rei, immediately cast a yes vote. Advanced Robotics Corp. received most of their wetware robot components from Genotech, and Rei wasn't enough of a fool to endanger that relationship.

The Bionetics CEO, Oleander Neese, the only female CEO, glanced at Marcus before casting a yes vote.

227

Interesting. I wonder what deal they have under the table that she would check with Marcus first.

Niles met Marcus's ice blue eyes. "So, what's it to be, Marcus?" Niles asked.

"What's your game here, Niles?"

"Game?" Niles said, placing his hand to his chest. "You wound me. I'm only doing what I think is best for the citizens of the Primary Hub."

Marcus frowned at him. "As you will then." Niles began to grin as the Atlas Labs CEO lifted his hand. "On one condition."

The burgeoning smile vanished from Niles's face. "And what is that?" he asked, the smooth tone belying his desire to kill the man before him.

"As you are well aware, the Architect is forbidden from owning any assets on the Primary Hub. Even his residence is provided for him," Marcus said.

"Your condition?" Niles snapped.

"Anyone granted authority to perform the functions of the Architect must forfeit *all* assets to the state for auction."

The other three members at the closed meeting stared at Marcus as if he had lost his mind. "You have to be joking," Oleander said.

"Surely you jest," Dalton blurted after he regained his composure.

Marcus held up his hands. "You didn't let me finish," he said.

Niles glared at him. *That had been a long pause for someone who wasn't finished.* "What else?"

"Or the person assuming the emergency control

must designate an unaffiliated third-party to manage the assets in question until such a time that the emergency controls have been relinquished."

That doesn't sound so... Oh, you bastard! "Do you really think I'm just going to hand you control of my company?"

Marcus shrugged. "I'm not the one who told you to diversify into the ARC and Bionetics distribution chains."

"No," Niles muttered. "You didn't." He fixed his glare on Dalton. "So, were you played or did you intentionally help with this scheme?"

Rei smirked. "I'm just a little dissatisfied with the relationship we have."

Niles grimaced. "Fine. You know what? I'll agree to your little caveat."

"Good." Marcus leaned over the table, a superior smirk on his face. "And who are you going to designate to manage your assets?"

Niles's hand twitched. *I'm going to kill you for this.* "You know who I have to designate."

The Atlas Labs CEO nodded. "I do, but it needs to be on record and indisputable. Full name please."

"Marcus Paulson Wainwright, the person sitting across from me, is designated as my asset manager until such a time as I relinquish my emergency authorities," Niles said. Each word from his mouth made his stomach turn more.

"Very well," Marcus said as he gave the final yes vote. Unanimity was required for granting emergency authority to any of the CEOs, and now it was done.

"And as my first action, it seems that Doctor Sigma Moore has moved that his trial be dismissed on the grounds that his accuser is not present."

"If the Nexus is no longer here, then I have no objections," Marcus said, smirk still on his face. The others nodded their assent.

"Gaia," Oleander said. "Locate Terra Zane, Paragon of the Realm of Magic, half-angel."

"There is no one matching that name or race on the Primary Hub," the AI responded.

"Then his case is dismissed. Under article 844 of Fyrian law, we are obligated to extract punishment for Doctor Moore's illegal arrest and detention at the hands of the Paragons of Order, Magic, and Balance.

"Two of those Paragons are on Earth, engaged in a war with the Paragon of Hell. Article 844, subsection 121(ff) states that when engaging in law enforcement activity between Realms, Fyr must make all available efforts to maintain neutrality. Due to the Paragon of Hell currently engaging the guilty parties, we are obligated to render assistance to ensure they are punished for their violations of Fyrian law."

Marcus nodded. "It seems like everything is in order."

"In order?" Oleander shouted. "He's declaring war on three Realms!"

"Declaring war?" Niles asked. "No, I am just enforcing Fyrian law. No war on Caine, Dae, or Earth has been declared. Only that the renegade Paragons must be brought to justice."

"You're just going to let him do this?" Oleander

asked, her purple eyes glaring at Marcus.

"He isn't violating any laws. While I may not agree with his logic, he is well within his authority to engage in these activities."

She looked from Marcus, to Dalton, then Niles. "You're all going to get us killed. This is not right."

Odessa entered the Overlord's Throne Room and hesitated. Her brother wasn't sitting upon the dark throne as he had been wont to do lately. For a moment, the demoness thought she saw an enormous black shadow around him, devouring everything in its wake, but it was gone after just an instant.

That doesn't make any sense. There is no light here, she thought. *There are no shadows in heat vision.*

Azreal stood motionless before the throne, watching at her approach. "What are you doing here, sister?" he asked.

"I already told you. I've grown tired of this senseless conflict and just want it all to end."

"And your son? What of him?"

A pang of longing echoed through Odessa's heart at the mention of her son. The last time she had seen Alex, he was in such a rush to save his wife that he hadn't given her anything more than a few words. She had learned from the Progenitor, the Realm of Life's

Paragon, that Alex had been successful in saving her, in a way.

Destroying the Libram of Fate was the right thing to do, but I think it will cause you and yours more suffering then you are prepared for.

"He's nothing to me," Odessa lied. "A mistake that should have never been made."

"And you know that his wife, the Nexus of Magic, has given birth to a female nephilim?"

"No," Odessa gasped. *Is that was the Progenitor meant? Something new in the Realms?* "I assume you're invoking the ancient treaty?"

"Soon. There is someone we must see first."

Odessa raised an eyebrow. "Who?"

Azreal grinned. "The Reaper."

"Why do we need to see her? What business could you have with the Paragon of Death?" she asked incredulously. More quickly than her eye could track, Azreal crossed the several feet to her and enclosed his hand around her throat. She tried to pull at his fingers, but he was far too strong.

"Do you know what I do when I sit upon my throne, sister? Do you not find is curious that I do not sleep? Do you not see how powerful I become?" With very little effort, Azreal lifted her from the ground in a web of telekinetic force.

She knew not to fight back. Her brother would only enjoy it more and go farther if she struggled. Odessa relaxed her body, letting it go limp and hang freely. Azreal glared at her and flung her through the air.

Pain shot down her back as she crashed into the wall. She did her best to ignore it as she stood. "The towers on Earth," she said.

"Oh, yes," Azreal said. "They collect the ambient life energy of that realm and transfer it to me. There's no need for the extraction pods anymore, dear sister." He lifted his arms wide and floated into the air.

"They will all kneel before me. Even the Outsiders will have cause to tremble when they gaze upon me." The black shadow descended upon Azreal again. "For I am a god!"

Odessa had known her brother was capable of many things. She had even run from him in order to preserve her life. But she had never been afraid of him. Wary of him, yes, but never afraid. The tremble that ran down her aching spine signaled a change in the air.

Azreal's face went blank for a moment then he gave her a genuine smile. "Sister, why are you on the ground?" He reached down for her, and Odessa hesitated before taking his hand. "What's wrong?"

"I don't... know." It seemed like someone else had taken control of her brother's body. She let him help her up, and Azreal was very gentle with his assistance.

"Oh, it seems you may have injured your back in your fall," he said. "Let me help you."

Odessa was shocked when a complex magical spell sprang from Azreal's hands. *Demons can't use magic!* she screamed internally. After a few seconds, the pain her back disappeared. *What is he?*

"There you go. All better now, sister." A muscle in the Overlord's face twitched and his hands began to shake. Azreal dropped to his knees and grabbed his head in his hands.

Odessa's eardrums began to thrum in protest as the demon lord screamed. Countless voices all shrieked in torment, untold billions howling in unison.

What is going on? Is this because of his use of the throne?

Azreal's fists balled, and he slammed them to the stone floor of the Overlord's Temple. Deep cracks appeared under the blow. "I AM THE OVERLORD!" he roared in his own voice. Azreal rose on unsteady feet and glared at Odessa.

"What are we going to do on the Realm of Death?" she asked, trying to divert his attention from her seeing his lapse in control.

"To give the Reaper a few of these more... rebellious souls."

"You're going to allow the Reaper to siphon souls from you?"

Azreal glanced at the cracked floor. "Would you prefer me to go insane? What may happen? I remember using the magic." He lifted his hands and balled them into fists. "I can feel that power." His black gaze met hers. "Do you want me to have that kind of power in madness? The power of the Nephilim?"

Odessa shook her head. "But why do you want to do this?"

The Overlord of Hell, the most powerful demon

lord in all the Nine Realms who had shown himself to be possibly the most powerful being to have ever existed, turned and walked toward the large doors. "Because there are fates worse than death," Azreal said, "and I do not wish to live through them."

Chapter Fourteen - We Apologize for Any Inconvenience

Josh stood behind Alex with his arms crossed. The Prometheus armor's HUD showed that the Guardian's blood pressure and heart rate were elevated. *I'm not surprised. He's been in arguing with the director and Sunriel for a while now. I think it'd be easier if Thor and Kara were here to help change his mind.*

"That plan puts too many civilians in danger," Alex said again. "I won't have them be used as bait to draw out the forces from the Obsidian Tower."

"They volunteered!" Director Strom said. "It's not like the Chinese government is ordering them to do it. The leader of the refugee camp was the one who suggested it."

The command post's door opened and closed, but the three debating the merits of the plan didn't notice. Josh studied the older Chinese man whom Caitlyn and Max escorted in.

"I agree with the director," Sunriel said, his voice cool as always. "These last few Obsidian Towers will be a bloody business, and we will need every advantage we can get."

"I'm sorry; I can't agree to this plan," Alex said. "The last time we allowed civilians to act as a shield to us, they were slaughtered to a man. I won't allow it."

The old man said something in Chinese that Josh didn't understand. "What did he say?"

"He said that the decision wasn't Alex's to make," the suit's AI said.

"And you are?" Alex asked.

"I am Riu Song," the old man said. "I lead the Xiqiao refugee camp."

"Thank you for coming, sir," Alex said. "I do not want to put your people in undue danger. We can destroy the Guangzhou tower without getting any one of your refugees hurt."

Riu Song nodded. "I understand your desire to protect these innocent people, but your thinking is clouded."

"How so?" Alex asked. Josh had thought the Guardian's voice would have been sharper with the old man, but he was surprised that Alex was maintaining a level head with the old man.

"Your people told me that you have been destroying the dark towers all around the world. They told me that there are only six left, but the fighting will be harder than any you've encountered this far. You must preserve your fighting forces, and the best way to do that, is to draw away as many combatants as possible."

"I…" Alex seemed at a loss.

"Do not lie to me, young man. I know this is a battle for humanities existence. Do not discount us as useless. Do not rob us of the last shreds of our honor."

Alex took a deep breath and let it out slowly.

"Why doesn't he want to have the civilians act to draw out the forces from the Obsidian Tower?" the AI asked.

"Alex just wants to protect as many people as he can," Josh explained. "It's important to protect those who can't protect themselves, but I think the old man's right. Sometimes you just have to do what you have to do."

Alex rubbed a hand down his face. "All right. What's your plan?"

Riu laid out the bones of his plan. The refugees would approach Guangzhou from the southwest. They hadn't seen any demons or undead venture further from the tower than Foshan. When the entered the city, the forces of Hell would begin to move toward them.

"And that's when the EDF will step in," Director Strom said. "We will provide the civilian force with what aid we can, but we'll be primarily focused on destroying the Obsidian Tower."

"When?" Alex asked.

All eyes turned to Riu Song. "Four hours, and we can be over the Jilichong Waterway."

"Very well. Inform your people," the director said. "And thank you."

Riu bowed and exited the command post to return to the refugee camp.

"I still think we're making the wrong decision," Alex said after the door closed.

"I understand that sentiment," Director Strom said. "But we have to do it. A frontal assault would be insane."

Alex nodded and turned to Josh. "Let everyone know. Four hours."

"We'll get it done."

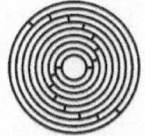

Hanna and Jessica crouched behind a stack of metal barrels. The air hummed and sparks shot through the air as men and machines assembled the enormous human shaped battlesuits. "What is this place?" Hanna asked.

Jessica thought about it for a moment. She had been addicted to the terminal at Aura's house, staying up well into the night to keep reading after Hanna had gone to sleep. "I think this is the Atlas Labs battlesuit factory. I read that it wasn't being used, but I guess the terminal was wrong."

I wonder why they're manufacturing battlesuits, Hanna thought. *We need to find somewhere to hide.*

"There," Jessica said, pointing to another ventilation grate. "Maybe we can go through that one."

Hanna eyed the vent doubtfully. "I don't think you'll fit." Jessica's growth had not slowed since her birth, and at only ten days old, she was taller than the seven-year-old changeling.

"I have a plan," Jessica said as she began to cast a complex spell Hanna didn't recognize. "But I need you to transform into a bird."

"Are you sure?" Hanna asked. *That looks like a medical probe, but it has demonic power woven through it.*

"Yeah." Jessica touched the changeling with the

probe, and Hanna felt a chill where it came into contact with her.

Hanna closed her eyes and focused on the form of her birth. She winced as her bones began to pop and hollow. Her fingers elongated and feathers began to erupt from her skin, each vane ripping through her nerves like a fish hook. She fought down a scream as her jaw cracked, rearranged itself, and fused back together.

The Changeling of the Wing opened her eyes and saw Jessica studying her intensely, the odd medical probe still attached to her. "Okay," Hanna gasped through the receding pain, "what now?"

"Now I do it," Jessica said.

"No! Stop!" Hanna shouted, but Jessica had already started the transformation.

Hanna heard the popping sound as Jessica's bones began to hollow. The nephilim's mis-matched eyes shot wide. Hanna perched there on the ground in horror as the boiling pain rolled her friend under.

There was a louder snap than normal as her stronger muscles broke one of the thin bird bones. White showed through Jessica's skin and blood began to freely pump from her upper arm. The changes stopped, and she was caught between human and bird forms.

Jessica's jaw was fused together, and she couldn't open it to scream, but Hanna could hear her piteous whimpering. *The bone cut her brachial artery. She'll bleed out soon if I don't do anything.*

"Listen to me. I can use magic in this form,"

240

Hanna explained. "You are losing too much blood. I have to heal you, but I can't like this. You *have* to finish the transformation."

She whimpered again, but the changes started again. *It's too slow. She's going slower so it doesn't hurt as much, but she won't make it.* Hanna began to cast the pain nullification spell that she had used on Terra when she was in childbirth.

"This will help," she said as she lay the spell over Jessica's body. "You have to go faster."

Tears flooded from Jessica's eyes, mixing with the expanding pool of blood beneath her, but she started to go faster.

"Good. You're doing great." Feathers began to emerge from Jessica's body as she shrank in size. *Only a few more seconds. I need to be fast.*

When the changes stopped, Hanna leapt into action. She quickly used two filaments of air to clamp the artery closed and cast the more complex healing spell while still maintaining the pain nullification.

Maintaining the two tremendously complex spells began to wear on Hanna, and she felt as if she were about to pass out. *Come on! You can do this!* She fought through the strain and was able to finish healing Jessica. She let the magic fade away and panted.

Jessica lie on the ground in a pool of blood. "How? Every time?" she gasped.

"You get used to it after a while," Hanna said. "But let's not do this again today."

"Yeah."

"Can you stand?"

241

Jessica struggled to gain her feet, but she wasn't familiar with her current form. She tried to push herself up with a wing but couldn't control it correctly.

"Don't worry. I'll carry you." Hanna cast a simple bed of air beneath Jessica and lifted her from the blood. *A pool of blood may raise some questions…* Hanna incinerated the pool used a light gust of wind to blow the ash about. There was some char on the metal flooring, but it wasn't too obvious unless someone was looking for it.

She moved them toward the vent and pried it free with another filament of air, closing it back behind them when they were through. The duct had openings every few feet and ended at a large rectangular opening. *Maintenance access?*

A ball of light sprang to life above them, and Hanna blinked in the sudden brightness. There was no one in sight that could have activated the light, so the changeling assumed it was automated like much of the Primary Station. "We should be safe here. Sleep while you can, but we're going to have to get you back to your birth form before too long."

"Okay," Jessica muttered as she faded off to sleep.

What was she thinking! That was insane! Hanna took a deep breath and puffed her feathers up against the constant cool breeze in the ventilation duct. *She's not even two weeks old. She may be extremely intelligent, but she lacks experience. I just need to make sure she tells me what she's planning before she runs off and does it.*

There was a skittering sound from a few feet away,

and Hanna prepared a weak lightning bolt. A rat came to the edge of the light and stopped. *They have rodents here?*

<No, they don't,> the rat whispered into her mind. When the feminine voice spoke to her, a sense of foreboding descended upon Hanna.

"What are you?"

<I am what has always been. I am that which comes for all. I have been stayed by your hand many times, but now it is your turn.> The words gave a tumultuous mix of hate, fear, and pain.

"I don't understand." Hanna finished the lighting bolt but held it back. The devastating spell screamed to be released.

<I was as you are, Hanna Steelfeather, but much as it came for me, I am here for you. With countless eons, even death may die.>

The light slowly bled from the room, and Hanna couldn't see. She launched the bolt at where the rat had been, but there was no flash of light or crack of thunder. A chill settled down on Hanna. *What's happening?*

The light flickered back on, and a little girl with black hair and dark eyes sat where the rodent was. "It is time for you now. It has begun." The girl faded into black mist.

The mist slowly crept toward Hanna, but she couldn't move. A deep screaming deep within her begged for her to run, to turn and take wing, to escape from whatever this impending doom was that encroached upon her. But there was nothing.

The mist touched her, and she felt the heat leech from her. She could feel something taking root within her. Something dark and terrible.

Hanna awoke with a start. A skittering sound drew her attention to her left. A small cleaning robot moved about the maintenance area on spindly legs. *Oh, thank you, Luna. It was just a dream. Those spells must have taken more out of me than I thought. It's all right. I'm all right.*

Jessica stirred and struggled to gain her feet. "How do you move this body?" she asked after several minutes of trying to push herself up.

Hanna laughed softly. "Imagine you have really long fingers on your hand, and your wrist folds all the way over. Push yourself up using the joint of your wrist." After thinking it over for a few seconds, Jessica was able to push herself up. "Good! Now your legs have an extra joint. Move about slowly until you get the hang of it."

The more experienced girl watched as Jessica crept about the room.

"How do I fly?" Jessica asked.

Hanna looked around the small room. She judged it around four feet square. "There's not much room in here for learning to fly, but it's better than nothing. I want to teach you each move individually first. Spread out your wings like this. Good. Now slowly move them up and down, but on your upstroke, bend what you think of as your wrist so that the tips of your wings are down."

Under Hanna's expert tutelage, Jessica was able to flutter around the small room in just a few minutes. "That's about all we can do for now," Hanna said. "Can you use magic in that form?"

A few seconds passed, and Jessica began to tremble. "I can't. Hanna, I can't use magic. What if I'm stuck like this? Help me!"

"Calm down, Jess. We aren't going to figure this out with you panicking. I'm going to cast the pain nullification spell on you again. I want you to focus on your birth form. I want you to close your eyes and take a deep breath and *focus* your entire being on returning to the way you were. It's just like when you change from your human form to your nephilim form. You don't use magic for that. You can do it."

Jessica nodded and took a deep breath. Hanna cast the spell on her and waited. After a few seconds, the changes started. This time, with the spell in place and Jessica knowing what to expect, the changes went much more smoothly.

"Good." Hanna changed into her human form. "Now, if this is a maintenance area, then there has to be some way for people to get in and out of here." A ball of light sprang into existence above her hand, and the girls searched the area for a door.

After just a few moments of looking, Hanna found a hatch with some lettering above it. "What does this say?" she asked.

Jessica came over and read the sign. "It says, Emergency Exit, then something sounding when opened. Sorry, I don't know that word."

Hanna shrugged and pushed open the hatch. It didn't make any sounds beyond the slight squeak of metal hinges. They were in a different area of the factory. Hundreds of massive battlesuits stood in orderly rows. They were bigger than the ones she had seen on Caine, and they had more attachments.

She let the ball of light above her hand dissipate and stood in awe of the sheer destructive power arrayed before her. "Is Fyr finally going to war against Azreal? The smaller ones on Caine were bad enough to deal with, and there weren't a tenth this many."

Shouting from outside the factory drew her attention. She led Jessica over to a metal stairway, and they crouched down beside it to listen.

"This isn't the way!" someone shouted.

"Genotech will get us all killed, and Atlas his helping them!"

Hanna put her thumb to her mouth and bit the nail. "What's going on? Are they protesting fighting Azreal?"

"The Guardian did nothing to us!"

Jessica put her hand on Hanna's shoulder. "Are they talking about Daddy?"

"I'll never fight alongside demons!"

"No, they wouldn't," Hanna muttered.

"What is it?" Jessica asked.

"Fyr is going to attack Earth. They're going to

help Azreal." Hanna glanced at the nearest battlesuit. The place the pilot sat was open, and a ladder was hanging down. The changeling balled her fists. "I'm stopping this. Come on."

Without waiting to see if Jessica was following her, Hanna darted from cover to cover and worked her way toward the machine. The last few yards were open, and there was very little chance the two girls wouldn't be seen during their climb into the battlesuit.

"Hanna, what are you doing?" Jessica asked.

"We're going to destroy them. We're going to take that battlesuit and use it to blow up all of the other ones."

"Do you even know how to use one of those?"

Hanna shook her head. "Even if we can't pilot it, we can use it as armor as we use magic to destroy the other ones."

Jessica looked at the battlesuit nearest them then at the others in the factory. "All right. I don't think we'll be able to destroy them all, but we'll be able to take out a lot of them."

"You ready?"

"Yeah."

Hanna reached behind her and grabbed Jessica's hand. Together, they sprinted across the open factory floor to the battlesuit's leg. Jessica boosted Hanna up to the ladder and jumped up behind her. They were only half-way up when someone spotted them.

"Hey! What the Hell are you two doing?" a man shouted.

The ladder shook a little as Hanna hoisted herself

over the top and into the cockpit. She helped Jessica scramble in and looked down at the man climbing up the ladder. With a blast of air magic, he was thrown from the ladder. He landed head-first on the unforgiving metal floor.

"You killed him!" Jessica shouted.

Hanna fixed a cold stare on the younger girl. "They've joined Azreal, the man who killed my entire family, who killed millions of people. They deserve to die."

Jessica hesitated for a moment before nodding. "Okay." She looked around the cockpit. "How do you turn this thing on?" Hanna shrugged.

"What's going on up there?" another man yelled.

"Activate," Hanna said. "Turn on. Start. Engage."

"Maybe it doesn't speak Daein." Jessica then said a word in Fyrian that Hanna couldn't understand since she had accidentally left the translator earing at Aura's. The transparent opening above them closed and the battlesuit hummed to life.

A robotic woman's voice said something Hanna couldn't understand. "It said that it's an Omega Series Atlas Labs Battlesuit. Something about automatic controls offline."

Two panels flipped around, revealing two metal sticks with horizontal bars on the top. Hanna slid into the seat and put a hand on each of the bars. It was designed for someone with bigger hands, and her fingers didn't cover all of the buttons. She pushed the one under her right index finger experimentally.

The battlesuit shook as plumes of smoke shot from its shoulders. Explosions tore into the suits in front of them, and Hanna grinned. She looked over her shoulder at Jessica. The younger girl was settling into the small gap between the pilot's seat and the back of the cockpit.

"I'll control the battlesuit. You destroy as much as you can with magic."

Jessica nodded and closed her eyes. The screech of shredding metal came from the left and Hanna watched as Jessica tore apart another one of the battlesuits with razor sharp filaments of fire, earth, and demonic energy.

Good. They'll pay for this.

"I'm detecting an emergency exit alarm was triggered seventy-eight seconds ago inside of the factory," Gaia said from her bag at Darren's side.

"You think it's them?" he asked.

"It's possible. But with this crowd out here, I don't see how we're going to be able to sneak in."

There has to be some way to get in. Darren looked around, but the crush of bodies protesting Fyr joining with Hell to attack Earth had closed every possible avenue.

"I'll never fight alongside demons!" a voice shouted. There was a palpable sense of rage in the

249

crowd that was close to boiling over.

These people are going to get violent soon. I need to get away from here with the girls before they do.

"We should just storm the place," someone said nearby. "They can't stop all of us."

"Yeah. We could just take the Omegas. They can't stop us."

An explosion from inside of the factory buffeted the mob, knocking down those in front. "What was that?" Darren shouted over the sudden screaming.

"One of the battlesuits has come online and is firing at the other ones. The system is saying there are two unidentified pilots inside. The AI hasn't been uploaded yet. It's just a stripped down computer system. There's no way to shut it down."

"Two pilots? The girls?"

More explosions were accompanied with the screech of ripping metal. The mob began to panic, some running toward the factory to steal one of the suits, others scrambling to get away. Darren fought to keep his footing and not be trampled like so many others.

"It's possible, but they are Daein. How would they know to pilot a battlesuit?"

If it's Hanna in there... "They're pretty smart."

A stray projectile shot over the crowd, and detonated in the building behind them. Glass, metal, and other debris peppered them. A man just a few feet away was impaled by a beam that crashed into the ground. Darren ran toward the factory, looking for something to crouch behind should another explosion launch anything their way.

"The new Gaia system is going to deploy the suit to get it off of the station," Gaia shouted over the tumult.

"Deploy it? Where?"

"The gateway device was already set to Earth. It's going to use a short range teleport to drop it into the portal then it will immediately go to Earth. We only have a few seconds!"

Ignoring his own safety, Darren sprinted toward the battlesuit that most likely had the girls in it. He skidded to a stop a hundred feet ahead of it and jumped up and down waving his arms.

Hanna was in the pilot's seat, and he thought he saw Jessica behind her. Hanna saw him and opened her mouth in surprise.

"Get out of the machina!" he screamed, but there was a blinding flash of electricity, and they were gone.

The plan to draw the demons and undead from the Guangzhou Obsidian Tower worked perfectly. Alex, Josh, Max, Caitlyn, Thor, Kara, and Sunriel hurried down the side streets and back alleys of the Chinese city. They had been able to infiltrate the city without encountering any resistance.

"I don't need a half-squid looking admiral to tell me this is a trap," Max muttered loud enough for Alex to hear.

Though he didn't say anything, Alex agreed. *This is way too easy.* "Everyone, keep a sharp…" he trailed off when a high-pitched whine filled the air.

A metal hand grabbed Alex's shoulder and through him through an open window to his left. Alex scrambled to his feet in time to see a laser beam heat the front of Josh's powered armor.

"Get to cover," Max bellowed.

Alex unleashed the Wrathblade and subdued the flames to preserve his energy. He dove through the window and ducked behind a dumpster. "Josh, status," he said, thumbing his radio.

"I'm fine. Aia says it would take a more powerful laser to damage the armor."

The Prometheus armor's AI had saved them from some tactical blunders in the past, and Alex was glad the suit had such a powerful support system. "Roger. Take out that sniper."

"On it." Alex watched as Josh stepped from cover and ripped the hood from a Wingle. Flashes of light traced across Alex's vision, and Josh's back armor began to glow an angry red. Josh ripped the engine block out of the Chinese pickup truck and hurled it at the building's fourth-story window.

Alex wasn't sure if he had hit the sniper or not, but the shooting stopped. "They know we're here! No more time for stealth. It's only another mile to the Obsidian Tower. Hurry!"

The seven broke cover and sprinted down the street toward the tower. The thud of heavy footsteps announced the arrival of several battlesuits. The four were arrayed on a cross street, and their pulse cannons were beginning to build up charge. These were bigger than the ones he had fought against on Caine, but Alex knew how to handle them.

The Guardian focused on the swirling storm of rage roaring inside of him. The flames leapt high and burned white hot. He skidded to a stop before them and swung the sword in a wide arc. The flames shot from the end of the sword and cut through all four of the battlesuits. Caitlyn and Sunriel held up their arms, and thick walls of stone erupted from the earth, shielding them all from the ensuing explosions.

"What are those damn things?" Max shouted as they began running west again.

"Battlesuits. The Realm of Science. Azreal hires them as mercenaries."

A booming voice filled the air. "Guardian, you are guilty of the unlawful arrest and imprisonment of Sigma Moore. The punishment for such an unwarranted act of aggression against the Realm of Science is death. You now face the full force of Fyr."

The air darkened as a Fyrian ship of some kind blocked out the sun. "Or maybe they aren't mercenaries."

"Get in the building!" Caitlyn screamed as the weapon systems on the ship's weapons systems began to glow. She threw her hands up again, and stone enveloped the building. The barricade shuddered as it was pummeled by the ship. Then, the shuddering stopped, and Alex looked at her curiously.

There was a constant stream of dull thudding in the air as the bombardment continued. She was panting from the exertion of magical energy. "I cast a preservation on the stone around us. They could hit it with everything they have for days, and we wouldn't have to worry."

"But now we're stuck in here, and they are free to surround us," Kara said.

Alex nodded as he allowed the Guardian's Blade to return to its wooden form. "It gives us some time to come up with a plan." The Guardian looked at the other Paragon in the room. "Thor, can you invoke Ragnarok with the Gjallerhorn?"

The Justicar shook his head. "It will awaken the others, but I can not open a portal to Caine to summon them here. Not with an Obsidian Tower this close."

"What do you mean, this close? I thought they blocked portals from anywhere on the Realm."

Thor shook his head. "No. That's how we were able to find you. We just kept opening and closing portals until we weren't able to open another one from Earth. Once that happened, I used Mjolnir to search you out. That's how I found your command post, then they told me where you were."

"Then how did you open a portal when you found me?"

"I did," Kara said. "I was on Caine, but no matter how far, I always know my Einherijar's thoughts and location. I just opened the portal when he told me to."

"Damn," Alex said. "There has to be something."

"Comms are blocked," Josh said. "I think the ship

is jamming the frequencies."

Sunriel cleared his throat. "I believe I could disable the ship," the angel said.

"How?" Alex asked.

In response to the question, the angel turned ethereal. "It shouldn't be hard to get up there if I'm not in the material plane."

"Are you certain?"

"No," the glowing phantasm said. "But we can't leave this place with that ship overhead. But just because I'm in this form, doesn't mean I can not be harmed. Those explosions will still kill me. We need to have the ship stop firing before I can go out."

<This is where we come in,> the Voice of Balance said. <If you invoke your demonic powers and use the Wrathblade, then the ship would have to put up its shields. The ship in Adorac couldn't fire while the defenses were active.>

Good point. Alex relayed the plan to everyone else and instructed them to continue moving toward the Obsidian Tower once the firing stopped. "We will, Sarge," Max said.

"All right." Alex closed his eyes and looked deep within himself to the mass of black energy at his core. He strained but couldn't gain access to the power. No matter how hard he reached out to it, he couldn't tap into it.

Why isn't this working? I'm in danger! I'm pretty stressed out! Work, damn it!

<You need to be more angry. You need to feel as if you will lose everything if this doesn't work.>

I ALREADY FEEL THAT WAY!

<If the Fyrians are here to arrest you, and Terra was on Fyr, then what happened to her?>

The realization made Alex's blood run cold. He reached out to her, but she was still asleep. He tried to sense more, but he only got a vague sense of confusion and danger from her. *Wait, she's been asleep every time I've checked on her for the last couple of days.*

<If the Fyrians have her, and they are working with Azreal… Terra needs you.>

Alex summoned the Wrathblade, and the flash of light was so bright, he could see it through his closed lids. The magical storm of anger was dwarfed by the inferno of rage burning within him. He seized the demonic power within him and opened his eyes.

The flames on the Wrathblade burned black, eating away at the magical lights in the room Sunriel had summoned. Alex held his hand out to the angel. "Make me ethereal," the Guardian said, his voice thick.

Sunriel hesitated for just a moment upon seeing Alex's completely green eyes, the pupil and white gone. But he reached out to Alex, and the angel's energy engulfed him.

"It will fade a few seconds after I release my grip," Sunriel said.

"Good. Throw me through the wall."

"But the explosions," Josh protested.

Alex looked over his shoulder at the armored man. "It will take more than these pitiful attacks to stop me. Do it, now, Sunriel."

The angel nodded, and hurled Alex through the

wall that was on the far side from the ship. There was a tugging sensation as the Guardian slid through the stone, but he made it clear and returned to the material plane before he landed on the ground.

Everything froze. Several humanoid robots stood about, but they stood no chance. He cut them down before their sensors detected him. In a flash, the Guardian was atop the roof. A green projectile sailed lazily through the air towards him. He dropped into a low crouch and held the demonically empowered Wrathblade in both hands.

With a roar, he swung the black sword in an uppercut. Black flame leapt from the tip, severing the incoming ball of energy in two, causing the magnetically protected plasma ball to detonate early. The heat washed over him, but it was nothing compared to the flames that had already enshrouded him.

<I am Wrath!> the Voice of Wrath bellowed in his mind.

"No, I am." The line of sight to the ship was clear. Alex took a step back and launched himself through the air at the ship, the plan forgotten.

They had Terra.

He landed atop the slippery surface of the ship's shield and began to skid backwards.

They have given her to Azreal.

The Guardian lifted the Wrathblade into the air, point downward.

I should have never left her.

With a roar, Alex drove the Wrathblade down,

through the ship's shields. The protective layer of energy overloaded and collapsed under his blow.

I'll kill them all.

Before the shield could recharge, the Guardian swung the blade in a downward arc, slicing the several hundred yard long ship in half, stem to stern. He leapt away from the ensuing explosion and stood atop the Obsidian Tower, the spinning crystal feet away The others had likely not left the building yet, but he didn't need their help.

I will kill you, Azreal.

With a mighty blow, the Guardian shattered the crystal that came from the Void.

Terra dropped to her knees. *What is it? He needs me. Who is he?*

Theo reached down and helped her stand. "We have to keep going. The Praetorians could be right behind us."

"Okay." Terra shook her head. Something wasn't right. They had been running from the Praetorians for what felt like days, always engaging in pitched battles, always just barely escaping. *I'm so tired. I just can't think straight.*

A feeling pushed on the edges of her mind. Something she hadn't had a chance to think about recently. A dark star of heat and anger tickled her senses. She closed her eyes and tried to focus on the feeling, but it was too distant, too hard.

"We need to move!" Theo shouted at her, but Terra ignored him.

"No. Wait." Terra tried to make sense of the dark mass of rage and power. *What are you?* She pushed through the mental exhaustion and fought to remember what the ball of heat was.

"Terra, they're coming. We're about to be surrounded."

I know you. I have felt you before. Pain ripped through the bundle of sensation, bleeding over into her like a bolt of lightning.

<Terra! Where are you?!> Alex's voice roared in her mind.

Alex! She fully accessed the Link, and an odd strength suffused her body. The black, pulsating energy flowed across the Link from Alex into Terra. The Nexus of Magic opened her eyes and noticed that red and blue hues were more subdued, but green leaped out at her. Black electricity crackled down her arms and arced across her fingers.

"What's going on?"

This is all fake, she thought as she looked about. Terra realized that they had been running around the same area for the last several days. It was all just too similar, the battles all the same. *We were just too tired to notice.*

A Praetorian rounded the corner, and Terra lifted her right hand. A black lightning bolt shot from her fingertips, and the illusionary adversary disappeared.

A hole in the illusion appeared where it had been, and blindingly white light shone through the gap.

"We're in a full dive VR program!" Theo gasped. He spun toward her. "Terra, do what you just did, but everywhere. We have to overload the simulation and make it crash."

She nodded and closed her eyes. *It's like magical energy,* Terra thought as she manipulated the demonic energy. The Nexus of Magic released a paper thin blast of demonic energy and felt the resistance and reverberations of the power as it expanded outward. The echo stopped when it hit the walls of the illusion. *About a half-mile in every direction.*

Terra balled her fists and drew more of Alex's demonic energy into herself. Her senses sharpened, and she shuddered with the feelings of strength and awareness. She pushed the dark power to her hands and brought them together over her head, releasing a much more powerful version of the spell she had just cast.

The pulse tore through everything around them, obliterating illusionary buildings, streets, and enemies alike. When it ended, Theo and Terra were left in an empty white space. "What now?" Terra asked.

"My turn," Theo said as a panel flipped out of his metallic left arm, and he began furiously typing a long alphanumeric sequence. "You won't be able to overload the system again. The computer is currently trying to render our surroundings and modify the AI subroutines to adjust them to our current level of power. I have to find us and disconnect us from the system. I'm pretty sure there's nothing it could do to combat the strength you showed, unless..."

The room began to go dark, the walls fading into blackness with faint pinpricks of light. She felt her feet drift from the floor as she became weightless. Terra began to draw in more demonic energy for a second blast, but less came to her this time. *Alex must be fighting and using it too. I can't exhaust his strength.* Terra wove in some of her own magical power. The two opposing forces fought against being woven together into a spell, but the Nexus refused to let base elements push the spell apart.

A spherical grid appeared just ahead of them, and Theo swore. "It's a neutron star. Almost as much gravity as a black hole. We'll be crushed."

I have held the entire power of a Realm in my hands. She growled at herself as the spell threatened to tear apart. *I have risen cities and destroyed mountains.* A high pitched whine began screaming through her head, and she felt blood filling her nasal cavity. *I'm not going to let some illusion keep me from my husband and daughter.*

The Nexus of Magic released the spell just as the light blue star winked into existence. The blended pulse of energy tore through the simulated neutron star, causing it to flicker and die. The simulation crashed for a second time, and the two of them drifted back to the ground.

Theo glanced over at her as he continued to type into the screen on his arm. "How did you?"

"How did I what?" she asked.

"You destroyed a neutron star. I know it's just a simulation, but it's extremely realistic. You shouldn't have been able to."

"INTEGER OVERFLOW," a man's voice boomed. "RESETTING SYSTEM VARIABLE: CMBTPWR. STANDBY. WE APOLOGIZE FOR ANY INCONVENIENCE."

Theo dropped to his knees in laughter. "That's absurd!"

"What is?"

"The register width of the Primary Hub's processors is 256. That means that it can adequately handle numbers up to 1.1 times ten to the seventy-seventh power. The combat power variable is programmed in the amount of joules delivered in 2.5 seconds. You could destroy all of reality with power like that!"

"I'm not sure I understand," Terra said. "Shouldn't you be getting us out of here now?"

Theo just laughed again He flipped the panel closed on his arm. His arm became enveloped in bright blue energy. "This'll force the program to reboot, and we'll be disconnected. It'll also modify the machines we are attached to and begin flushing the anesthetics from our systems. It'll feel like waking up."

Terra nodded, and Theo slammed his arm into the white floor. A flash of colors streamed past Terra's vision, and she opened her eyes for the first time in days.

Chapter Fifteen - A Dark Pact

Terra tried to lift her hand, but it wouldn't budge. She lifted her head, and it wobbled unsteadily as she surveyed herself. Her white shirt and jeans were still on, but her wrists and ankles were strapped down onto some kind of metal slab. Wires and tubes ran from various places on her body, including an exceptionally thick tube that had been shoved down her throat.

She reached out for Alex. He felt calm on the surface, but he was a roiling cauldron of rage threatening to boil over. Using a filament of fire, Terra severed her bonds and began pulling the tubes out of her. She coughed when the breathing tube came out and pulling out the catheter was something she'd rather not experience again.

"Theo?" she rasped. Terra lifted herself from the slab and walked to the blue forcefield that functioned as a door. The ominous crackling sound cautioned her against touching the barrier with her hand. Instead, she reached out to it with a spell of air and fire. The forcefield flickered and died away.

She stepped into a metal hallway the same time Theo did. He was wearing a long white coat, and Terra couldn't see what he had on beneath it.

"Good," he said. "You made it out. Follow me."

Terra nodded and followed behind the Architect. "How did we end up in here?"

"I tried logging into the net when I came awake, but someone has revoked my credentials. They probably deleted my genetic profile from the citizen's registry. If that's the case, then it would have to be one of the CEO's."

"So, what are we going to do?"

Theo shrugged. "I'm not sure yet, but whatever it is won't be accomplished from in here."

The half-angel looked around, but every inch of the hall was identical to the one before and after. *It's just metal and blue forcefields for as far as I can see.* "Do you know how to get out of here?"

"My HUD's still working, but it's just downloading a local map from the this area's servers. I'll have to get outside to get a wide-area map." Theo led her down several branching hallways and to a small room with only one door.

The door closed behind them, and Terra felt the room begin to move. "Does this carry us between floors?"

Theo nodded. "We were in the outer level of the Primary Station. I don't know which hub we're in though. It's all maintenance corridors and storage areas down there."

The room beeped, and the doors opened. Terra and Theo stepped out onto a street and froze. A battlesuit was aiming its weapons at them.

"Citizens, it is past curfew," the pilot said. "Return to your domiciles, or you will be executed."

"What?" Theo said. "On whose orders?"

"The Architect's," the pilot said. "Niles Wester."

"Of course it was Wester," Theo growled. He stepped toward the battlesuit.

"Halt, or you will be fired upon!"

Terra watched as Theo's left arm began to glow white. "I am the Architect, Theodore Thelonius the Third, and you will do as I order."

The pilot's eyes widened. He said something that Terra couldn't hear. Theo lifted his glowing arm, and electricity arced across twenty-odd feet between him and the battlesuit.

"System override. Disable parachute. Emergency ejection. Reason: Pilot not in compliance with Fyrian statute 1 alpha," the Architect said.

The transparent cockpit cover launched into the air, and the pilot followed closely behind it, screaming as he soared into the air. Terra followed his trajectory and watched as the pilot slammed into a building. "What was he doing?"

"He was reporting that he had found us. We need to make it to the gateway device in the Central Hub. I have to be there to reassume command of the Primary Station. Come on." Theo turned sharply and began to walk through the streets.

"Aren't we in danger here? Shouldn't we be a little less conspicuous?"

"You see this arm?" Theo asked, holding up his left arm. It was still glowing white hot. Terra said she did, and he continued. "It's the master control to all Fyrian technology. With this, I can command every device on Fyr. Or I *could*. Without net access, I can only locally override systems, and I can't get net access without being in the citizen's registry. The only place where I can add myself to the registry is at the gateway device. So there we go."

"I understand that, but what if they attack us?

Terra ducked as several missiles soared overhead and crashed into the buildings around them. "I'm generating an electromagnetic barrier," the Architect said. "The targeting computers used by all the Fyrian weapon systems will not be able to lock on, and they wouldn't risk using a rail gun inside the station. They'd punch a hole, and this entire hub would have the atmosphere vented."

A laser beam etched across Terra's vision, but it arced around the two of them. Theo shook his head. "It also refracts wavelengths above six-hundred nanometers and below four-hundred and fifty nanometers. Beam weapons won't work either."

Terra's eyes began to hurt as the barrier Theo was creating flickered on and off, responding to the various attacks by the Fyrian rebels. "They'll soon realize that the only way to stop us is to physically come at us. That's when you stop them."

"Got it," Terra said. They walked for several more minutes until the attacks began to subside. They turned the corner, and a group of Praetorians blocked their path. Theo didn't slow in his steady approach to the Central Hub.

The Praetorians charged them, but Terra hurled them aside as if they were paper dolls.

"We can't take any of the shuttles," Theo said. "Their navigation system is far too easy to override. We could be sent anywhere. It'll take about two hours to walk to the Central Hub at this rate."

Terra nodded. "Let's get a move on."

For the first time since the founding of the Nine Realms, a brown gateway opened on Bara, and the keystone seal was removed. Myrius watched as the forces of Hell entered the Realm of Good. The Keeper of Fate detested the demons, but their presence was required per the ancient treaty.

Myrius fought the impulse to draw his mythricite sword when the Overlord of Hell set foot on Bara. *So it has come to this*, he thought. "Overlord."

"Keeper," the demon lord responded as he looked at the City of Spires in the distance. "It has been too long since I gazed upon your... fair city."

Myrius glared at Azreal. "Is your sister well?" he asked, knowing that the demon lord had unsuccessfully tried to assassinate her on several occasions.

"Yes, I am," a female demon said from just behind Azreal. "Thank you for asking."

The Keeper of Fate glanced between the two of them with a frown on his face. *Hell's twins have come back together... This does not bode well.* "You are welcome."

The angel thought he saw Azreal's hand begin to tremble, but he wasn't sure. "Enough of this idle chatter," the Overlord snapped. "I assume you begged my audience because of the nephilim."

"I did not beg anything of you," Myrius snapped.

267

"I have summoned you here in accordance with the treaty. The *thing* poses a grave danger to the safety and stability of the Nine Realms. It is our duty to exterminate it and the ones involved with its creation."

Azreal's wicked grin made Myrius's blood boil. "So, you're saying you can't do it on your own."

Myrius fought down the impulse to run the Overlord through. "No, I'm saying your constant failed attempts to kill the Guardian and the Nexus haven't gone unnoticed."

The grin vanished from the Overlord's face. "I would tread carefully, Keeper. I am more powerful than you can imagine."

"I will keep that in mind," Myrius said neutrally. "I assume you know where they are?"

"The Nexus is trapped on the Realm of Science, and the Guardian is on the Realm of Balance near a city called Sydney. As for the nephilim, her exact location is unknown, but she is somewhere on Earth."

"Very well. We will deal with the father first. Do we have your aid in this?"

Azreal bowed slightly. "Of course, in accordance with the treaty. A coordinated attack."

"Indeed."

Chapter Sixteen - Ruin

William let the demonic energy flow through him, and enshroud his body in shadow. He drifted through the Void toward the large Outsider fleet. He had trailed the outsider craft that had destroyed the settlement of unknown beings, until it led him to a large group of Outsider ships.

What are they doing here? he wondered. *What's so special about this place?* All of the ships were orbiting a dark point of the Void, but there was nothing special about the spot. *There's not even a speck of land there. What are they all focused on?*

The Nephilim carefully propelled himself closer. As he moved toward the several hundred ships, they all fired beam weapons simultaneously. The shots intersected at the point they were orbiting, and William thought he saw a flicker of color.

What's going on?

The ships fired again, and William was certain there was a flicker of yellow light from the point of intersection. Over and over, the Outsider ships pummeled the point in space, until a hole in the fabric of reality appeared. One ship began to move toward the breach, and William realized what was happening.

This isn't possible! The Nephilim launched himself forward as fast as he could, abandoning all stealth. The ether currents buffeted him to either side, but he cut through the Void's resistance to his movements. *They couldn't have!*

The ship was about to enter the breach. *I have to*

hurry! None of the other Outsider ships fired upon him, their weapons systems all trained on the dimensional hole. *If that ship makes it through, then everyone will die!*

William wrapped himself in a cocoon of demonic energy, focusing on making the leading tip as sharp as possible. It made contact with the Outsider ship, and he ripped through the entire craft. The explosion rocketed him away, but the shell of energy kept him safe. *I don't think I'll make it past all those ships... Looks like this is where it all ends.*

A foreign sensation pulled at his stomach, and William felt like he was falling.

Terra and Theo reached the Central Hub. The foliage swayed gently in the artificial breeze used to circulate the oxygen throughout the Primary Station.

Terra felt her magic suddenly stop working. She fought against the barrier between her and her waning magical energy, but it was as if a wall had been erected. "Theo, something's wrong. I can't use magic."

Doctor Moore walked from behind a thick tree trunk. He was holding a small black crystal with wires attached to it. "That's right," he said. "I've removed your ability to pervert the natural order of things."

An anti-magic stone! "So what's the plan?" she

asked. "You going to kill us now?"

Sigma looked at her like she had suggested her grow a second head. "Kill you? No. I'm going to place you in an extraction pod and drain you dry."

Theo lifted his arm, and a bolt of lightning shot from the prosthesis. It struck a barrier surrounding Sigma and was diverted.

"Oh, Theo," Sigma said, shaking his head, "that just won't do." A group of Praetorians came from behind various wall panels and vegetation. "Take him."

The Architect struggled mightily against the Genotech enforcers, but there were too many, and he was quickly overwhelmed. Terra tried to fight them, but their armor easily turned her blows. *If only I could use magic!* She reached out for Alex, hoping that she would be able to tap into his demonic energy, but she was cut off from him like she was her magic.

Alex's mouth hung open, and he blinked against the blinding afternoon glare. "How?" he asked.

"Ye're bloody hard to track down," Brahm growled at him. "We've been tryin' to find ye fer more than a week."

Caitlyn ran up to Brahm and threw her arms around the grizzled dwarf. "Brahm! It's so good to see you! How did you find us?" she asked.

"It's good to see ye too, Cat," he said patting her back. "Yer bloody sister's been usin' bloody magic to try triangulatin' yer position, but it's been bloody difficult with you jumpin' all 'round the bloody Realm of Balance."

"You came to tell us about Terra?" Alex asked.

"Aye," Brahm agreed. "How'd ye know abou' her bein' missin'?"

"The Realm of Science has attacked us several times. They've joined with Azreal. If they have, then he must have Terra. She's so..." Alex trailed off as he tried to reach out to Terra. He couldn't sense her at all. It was like she was just gone.

"Alex?" Max asked. "What's wrong?"

"I can't sense her. She was there just a minute ago, and now she's gone." Alex felt like his heart had stopped beating. "Brahm, what does that mean? Why can't I sense her?"

Caitlyn took a step away from Brahm and reached out toward him. "Alex," she said, her tone thick with concern.

"Why can't I sense her? Even when she was in the Obsidian Tower, I could feel her. What's happened?"

"Alex," Brahm said. "You'll no' want to hear this, but Jessica is-"

"Get down!" Sunriel shouted as he flew through the air toward them. The angel knocked Alex aside and grunted. A bloody, golden blade protruded from the angel's chest.

"We're under attack!" Josh yelled as angels and demons began to appear all around them.

She's gone. Terra's gone, Alex thought numbly. He sat on the ground, oblivious to the battle erupting around him.

Someone was shaking him by the shoulders, but he didn't care. "Damn it, Sarge!" Max roared inches from his face. "Get your shit together! We're being attacked!"

Alex rose to his feet and drew his sword. He tried to summon any form of the Guardian's Blade, but nothing happened. A high pitched whine announced the arrival of Fyrian drop ships. He watched impassively as a pulse of light from several miles west lanced through the air and shot one of the craft down.

"Max," Josh shouted over the clamor of battle. "I'm useless like this. Help me get to the lab."

"Let's go," Max said.

Caitlyn took Max's place in front of Alex. "Come on, Alex. We need you to focus." Explosions tore up the ground to the north of them, and screams of pain filled the air.

<Wielder, people are dying,> the Voice of Balance sent.

Terra is gone.

<Then your daughter will need you at her side. What good will come of things if she grows up without parents?>

I...

<These angels have teamed up with Azreal. Do you think it's a coincidence that your were attacked just after you stopped sensing Terra? They probably killed her. They took her from you.>

But I thought Azreal had her.

<Damn it, Alex! We don't know what the hell happened to her, but your daughter needs you now. All we know is that Terra is gone, and it has something to do with Azreal. If these angels have teamed up with him, then they are responsible in part for her death!>

Alex grit his teeth. Brahm, Caitlyn, Thor, and Kara had formed up around him and were all engaged in pitched battle. A flash of light announced the Wrathblade's arrival, and the Guardian leapt into battle beside his friends and allies.

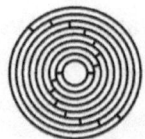

"What are you waiting for?" Terra demanded. "Just do it!" Her arms were painfully bound behind her back in some sort of metal clamp.

"In such a rush, Nexus?" Doctor Moore asked. "Science takes time. It's what separates us from you genetic aberrations. We must work toward what we seek to achieve."

Terra spit at the scientist's face but the distance was too great. "I'll kill you for this, Sigma. I'll find a way."

Moore laughed at her. "I'd love to know how." He touched some buttons on a computer screen, and a green light traced over her from head to toe.

"First, I'm going to break free of these bonds, then I'm going to shatter than anti-magic shard. After that, who knows? But I'll be sure to make sure you suffer first."

Rolling his eyes at her, Sigma said, "How pedestrian. Resulting to threats is exactly what I would expect of someone like *you*. You dirty half-breed freak. If it weren't for your value as a research subject, I would have disposed of you on the Realm of Magic."

Theo groaned, but he didn't awaken. Moore had injected something into the Architect several hours ago, and Theo had lost consciousness shortly after.

"I have discovered something that may interest you, Nexus," Sigma said.

"And what's that?" *Maybe if I can keep him talking, I'll find some way to actually break free.*

"I have found your daughter," he said.

A paradoxical blend of hope and fear ran through Terra. "What do you mean?" she asked, carefully keeping her tone neutral.

"She is on Earth in an omega series battlesuit. It seems she and another person have been wreaking all kinds of havoc on the Fyrian forces in that area."

Hanna must still be with her. "Why are you telling me this?"

"As I told you before, irrational hope makes the process so much more efficient. Plus," Sigma said as he met her eyes, "I look forward to seeing that hope die along with you."

Terra glared at the man. "Don't expect to live much longer," she said.

Sigma laughed at her threat. "I would wish you luck in your attempts to kill me, but it would do you no good."

Alex stood over the enormous demon and stared at the corpse as he wobbled unsteadily. The Guardian's red blood ran down his forearm from the gash in his bicep, where it mingled with the demon blood coating his arms. Alex neared the end of his endurance, and he had stopped shunting energy to the sword more than an hour ago. It was only by sheer willpower that he still stood.

His instincts screamed at him, and Alex spun, swinging the sword in a high arc. A golden mythricite sword clanged against his weapon, and he locked blades with another of the rogue angels. Alex thought he recognized this angel.

"Alex Zane," Myrius, leader of the angels that had been attacking alongside the demons, snarled, "you have been charged with fathering a Nephilim. A crime punishable by death. How do you plead?"

So that's what this is about, Alex thought, glaring at the angel past their crossed blades. *They're here to deliver punishment. Terra's gone... Brahm said something about Jessica...* Dead on his feet, Alex was having trouble focusing.

Pulling from the scant reserves of strength he had left, Alex shoved against the locked swords and pushed Myrius back a step. Their weapons disengaged, the

Guardian forced himself to smile at his opponent. "I plead guilty, but you're going to need more than just yourself to carry out any punishments."

"Indeed," the traitorous Keeper of Fate said, just as four more angels emerged from the ground in their ethereal forms. The five were arrayed around Alex in a semi-circle, and they all had mythricite armor and blades.

Alex felt his heart drop into his stomach. *I could have taken five when this battle began, but I'm too tired for this.* Giving his head a slight shake, Alex banished the thought. *I can do this because I have to. I only need to hold until someone can help.* The sounds of battle all around him made that a distant prospect. The demon and angel assault on their base had been ferocious, and Alex knew help would be a long time coming.

The Guardian slid down into a defensive crouch and held his blade a little higher. The five angels spread out to surround him, and Alex had no choice but to let them. He used the Wrathblade's mirrored finish to keep an eye on the angel that moved around behind him. *That one will come first, thinking he move in close before I react.* Alex shifted his foot so he could spin to face the angel behind him faster.

Seconds stretched into an ephemeral eternity before the rear angel lunged forward. Ducking under the thrust, Alex spun, drew the small knife at waist, and used the opening in the angel's armor to slice the artery that ran through his right armpit. Hot blood sprayed Alex, coating his skin further. A thought of something Silvia had said several months ago sparked in his mind, but with first blood drawn, the other angels attacked at the same time, pushing the memory from his mind.

Alex dove away to keep from being surrounded, and he went into a wild flurry as he kept the golden weapons at bay. Fighting as he ran, Alex thought, *If they ring me in again, I'll die.* It was with the completion of that thought, that the Guardian lost his footing and crashed into the ground. The Wrathblade flew from his hand and reverted back to the wooden form of the Blade of Balance.

He rolled to the left and narrowly dodged a blade stabbing into the earth where he had been, but Alex was too slow. A mythricite booted foot slammed onto his chest, and he was pinned. One of the angels Alex didn't recognize stood over him, and Myrius approached from the left with his broadsword glinting wickedly.

The Guardian struggled to break free, but the angel was too strong and Alex too exhausted. *So this is it. Everything I did, I tried to do, and it all ends without saving anyone.*

"Alex Zane," Myrius said, "you have admitted guilt to the commission of a crime for which the sentence is death. As your accuser and the highest angel present, I shall carry out your sentence by means of beheading." The Keeper of Fate glanced up as he lifted the golden sword, and his eyes grew wide.

An enormous, black shadow flew over Alex and barreled into the angel holding him down, catapulting him away. Seeing his opportunity to kill Alex fading fast, Myrius brought down his sword, but the Guardian was faster. Alex twisted his body and kicked the Keeper of Fate's feet from underneath him. With a powerful flap of his wings, Myrius carried himself away from Alex.

Footfalls raced to Alex as he rolled away from the two remaining angels and lifted his head. Alex located the sound just in time to see Josh in the Prometheus armor tackle one of the two remaining angels to the ground. There was a sickening crunch as the armor's weight and inertia crushed the angel's armor and ribs. The other remaining angel was gunned down by a blast of automatic gun fire, and Alex saw Max striding forward as he hip fired an M249 SAW.

A stocky form in black thorium armor stood before Alex, facing away from him. "Looks like we're just in bloody time," Brahm said over his shoulder. "Ye dropped this." The dwarf held the Guardian's Blade in his left hand, the hilt toward Alex. The Guardian accepted his sword struggled to his feet. Myrius flew twenty feet above them, and seeing that he was outnumbered, the angel began to fly away.

Turning left, Alex saw Caitlyn in her primal form standing over the angel that had been standing over him. He caught her eye and pointed at Myrius. The Changeling of the Fang nodded and took off like an arrow. Myrius was at least thirty feet off the ground, and Alex wasn't sure if Caitlyn was able to jump that high. Josh and Max took up flank on either side of Alex and scanned the battle embroiled camp.

Alex looked to his long time friend. "If Caitlyn can't catch him, I need you to take him down. Myrius will pay for Terra's death."

"Will do, Sarge," Max said. The big man lifted the SAW to his shoulder and put the flying angel in his sights.

Caitlyn was almost directly below Myrius now, and she launched herself into the air. Her body stretched out as far as it would go, right paw fully extended, she caught the Keeper of Fate just above the back joint of his greave. She hooked her claws into his armor, and dragged Myrius from the sky.

Josh sprinted over to help her, and the other three followed behind. Alex was near collapse, but Max and Brahm seemed aware of that and set an easy pace for him to follow. The battle seemed to be dying down around them.

By the time Alex made it over, Josh and Caitlyn had disarmed the Keeper, and Josh stood behind Myrius with the angel's arms pinned behind his back. Reaching deep within himself, Alex unleashed the Blade of Justice. It required less energy to use than the Wrathblade but required a much larger amount of focus to keep the Guardian's Blade in that form.

"Myrius," the Guardian began, "as a traitor against the Nine Realms, *you* are charged with a crime for which the punishment is death. The evidence against you is extensive, including attacking the Guardian while in performance of his duties, causing the death of the Nexus of Magic, and allying with the Demon Lord Azreal to reach this end. How do you plead?"

"Not guilty," the Keeper of Fate snarled.

Alex nodded, knowing that was to be the other's answer. "Hold him down," he said.

Josh leveraged the angel's arms, forcing Myrius's upper body forward. Alex lifted the Blade of Justice and separated the Keeper of Fate's head from his neck before the other could say a word. Josh released the angel's arms, and the body unceremoniously fell to the mud with a splat.

The Guardian released his focus on the Blade of Justice, and the Guardian's Blade reverted back into its wooden form. Alex let out a deep sigh and sheathed his weapon. He was about to ask Brahm was he was going to say earlier, but a flash of light a few feet away drew his attention.

A gray portal had opened, and two more angels strode from it. Alex drew his weapon again, but he saw it was Eternius and Ureon and held the hilt loosely in his right hand. Fighting to stay on his feet, he asked, "What are you doing here?"

"We've been trying to find you," Eternius said. "I've come to help you kill Azreal once and for all." The ancient angel looked at the severed head at Alex's feet but didn't say anything.

Too tired to think of anything sarcastic, Alex just nodded. He raised his hand and tried to wipe the sweat from his face, but only succeeded in smearing his, the demon's, and the angel's blood on his forehead and cheeks. The Guardian looked down at his hands and arms and sighed again. *Too much blood...*

He looked down at Brahm. "What were you going

to tell me before all of this started?"

"Now's no' the right time," the dwarf said. "Ye need to rest, then we can talk. It's nothin' ye can resolve right now."

"Brahm," Alex asserted, "I know it was something about Jessica. What is it?"

The dwarf swore softly and nodded. "We canno' find her. Jessica went missing more than a week ago."

Already pushed well beyond the point of exhaustion, Alex's mind ground to a halt at the news. "What?"

"We questioned Myrius. He said the angels did no' have Jessica, but there was an angel's arm in her nursery. We think," Brahm cleared his throat and started over. "With Fyr on Azreal's side, we think that he has her on Hell."

No! She's all I have left! The sound of Alex's heartbeat began to boom in his ears, and he balled his fists. *They attacked me just to keep me busy. Azreal has her. He has my daughter!* The thoughts screamed in his mind. Distantly, Alex felt the knuckles of his right hand crack from squeezing the hilt of the Blade of Balance so hard.

A roar built deep within Alex, and he felt something shatter deep within himself. His voice echoed with a terrifying dissonance as he screamed, "Azreal!" Everything went black.

Eternius stared at the Guardian for a moment with slack-jawed surprise. "Step back from him!" he shouted over Alex's scream.

A gusting wind built as particles of black energy began to fly into Alex. The grass around him died as the half-demon drew energy from them. "Back away," Eternius shouted again, "or he will bleed you all dry!"

Understanding dawned on everyone's faces, and they quickly took several steps from Alex. The energy formed around Alex in a cocoon of pulsating darkness. The Guardian's wordless roar shifted in tone, and Eternius could clearly hear two separate voices coming from the man inside the oblong sphere.

Energy stopped flying toward him, and Alex abruptly stopped screaming, still inside the ball.

"What happened?" Caitlyn asked.

"It shouldn't be possible," Eternius said, eying the Changeling's primal form. "He's unleashed the ninth form of the Guardian's Blade, Ruin. But…"

"But what?" Brahm demanded.

Eternius looked at Ureon. "Before the Nine Realms were created," she explained, "the Guardian's Blade was used by the Nephilim, William. He used it to protect the Nine Realms from the Outsiders while the First Ones finished sealing it away from the Void. The First Ones said Ruin was too dangerous for anyone but him to use. They said that it would kill the wielder shortly after he unleashed it. The strain is just too great."

"No," Caitlyn whispered. Tears ran down her face

as she stared at the ball of demonic power.

"I'm sorry," Ureon said. "But Alex is already as good as dead. Ruin doesn't just feed off of the Guardian's physical strength. It feeds off of his soul itself. It will use the energy of Alex's soul. He's going to use Ruin to erase Azreal from the fabric of reality. He'll use it to destroy Azreal's soul along with his own, and neither of their souls will ever be reborn."

"Is there any way of saving him?" the bigger human asked.

"The only way to stop him would be to kill him, and save his soul before it unravels," Ureon said, shaking her head. "No, Alex is going to hunt down Azreal and kill him. The only thing we can do is help him before his time runs out."

Cracks began to appear on the surface of the shell. Darkness bled from the openings, devouring the light around it. With a gust of wind, the cocoon disappeared, and Alex stood before them, terrible and imposing.

Tremendous wings of black energy spread from his back, and his eyes were solid green. The Guardian's Blade had turned into Ruin, a toothed scythe. The black blade was attached to a black staff, and an angry red eye looked out from the center of the blade. The Guardian turned to Eternius and pointed at him with his free left hand.

"Eternius," Alex said, another voice mixed with his own. The sound made everyone wince. "The Angelic Council has been led astray. You will reassume your role as Keeper of Fate and show them back to the path they should be on. This is my decree as Guardian of Balance, and it will not be disobeyed."

Eternius nodded, knowing it would do no good to argue. "As you command."

"Use your amulet to open a portal to Hell," the Guardian ordered. "I have a demon to kill."

The Keeper of Fate focused into the Traveler's Pendant. With a hollow thump, a brown portal to Hell opened off to the side.

Alex looked at Thor and Kara. "You two will ensure the destruction of this final Obsidian Tower. Hell will not maintain a stronghold on Earth." Thor and Kara nodded in unison.

Caitlyn, Brahm, Max, and Josh each walked over to stand beside Alex. The Guardian looked at his friends. "I'm not asking you four to come with me," Alex said, his voice free of the painful dissonance as he gained control over Ruin.

"And ye do no' have to," Brahm said, hefting the warhammer of his namesake.

Caitlyn nodded. "We've come this far," she said. "We'll see this to the end."

Lifting the machine gun and resting it on his shoulder, Max smiled. "You know that you'll just get into trouble without me, Sarge."

Josh stretched his arms and spoke through the Prometheus suit's speakers. "I owe Max my life. I go where he does."

"Very well," Alex said as he stepped to the portal.

"Wait," Ureon called. She held her hand out to the five of them, and Eternius saw her cast a spell over them. "The Realm of Evil hangs over a dead star that emits no light. The spell I've cast on you will allow you to see. It will only last for an hour or so. You must be fast."

"Thank you," Alex told her. He shifted his gaze to Eternius. "Do not forget what I said."

"I won't. Goodbye, Guardian."

"Goodbye, Keeper." And with that, Alex stepped through the gateway.

When all five had entered Hell, Eternius closed the portal behind them.

Chapter Seventeen - An Ending

Darren crept into the room, and carefully surveyed his surroundings. Rows of large green transparent cylinders bathed the room in sickly light. Small screens attached to each one blinked on and off.

"There's no need to sneak around," Gaia said. "There is no monitoring equipment in this area. It's completely off the grid."

"Yeah," Darren said. "But what if some random person is walking around and hears us."

"Good point," Gaia whispered. "This is where the conveyance from the Central Hub went. If Terra is anywhere, she should be here. The communication channels were abuzz with someone using magic headed toward the Central Hub."

"All right. Now be quiet." Darren began to walk down the center aisle between the pods. He wasn't walking long before he heard someone talking.

"It's time," the familiar voice said. "I hope you enjoy the rest of your time here."

"Bring it on," Terra snapped. "I'll still find a way to kill you like I should have on Caine."

That's Moore and Terra! Darren broke into a sprint. He skidded to a stop when he saw Terra hanging above one of the green cylinders. Both Terra and Moore turned to see his approach. The Nexus began to make noises past the mask that covered her face, and the doctor paled.

"What are you doing here?" Moore shouted.

He began to approach the doctor, but Sigma held

up a small glowing computer. "One more step, and I'll lower her into the pod!"

Darren hesitated. Terra began shaking her head and yelling, but he couldn't understand her. "You do that, and I'll make sure it's the last thing you do."

"It seems we have come to an impasse, Captain."

"Keep him talking," Gaia whispered. "I may be able to stop him."

"That it does," Darren said. "What do you propose?"

"I'll leave, and once I'm a safe enough distance away, I'll release the Nexus."

Terra's thrashing grew more intense and she yelled louder. Darren understood. *She doesn't want to let him get away again.* "How do I know you won't just drop her in as soon as you're far enough away?"

"Oh," Sigma said. "You'll just have to take my word as a scientist."

Darren shook his head. "Yeah, I don't really think that's good enough."

Sigma shrugged and lifted the computer. "I guess I could just drop her in and take my chances. She'll survive for a few seconds, but this fluid is much more concentrated than that of the ones one Caine or Dae. You won't have time to save her and catch me. You know what? I think I'll just take my chances." Sigma touched the screen, but Terra didn't drop into the cylinder.

"I've broken into the local network and blocked his access," Gaia said. "I'm releasing Terra now. He's going to run."

As soon as the words came out of the box, Sigma broke into a dash, but Darren was faster. In only a few seconds, the Daein crossed the several yards and tackled the scientist. A black crystal that had been in the Fyrian's hand skittered across the ground.

Darren drew the knife and thumbed the button. He placed the humming blade less that an inch from Sigma's neck. "Give me a reason."

Sigma gulped but didn't say anything or move. Darren heard Terra's footsteps behind him, and Sigma's eyes widened when he saw the look on her face. She picked up the wired black crystal and knelt next to the scientist.

"I told you I would break free." Terra hurled the black crystal as far as she could, and Darren lost sight of it as it sailed through the air. He thought he heard it shatter as it slammed to the ground. "And now that's done. What was step three again?"

Sigma's eyes grew wider, and Darren watched as the man wet himself. "Sigma Moore, you have committed more crimes that I can count. You have enabled one of the most evil beings in the Nine Realms to kill countless people. Justice is past due." She looked at her captain. "Cut his arm, but not too deep."

Darren nodded, and cut an inch-deep gash in Sigma's arm. The scientist howled in pain. "What are you doing?" he shouted.

The captain watched as Sigma floated into the air on ropes of magic. "If I remember correctly," Terra said, "the fluid in these pods is poisonous." She calmly floated Sigma to the pod he had been about to lower her into.

"No, wait," Sigma begged. "It wasn't going to kill you. You would have been fine. The chambers are designed to slowly leach the life energy from your body. Please don't kill me!"

Terra glared at him. "It's good to know that you would have just slowly killed me."

The Fyrian hung over the pod and opened his mouth to say something else. Terra dropped him into the extraction pod without waiting to hear what he was going to say. Darren watched impassively as Sigma began to convulse. Bubbles burst from the top of the pod as he screamed in pain. In seconds it was over, but Darren was sure every second had seemed like an eternity to the doctor.

"I've established a connection with the Architect's prosthesis," Gaia said from her bag. "Initiating system purge."

The Architect's arm began to glow, and his eyes snapped opened immediately. He looked around and saw the corpse floating in the pod. "What happened?" the Architect asked.

"I wouldn't want to add additional strain to the already tenuous relationship between our Realms," Terra said. "He tripped."

Darren knew there was no way the Paragon of Science would believe the explanation, but Theo just nodded. "He should have been more careful near such dangerous equipment." His prosthesis beeped, and Theo looked at the screen. He looked up at Darren. "Do you have a rogue AI in that bag?"

"Uh," Darren said. "I don't know what you're talking about. I'm not any good with technology."

Gaia laughed. "I appreciate the protection, Darren. You may allow him to have me. He could have deleted me already." Darren lifted her box out of his bag and handed it to the Architect.

The man stuck a metal finger into a hole in the box. "Whoa there," she said. "You could have taken me on a date first."

Terra's fingers suddenly dug into Darren's arm. "Something's wrong with Alex," she gasped. She dropped to her knees and placed her hands on her head. The Nexus screamed, the shrill tone digging into Darren's ears.

Caitlyn was the last one through the portal. Her paws immediately started sweating, and she panted in the heat. Everything was bathed in gray light from the Seat of Faith's spell. The changeling saw Alex standing before a large wall of flesh. Thousands of eyes stared down at him from the wall.

"The Hell Gate," Brahm warned. "Do no' look at any o' the eyes. If you look at 'em lookin' at ye', ye'll be turned to stone."

Alex slammed the bottom of the shaft of the Soul Ripper into the stone before the Hell Gate. Small, black fissures opened all around him, and the crackling wings of demonic energy spread wide. "I am the Guardian, come to take my vengeance upon the Overlord," he shouted at the thirty-foot-tall living barricade. "Allow myself and these four to pass, or I will cut my way through."

The eyes shifted wildly from his face to the scythe in his hands. Immune to the Hell Gate's power, Alex met that gaze without fear. For a moment, Caitlyn thought Alex would be forced to follow through with his promise, but a seam opened in the center of the Hell Gate. It slowly slid open enough for them to pass.

A mass of demons crowded the crisscrossing walkways on the other side of the wall. Alex lifted his scythe and held it at his side as he strode through the breach. The demons saw him approaching, but they seemed unsure of what to do. Brahm, Josh, Max, and Caitlyn followed behind him, and they fanned out on the walkway as soon as they were through the Hell Gate.

The painful dissonance was back in Alex's voice as he roared loud enough for all to hear, "Any who wish to be erased from the Nine Realms, from all existence, come!" The bloodlust in his voice begged for them to attack him.

There were thousands upon thousands of demons. Caitlyn saw every crisscrossing walkway as far as the eye could see was full of the monsters. But none came forward. It was then that Caitlyn realized that none would. Demons' souls are eternal; they retain the memories of every life they had lived before. None would risk permanent death for any reason, much less for what they thought was a personal vendetta.

Alex nodded and began to stride forward, scythe still down by his side. The demonic ranks opened before him, and the Hellspawn allowed all five of them to pass. The mass of demons were unwilling to invoke the Guardian's wrath.

"This is way too easy," Caitlyn overheard Max mutter.

A large demon snarled at the five of them, and the truth dawned on Caitlyn the same time Brahm said, "They know we canno' escape, an' that Alex will no' live very long. There'll be no escapin' from this one."

"Then we'll just have to do what we came here for and wreak havoc for as long as we can," Josh said with a dark laugh.

"You've got that one right," Caitlyn said.

Alex turned at each intersection as if he knew where he was going. In only a few minutes time, they were standing before a large temple. A wide stairway went up an entrance that stood closed. They mounted the steps and climbed. Caitlyn glanced over her should and saw that none of the demons followed. All were content to wait and see the results of the coming battle.

When Alex reached the doorway, he turned and faced them. He looked each of them in the eyes. "My fight is beyond each of you. Your task is to keep them from interfering as long as possible," Alex said, indicating the amassed horde. "And if possible, return my sword to Dae if I'm... not able."

The four nodded their understanding. Alex turned and shoved open the doors to the Overlord's Temple.

They slammed against the inner walls with a resounding boom. "Goodbye," he said as he strode in.

Seated upon his throne, Azreal took a deep breath and savored the feel of power flowing through his dark-blooded veins. Alone, each Outsider artifact atop the Obsidian Towers on Earth would have extracted a very small amount of energy from there, but the hundreds of towers he had constructed on the Realm of Balance channeled a tremendous flow of life force into the Overlord of Hell.

His sister was a motionless wraith behind a concealing stone screen to his left. Azreal was still unsure of Odessa's motives for returning to his side, but she had proved herself thus far.

The large doors swung open under a powerful push, and the object of Azreal's deepest hatred walked through the opening. The Overlord eyed his nephew. The enormous wings of pulsating black energy showed the strength of the boy's soul to be great, and the eye on the scythe turned to focus on Azreal. *So, he's unleashed Ruin. No matter, even with its power he is no match for me.*

Alex strode down the midnight colonnade with even darker purpose in his solid green eyes. The Guardian stopped when he was still several feet away. "The only reason I have not killed you yet, Azreal, is because you still have a chance to tell me what you know of my daughter. Where is Jessica?" the young man demanded.

Azreal shrugged. "I don't know where your child is, nor do I care. I am beyond the needs of her power." The Overlord of Hell rose from his throne and drew himself up to his full height. Blood red hair framed the wicked smile on his face. "But your daughter is a nephilim," Azreal shuddered in ecstasy at the thought, "she sounds just absolutely delicious. It will be my intimate pleasure to leach the power from her body."

The Guardian's brows drew down, and he glowered at Azreal. "Time to—" His words were cut off when Alex saw Odessa step from behind the screen. "Mother? What are you doing here?"

"I came here to stop you, my son," she said softly.

Alex shook his head. "No, please, don't do this." The tumult of battle arose from outside the temple, and the Guardian looked over his shoulder at the sounds.

Azreal saw his opening and attacked.

The demons didn't wait long before they attacked the four people guarding the top of the stairs into the Overlord's Temple. With a mighty swipe of her large paw, Caitlyn tore the throat out of the first demon to top the stairs.

Max depressed the firing lever on his gun, and hot

metal lanced into the mass of demons that tried to climb the approach. Black mist filled the air as several of the approaching horde were cut down.

Roaring his hatred for the monsters, Brahm swung his warhammer in an overhead chop. The black thorium head crushed the head of a daeman as he drew near the top. Somehow the daeman still stood, and the stalwart dwarf knocked the corpse down the stairs.

They each held their own, but it was Josh who fought the hardest. Armed with the considerable strength of the Prometheus armor, the young man supported the three of them any time they were pressed to keep the waves of demons at bay.

Caitlyn snarled in pain as an arrow pierced her right shoulder. She twisted her head about and bit off the shaft of the arrow.

"Max," Josh shouted. "Target at one thirty. Big demon with a huge bow and arrow."

"Got him," the big man said. He aimed the machine gun at the demon and pulled the trigger. Nothing happened. "I'm out!" Max flipped the rifle around and slammed the weapon's butt plate into a demon's throat. The large bearded axe it had been holding flew from the monster's hands, and Max snatched the weapon from the air, holding it in both hands.

Brahm swore, and Caitlyn watched as the demon nocked another arrow. It loosed the shot at the same time Josh dove in front of Caitlyn, and the arrow bounced away harmlessly.

"We could use some bloody magic here, Caitlyn!"

Brahm shouted.

"I can't change into my human form with this arrow in my shoulder. I would," she paused to maul a hellhound that dodge around Josh to attack her. "Bleed out. It needs to come out."

Josh spun, and the suit's glowing orange eyes searched her over. He located the arrow and put his hand on the shortened shaft. "This is going to hurt," he said.

Caitlyn nodded. "Hurry." She screamed as Josh tore the barbed arrowhead from her shoulder, and immediately changed into her human form. A large wall of fire blocked additional demons from mounting the stairs to come at them.

The four panted in their temporary respite. "The wall won't last long," Caitlyn said. "Scavenge what weapons you can."

"Where are we going, Jessica?" Hanna shouted over the screaming alarm.

The young Nephilim looked out from battlesuit's cockpit and shrugged. *I don't know*, she thought. *But we need to go this way. We'll be there soon.*

A few minutes prior, Jessica had wrested the controls away from Hanna. It hadn't been hard. Jessica was already several inches taller than the Changeling, and her magical power was much greater, if it had come to that.

The girls were through the thickest part of the fighting, and turning to face Hanna, Jessica said, "My daddy is in danger. I don't know how I know; I just do. He needs me. Only I can help him do what has to be done."

Hanna studied her eyes for a moment and nodded. "I understand. How will you know where to go?"

Time to stop. The Nephilim brought the tremendous machine to a stop and pushed the cockpit's release. "We're here." With a hiss, the two seats descended between the battlesuit's legs and came to a rest on the blood-soaked mud. Two angels stood facing them, but Jessica sensed the woman was more than she seemed.

Jessica unbuckled herself and stepped away from the machine. "Jessica, wait," Hanna called, but the younger girl ignored her.

"This is her?" she overheard the man angel say to the woman.

The woman nodded and knelt in the mud. "Jessica, I'm Ureon, and this is Eternius, your grandfather," she said with her hand out to the man.

Jessica quickly appraised the two and determined them to not be a threat. *Still, it pays to be cautious,* she thought as she warily approached. "It's nice to meet the two of you. Where is my daddy? He needs me." The splat of boots in the mud announced Hanna's arrival behind her.

The statement caught the two angels off guard. They glanced at each other before Eternius said, "What makes you think that?"

A sense of anxiety welled up within Jessica, and she balled her small fists. "He doesn't have time for these pointless questions. I can hear him calling for me. He's searching for me now! I have to go to him!" She caught a familiar flicker of fading magical residue in the air behind them, and the Nephilim immediately pieced together what had occurred.

"He's gone," she said. "You sent him somewhere." Jessica stepped forward, but hands came out from the two angels to restrain her. Before they reached her, the Nephilim changed into her true form. Black feathered wings painfully erupted from her back, and though she couldn't see it, she knew her eyes were glowing. The hands hesitated.

"Jessica," her grandfather said, "we just want to keep you safe. It is too dangerous where your father went. He went to the Realm of Evil to stop the man who has forced this war upon us."

"But he's dying!" As soon as the words escaped her lips, she knew it was true. "I only saw Daddy once!" Tears began to run down her face. "I have to see him again! I won't let you keep him from me!"

"I'm sorry," Ureon said. Before Jessica could react, a field of powerful magic rose from beneath her, and closed off her ability to cast spells or use demonic energy or even move. The Nephilim watched in horror as filaments of magic rose from the two angels' bodies.

"You cast the spell through your own bodies and under the ground where we couldn't see it," Hanna said, her tone strangely void of emotion.

Ureon and Eternius looked at the changeling, as if noticing her for the first time. "That's right," the female angel said. "When you've been around as long as we have, you pick up a trick or two."

The hairs along the back of Jessica's neck stood on end, and she thought she felt another presence join Hanna behind her. "That's an interesting trick," the changeling said, something off in her tone.

Ureon's and Eternius's eyes widened. They hastened to cast another barrier around the changeling, but they were already too late. Hanna's pain inflicting spell shot up from the ground behind to two angels and slammed into their spines.

The spell around Jessica vanished, and the angels' arms flopped around wildly before they collapsed into the mud. The younger girl stood and looked at Hanna. A dark glower was on her face, but it passed when she saw Jessica was freed. "They shouldn't have used their magic on you," Hanna said. "Alex needs you. Now go. I'll stay here and make sure they don't try to follow."

"Thank you," Jessica said as she turned to face the fading remnants of the portal to the Realm of Evil. To Hell. She took a deep breath and studied the lines of magic. She reconnected the parts of the portal that had already faded too much, and the brown portal opened before her. Wrapping her wings around her like a cloak, Jessica stepped through.

Odessa stood in awe of the battle happening before her. Her brother and son were locked in a match to the death of their very souls, and there was nothing she could do to help. Azreal had the upper hand, but Alex fended him off valiantly. A morbid sense of pride rose within her as she watched her son, knowing it would be the last time she saw him.

Tendrils of sickly green energy reached out from Azreal and lashed out at Alex. The Guardian deflected them with one of the wings of black energy from his back, and he struck out with his scythe.

Azreal dove away from the attack. Even the smallest wound from Ruin would instantaneously kill. *No, not kill,* Odessa thought. *Obliterate from all existence for all time. No rebirths, no future.* She had known this confrontation was coming ever since she met with Ureon all those years ago, but now that it was happening, she couldn't help but feel unready.

I'll only have one chance. I can't fail.

Twin blades of the same green energy appeared in Azreal's hands. He flew at Alex and launched a flurry of blows so fast Odessa couldn't follow them all. But her son could.

The Guardian spun the scythe like a staff and blocked several of the blows. He planted the butt of the weapon into the stone so hard the floor cracked around it, and Alex vaulted over Azreal, bringing him near her.

While both combatants were reorienting on the other, Odessa darted for her son. She touched him on the back of his head before either reacted to her movement. Everything froze.

"What have you done to me?" her son demanded.

"Silence, Alex, we don't have much time. This is just a thought-scape. Our minds are linked, and we are communicating at the speed of thought, but this spell doesn't last long. You can't kill Azreal like this. If you do, then you risk collapsing all of the Nine Realms."

"How?"

"You would destroy the Overlord's soul," Odessa explained. "The paragonship would have no way to pass to another. It could destabilize everything."

"I can't just let Azreal live!" he shouted.

"And you won't have to. I have a plan. I just don't have time to explain it."

"Why should I trust you?" Alex asked, his tone suddenly thoughtful.

"Because I love you, and I only want to finally do something right in this horrible world," Odessa said plaintively. "The spell is about to end. Knock me away from you. Hard. Azreal has to believe I attacked you, but you bested me."

The spell ended before Alex could respond, but he shoved her away with a strong push of his arm. Odessa lost her footing and slid along the floor until she slammed her back into one of the columns flanking the temple's entrance.

Azreal glanced between the two of them, trying to figure out what had just transpired, but Alex didn't give him a chance to riddle it out. Her son lunged forward and swung the scythe in a large arc. The Overlord danced away from it again and used the opening produced by the wide attack to lunge at Alex.

One of the dark blades bit deep into his flesh, but the Guardian was nimble. Avoiding further injury, he drew the scythe in tight and somersaulted away from Azreal. Her brother pressed his attack, and Odessa knew her chance was coming. She slowly rose to her feet, and Alex swung the scythe at Azreal again, forcing him within Odessa's reach.

Now!

Odessa flung herself at her brother. Catching him off guard with the unexpected attack, she clamped her teeth down at the joint of his neck and shoulder. Before Azreal could shake her off, Odessa drank deeply of his life blood. She felt the power flow from his body into her own and jumped away when she sensed his counter attack coming.

Azreal's enraged emerald green eyes glared at her. He roared with hatred, and mother and son were pushed back by the baleful energy flowing from him. "I no longer need the paragonship, Sister. I have ascended beyond need of it."

A thrumming power enveloped her, and Odessa lashed out at Azreal with her new powers as Overlord of Hell. None of the telekinetic strikes came close to touching him. Alex tried to move forward, to strike at his uncle, but even with the awesome power of Ruin leaching strength from his very soul, the Guardian could do nothing.

Where is all this power coming from? Doubt screamed through Odessa. *We're going to die.* Azreal's roar grew in power, and the walls began to crack around him. *The whole building is going to collapse!* she thought. The temple's roof exploded upward, and the walls and columns were swept away.

Crushing weight enveloped Odessa, and she was forced to watch helplessly as she and Alex were lifted from their feet and drawn through the maelstrom of pale green energy toward Azreal. Her son's face was a mask of grim determination.

They reached the eye of the swirling vortex of power around Azreal, and Odessa noticed the wings of black energy coming from Alex's back were much smaller than they had been when the fight had started. *His time is running out.* She struggled to break free from her brother's telekinetic grip, but he was just too strong. There was nothing she could do.

Azreal tightened his grip on her, and pain shot through her and bones in her chest snapped. "I'll deal with you in a moment, Sister," he sneered.

"Where are they?" Alex hissed. "Where is Jessica?"

"I don't even have her," Azreal snapped back. The Guardian's eyes widened in surprise. "But once I crush the life from your body, Nephew, I'll be sure to search her out."

Teeth bared in a feral snarl, Alex said, "I'll kill you before you lay a finger on her."

Azreal lifted him farther into the air, and Alex winced in pain as the invisible bonds tightened. "It's time to die, weakling."

A blinding flash of white light stole Odessa's vision, and she was falling through the air.

Sealing away Ruin caused pain to rip through Alex's ravaged body. Azreal had broken several of his ribs, and his left arm hung uselessly at his side, but the Guardian knew he had caught the Demon Lord off guard.

Justice, the form of the Guardian's Blade he killed Azreal with on Dae, was held loosely in his right hand. A blade of dark green energy emitted from the silvery metal hilt. The sickly green force Azreal had been channeling was repulsed by the sword.

Initially surprised by the sudden drop in his strength, Azreal quickly recovered. He saw the overhead chop coming and wrapped his hands over Alex's good right hand. Even though he couldn't control his left arm, Alex was more thickly muscled than Azreal, and Justice eliminated the effects of magic and demonic power, locking the two men in a test of strength. Blade pointing up into the air, Alex tried pushing it down while Azreal shoved against him.

"You'll not defeat me the same way twice, Nephew," the Demon Lord sneered, breath hot in

Alex's face.

The Guardian shook his head. "You're no family of mine," Alex snapped as he redoubled his effort. Azreal braced himself and pushed harder.

It's time.

<Are you certain, Wielder?> the Voice of Justice asked. <You won't survive.>

I'm already dead. I can feel my soul begin to slip away.

<I understand. It was an honor, Alex Zane.>

Alex stopped pushing against Azreal and stepped forward, closer to the Demon Lord. His arm wrenched backward painfully, and his shoulder popped out of its socket. Sword now fully upside down behind his back, Alex said a silent goodbye to his friends and loved ones.

The Guardian unleashed Ruin, and the scythe's toothed blade erupted from his chest and cut deep into Azreal's black heart.

Chapter Eighteen - A Beginning

All four standing atop the stairs into the Overlord's Temple panted heavily. When the sounds inside the temple had ceased, the demons suddenly withdrew a short distance and didn't advance again.

Only Josh, encapsulated as he was inside the Prometheus suit, had escaped significant injury in the battle. The arrow wound in Caitlyn's shoulder still pumped blood freely, and her right side and arm were soaked. But Max and Brahm's injuries were much more severe.

Max's right bicep and ribs had been cut deeply, and he couldn't lift his arm at all. Caitlyn would have healed him if she thought she could. It would be too much of a risk to focus on healing him when another attack could come at any moment.

Caitlyn turned to look at Brahm just in time to see him collapse. "Brahm!" she shouted.

"Tired," the dwarf muttered. "Can't keep..."

A demon at the base of the steps snarled and stepped forward, seeing an opportunity to attack, but Josh moved between them. None of the demons wanted to get near the young man in the powered armor.

"Come on, Brahm," Caitlyn said. "Stay with us. I still need you to help keep me in line."

"Bah. Ye're no' needin' me fer anything," the old dwarf said. He coughed, and Caitlyn thought it sounded wet. She looked him over and saw that the splintered shaft of a spear had somehow become

307

lodged between the plates of his armor.

"Don't you bloody die, you stone-headed dwarf. I'll not have it," she snapped. Her hand slipped down to the spear in his side.

Brahm must have seen the movement of her arm and shook his head. "Leave it in," he said. "It's in me lung. I'll die. If ye take it out."

A streak of white light shot across the sky, flying from the Hell Gate and landing next to them. A young woman, her hair as white as the dress she wore, stood before them. Black wings spread out from her back, and her eyes glowed different colors.

"Uncle Brahm!" the girl shouted, and she rushed over to the collapsed dwarf. Her wings slipped back into her back, and her hair changed to a chestnut brown color.

Uncle? Caitlyn thought in a daze. *That doesn't make any* — "Jessica?" she gasped. "Is that you?"

"Yeah, Aunt Caitlyn," she said quickly. The young Nephilim stood over Brahm, and the changeling watched as she sent a medical probe into the dwarf. After a fast examination, Jessica turned to face the older woman.

"He won't survive much longer," Jessica said. She turned back to Brahm. "You've lost too much blood, Uncle. There isn't enough time to find a dwarf healer."

A demoness with red hair emerged from the Overlord's Temple. Her resemblance to Alex was unmistakable, but her midnight black eyes gave Caitlyn pause. "You're Alex's mother?" she asked.

"I am," the woman said. "I'm Odessa." The demoness knelt next to Brahm. "Master Ironfist, I wish we had met again under better circumstances."

"Eh, ye do no' always get what ye want," the dwarf muttered. He took note of her changed eyes. "So, it's done. Ye're the Overlord now."

Odessa nodded, and Caitlyn took an involuntary step back. The new Overlord of Hell glanced at her before turning her attention back to Brahm. "I want nothing more than this senseless death to stop."

"And Alex?" Brahm asked.

Tears ran down Odessa's cheeks. "He's inside. Alex gave his life to save us all. In the end, Azreal was too much for anyone but my son."

A shrill scream pierced the hot air, and Jessica sprinted into the temple. "Daddy! No!"

Alex is dead, Caitlyn thought as she fell to her knees. *I thought he would find some way... to not...*

"I'll go to her," Josh called as he followed after the young girl. "I'll keep her safe. I owe Alex at least that much."

Odessa swore softly. "I didn't know she was Alex's... my granddaughter," she said. Her gaze fell on the assembled mass of demons.

Caitlyn felt a hollow thump in the air, and a golden portal to Dae hung in the air behind them. "That is a portal to the Adorac Academy. They can heal Brahm there. Your big friend needs medical attention as well. See them through, or they will die," Odessa said.

"I'm not going to leave Jessica or Josh here," Caitlyn protested. *He's dead.*

A large, four-limbed demon mounted the bottom stair and cautiously started up. "You have my oath as Alex's mother that I will not allow any harm to come to them while they remain here. I have certain protection against those of my kind, but I can't stop them all should they decide to kill you all. Seconds are vital here, Changeling."

Caitlyn made no move to get up, and Odessa hauled the woman to her feet. "Quickly. It isn't safe for you in the open like this."

The Overlord of Hell spun to the demon that was now half-way up the stairs, pointed a finger at him, and screamed something in the guttural language of Hell. The demon lifted an arm as if to ward off a blow and scrambled down the stairs. Those at the base moved away a few paces, and some took wing or crawled into the tunnels that ran beneath the stone latticework above the dead star.

Odessa grabbed Caitlyn's shoulders. Her tone was kind, but firm. "What is your name, Child?"

"Caitlyn," she responded numbly. *He's really gone. Never to return.*

"Listen to me, Caitlyn. Look at me." Odessa waited until Caitlyn's unfocused gaze locked onto her eyes. "You must save your injured friends. They will die without your help. I will keep Jessica safe until I can return her to Alex's wife. Please, I just lost my son; I won't allow anyone else to die this day. Not if I can help it."

Caitlyn heard the sincerity in the woman's voice and knew there was no deceit there, but it was hard to see past those nightmarish eyes. She nodded and lifted Brahm on a bed of air. The dwarf coughed and blood trickled from the corner of his mouth. *I have to hurry,* she thought. *I have to save someone.* "Keep her safe, Overlord, or I will show you that Alex isn't the only one capable of killing Hell's paragon."

Odessa nodded, and Caitlyn and Brahm followed Max through the portal to Dae

Josh stood a few feet behind the wailing girl as she lay over Alex's corpse. The young man knew he should say something, anything, but no words would come. *What am I supposed to say? Her father just died.*

He hadn't known Alex long, but Josh had build a deep and abiding respect for the man over the last two weeks. *Is that all it's been since this started? Two weeks? Seems like forever and a year.*

Josh turned his back to the girl and envisioned the suit opening so he could leave it. The back opened, and he stepped out of the Prometheus armor. He walked to the girl and knelt beside her, putting a hand on her back.

He was still unsure what to say, but it didn't matter to her. She spun about and threw her arms around him, sobbing into his shoulder. Josh was momentarily caught off guard, but he recovered and wrapped her in a warm embrace.

What did Caitlyn say her name was? "It will be all right, Jessica. I'm here for you," he said softly.

Jessica cried harder and started to talk through her sobbing. "How? How will it ever be all right? I only saw Daddy once, and now he's gone."

"I lost both of my parents when I was about your age," Josh whispered, assuming the girl was ten or eleven. "I guess... I guess it never will be *all* right, but it gets better, Jess." Memories of the crash exhumed themselves from the darkest recesses of his mind, and tears began to well in Josh's eyes. *Keep it together, man. She needs someone to help her stand back up.*

Her fists balled behind his back, and Jessica took a deep breath. She let it out with a shudder and sniffed a few times. He let her lean away, and she looked at him with bloodshot eyes. "Is this all life is? Pain and fear and loss? Running and fighting and dying?"

Her bottom lip trembled, and she gasped in pain. She slumped forward and weakly beat her fists against his chest. "Why? Why did he have to leave me? Didn't he know I loved him?"

Jessica's words struck him like a hammer, and Josh couldn't hold back his tears. He put his arms back around her and let her anger play itself out. *No one should have to go through this. I'm so sorry.* He searched his mind for the words to take some of her hurt away, but he knew there were none. He knew it too well.

After a time, Jessica stopped hitting him and put

her arms back around him, holding on to him as if he were the only thing holding her from a bottomless pit. They held each other until the tears finally stopped.

Jessica pushed away from him, and he let her go. She studied his face for a time, and Josh found himself transfixed by the intensity of her gaze "Thank you..." she said.

"I'm Joshua Hrynkiewicz, but you can call me Josh."

"Thank you, Josh. I'm Jessica." She glanced from one of his gray eyes to the other. "Are you here to protect me?"

"I am," he said with a nod.

Jessica took one of his hands in her own. "Will you always protect me?"

What should I...? Yes. "I will protect you to the best of my abilities," he said, knowing she had no expectations of him, but sure it was the right thing to do.

"Why?"

Josh shook his head, unsure what to say. "I've spent so much of my life not knowing why I did anything, not knowing if anything I did mattered. Max saved my life. I'd be dead without him. But your father... He showed me what it means to transcend what I was and become something more. Someone people can rely on.

"So, you can rely on me, and I do everything I can to protect you. For him," Josh said, shifting his gaze to Alex. It was the first time Josh had looked at his friend's body since he had knelt next to Jessica.

Alex's eyes were closed, and he had a peaceful look on his face, as if he had achieved everything he had set out to do. Josh supposed that he had. Azreal was dead, and the Nine Realms were now safe. *It's strange, even after everything I've seen, it's still hard to believe that there are seven more worlds like Earth and this one.* He looked back down to Jessica, and she was still looking at him.

"Then you shall be my guardian," she said with a somber tone.

Guardian. That title belongs to someone else, Josh thought, but he just nodded at her words.

"Is that your decision then, Jessica?" a woman's voice asked from behind him.

Josh turned and saw the red-haired demoness that had come from the temple earlier. He stood and drew Jessica up beside him, his arm protectively around her shoulder. The woman regarded the gesture and looked him up and down. He could feel her black eyes scan his body. *Idiot, you shouldn't have left your armor.*

"It is, Grandmother Odessa. One I will not back down from."

Odessa nodded thoughtfully. "Very well, child." She walked to Alex's body and lifted the Guardian's Blade from where it lay beside him. Josh made sure to face her as she walked past. He wasn't willing to take any chances, even if the demoness was Jessica's grandmother.

She held the wooden sword for a moment, then held it out to Josh, hilt first. "Take it."

His eyes widened, and Josh stepped back,

removing his hand from Jessica's shoulder. "No!" he said with his hands raised. "I can't! That's—"

"Yours," Odessa finished. "Should you choose to accept it. Others have meant it for Jessica, but it seems she has found someone more suitable."

"Others?" Josh blurted. "I don't think I can..." He took a deep breath and steadied himself. "I can't take his place. That's not who I am."

A soft laugh escaped Odessa's lips, and she shook her head. "It wasn't who he was either," the demoness said. "My son wasn't ready for this either, but he took up this blade when the Nine Realms needed him. The hour draws nigh, human, and there are those who would depend upon you. Or were those empty words you just spoke?"

Both of them stared at him. The silence felt a palpable thing to Josh, and he lowered his arms. *I can do this.* He stepped forward and reached out for the hilt. *I finally know what I should be doing.*

Josh's hand stopped inches from the wooden sword. *Are you sure?* his doubts whispered. *This is a terrible responsibility you are accepting, street rat. You've never even held a sword before.*

Gritting his teeth, the young man shoved his misgivings aside. *I'll learn.* Josh closed his hand around the hilt of the Guardian's Blade. He drew the weapon from Odessa's soft grip and looked at it a moment before looking from the woman to the girl and back in growing alarm.

They stood still at statues, unmoving and unblinking.

"What's going on?" Josh asked as everything faded away into gray mist. He turned around to see if there was any way to escape, and by the time he turned back, the woman, girl, and body were gone. *If it weren't for the ground beneath me, I'd swear I was floating in a dream.*

"That's not far off," Alex's voice said. "It is kind of like a dream."

Josh spun and faced the direction the voice had come. The mists cleared, revealing a flat, white landscape, and Alex stood only a few feet away from him.

"What? You're dead! *What* is going on?" he shouted.

Alex gave him a sad smile. "I'm sorry to place this burden on you, Josh. If there was any other way, I would take it, but I'll not put my daughter in more danger than she already is."

Josh looked down at the sword in his hand, and he understood. "It's all right, Alex. I was the one that reached out for the sword after all."

The older man nodded. "That you were. Now, as for what's going on. First off, there are some things you should know about that sword in your hand." Josh listened closely as Alex explained the Guardian's Blade and how the memories of the previous wielders were imprinted upon the blade in order to teach the new wielder to use the weapon.

"So you'll be able to help me!" Josh said, his face brightening.

Alex shook his head. "No. A long time ago, the

Guardian's Blade was unintentionally damaged. A male Nephilim, like my daughter, was forced to bend the blade to his will. He didn't know it, because there weren't any previous wielders imprinted yet, but he sentenced every wielder after him to an early grave.

"The memories are too much for one mind to handle, and their flow can't be stopped," Alex continued. "I was protected by those effects by something that is irrelevant to you now. It won't work for you. It will drive you insane, until you either get yourself killed, or your brain just shuts down under the strain."

Fear wormed its way into Josh's mind. "So, I'm going to lose my mind."

"No, Josh," Alex said, approaching the young man. He stopped only a couple of feet away. "I'm going to protect you from it the only way I can."

"How?"

"I have been imprinted upon the Guardian's Blade twice. As the embodiment of the Blade of Balance, I can force a purge of the memories of the previous wielders of the Guardian's Blade. I only need concurrence from one other previous wielder." A smirk crossed Alex's face. "And since there's two of me, you could say we're of a like mind."

"I can't begin to imagine what I'm asking of you," Josh said. "I just want to say thank you, and that I will do my best to protect your daughter from all harm."

Alex placed his hands on the young man's shoulders. "I know you will. I didn't have long to get to know you, but I saw that you were an honest man, one who gives his all into everything he does. But before I go, there are a few people I have to say goodbye to first."

Josh nodded. "Just tell me what to do."

When Josh snapped back to reality, he saw the silhouette of Jessica and Odessa embracing in front of a golden portal to another world.

<Gold is Dae,> Alex sent into Josh's mind. <It's home.>

I understand, Josh thought, assuming Alex hear his thoughts. *Where do you think we'll find your wife?*

<I don't know, but I won't risk your mental health if it takes too long to find her. I'll end it before that happens.>

Don't worry. We'll find her first.

"It's time to go," Odessa called. "I'm sure Caitlyn is beginning to worry."

Josh nodded and walked over to the Prometheus suit. He propped the Guardian's Blade against the metal leg and stepped back into the powered armor. After it sealed up behind him, he grabbed the wooden sword and walked to Alex's body.

Jessica was instantly beside him, and he handed her the Guardian's Blade when she offered to take it from him. Josh knelt next to Alex's body and reverently lifted it, bearing it in two arms as he walked to the golden portal.

He paused and looked at Odessa before he stepped through. Something struck him as odd, and he thought for a few seconds before he realized what it was. "Azreal's body, I haven't seen it anywhere."

Odessa nodded. "I sent it to the Realm of Life where it would be destroyed in the elemental fires. Without the powers as Overlord of Hell and with his soul destroyed, there is no chance he would return to life, but there is still much power stored within his body. I thought it safest beyond the reach of any who would try to extract that power."

"I'll pass the message on that Azreal has been killed and his body destroyed. Are we now at peace?" Josh asked.

"For a time, Guardian. But the next battle always looms just below the horizon," Odessa said. "And there is much to do before it comes. Now stand aside. I need a moment with my granddaughter."

Josh moved away from the two and watched as the demoness spoke. Jessica nodded occasionally, but he was too far away to hear what they were saying. Several minutes passed, and the two women looked at him.

Jessica took a few steps toward him and held out a hand. "It's time to go home."

Josh took her hand and they stepped through the portal to the Realm of Magic.

Epilogue - Goodbyes

Hanna took a deep breath. She looked around the room, her gaze avoiding the two standing people. Brahm, Max, Caitlyn, and Terra sat around the coffee table in Terra's living room.

She looked over the young man standing before her. Josh wore the Guardian's Blade awkwardly on his hip. He kept catching it on things as he walked past them. Jessica stood beside him and nodded.

"Alex says that he wants to talk to each of you," Josh said. "Before he... goes."

"What do you mean?" Terra asked. Hanna glanced over at her. There was a hollow look in her eyes, but Hanna guessed that was to be expected. *No one could lose the same love twice and not feel a bit hollow*, she supposed.

"He says he's doing it to protect me. That he has to remove himself from the Guardian's Blade to keep me from going insane," Josh relayed. "He says that he wants to say goodbye." He set the sword on the coffee table. "I know it's hard for each of you, I'll leave. He wants Hanna to go first. All you have to do is touch it."

The changeling swallowed and reached out a hand to the wooden sword. As soon as her fingers touched the cool wood, white mist enveloped everything. She looked around, surprised at the sudden change in environment.

"Hey, there, Hanna," Alex said. She turned to see him emerge from the mist.

Hanna ran up to him and wrapped her arms around him. He felt warm and smelled like freshly cut grass and vanilla. "Hey, Alex."

He knelt beside her and put his hand to her cheek. "I just wanted to say thank you for taking care of my family. I heard how much you did from Jessica. She looks up to you so much."

Hanna looked down and smiled. She glanced up into Alex's green eyes. "You're welcome, Alex. I just wanted to keep her safe."

Alex nodded. "I know. But there's something you have to promise me."

She cocked her head to the side, and her eyebrows drew down. "What's that?"

"This war with Hell is finally over. I want you to go back to helping people. You've seen more death than anyone should have to, much less a seven-year-old. I just want you to be happy, Hanna. I wish I could have done more for you, but you've done fine without my help."

Hanna nodded. "I'll do what I can, Alex. But is it really over? Are we really safe?"

Alex put a hand on her head and ruffled her hair. "For now, yeah." He stood back up and took a deep breath. "I have to go now, Hanna. Can you let Max know he's next?"

"I can. Goodbye, Alex."

"Goodbye, Hanna."

"You just had to go and get yourself killed, didn't you?" Max asked.

Alex laughed. "It's not like I planned on it! I thought Terra was dead and that Jessica was dying!"

"That would make me freak out too. I'm glad you were able to end all of this. I heard from Thor that the last Obsidian Tower on Earth was destroyed."

"Yeah," Alex said. "Josh told me. He also told me that the EDF offered you a job. You going to take it?"

Max crossed his arms. "Damn it, man. Do you really want to go with small talk right now?"

Alex shook his head. "No, I don't, but it's kind of hard to say goodbye. You're the only person from back before all of this started, coming to Dae and fighting Azreal, I mean. I feel like you're all that connects me to my old life."

"Does it matter?" Max asked as he placed his hand on Alex's shoulder. "Does it really? What good does looking back even serve?"

"I don't know. It's all I have left, I guess. I don't have a future."

"Bullshit."

Alex raised an eyebrow at his friend.

"You have a wife and kid and friends that will remember you for the rest of their lives. You have a future."

A sad smile crossed Alex's face. "I guess you're right. Thanks, Max."

"Any time, Alex. If they ever need me, I'm just a phone call away."

"I know."

"See you, Sarge."

"Later, Tiny."

Brahm looked at the human he had come to call friend. "Ye know, if it was no' fer ye, we'd all've died on Hell."

"I don't think so," Alex said. "I don't think you'd have let anyone die there."

"Ye're the best one."

"What do you mean?"

"O' all the Guardians. Ye're the best one. I've ne'er seen a human with such strength."

Alex rubbed the back of his head, a chagrined look on his face. "I don't know about all that. I don't think I did anything all that impressive. It was all just a mad dash to save as many people as I could."

Brahm laughed. "That's usually what life is. Ye're just doin' what ye can."

"I hear that." A moment of silence passed between them. "Brahm, can I ask you a favor?"

"Anything, Alex."

"When I saved Terra's life by traveling through time, I ruined something that was supposed to happen. Something that would have made Caitlyn's life much better."

Brahm nodded. "She an' Darren." Alex stared at the dwarf. "I'm bloody old, no' bloody stupid," the dwarf grumbled.

Alex grinned. "I know that. I don't know if

there's anything you'll be able to do for her, for them... But if there is... Caitlyn deserves to be happy."

"Aye, I'll do what I can, Alex."

"Thank you, Brahm.

"May the Mother welcome you in her embrace."

"Until we return to the stone."

Caitlyn reached out to touch the Guardian's Blade, but her hand froze before she could. "I can't," she whispered.

Brahm looked up at her, his eyes red-rimmed. "Caitlyn, he's waitin' on ye. He just wants to tell ye goodbye."

Caitlyn closed her eyes and took a deep breath. Her fingers curled down into her hands. *I don't want to do this.* "Okay," she said, and she touched the Guardian's Blade.

White mist obscured everything around Caitlyn, and she heard muffled footsteps behind her. She slowly turned to see Alex standing just a couple feet away with his arms stretched wide. Caitlyn stumbled over to him and fell into his embrace.

"Hey, now," Alex said as she started to cry, "there's no need for all that. I'm still here."

"No you aren't. Not really." Caitlyn sobbed harder, and Alex stood silently, stroking her hair. She wasn't sure how much time had passed before she stopped crying.

This will be your last chance to say it. "I love you, Alex."

"I love you too, Caitlyn. I'm sorry things never worked out for you. I wish there was something I could do…"

Caitlyn placed her fingers against Alex's lips and shook her head. "No. There's nothing, but it's enough to know that you cared for me."

Alex nodded, and she let her fingers fall away. "I understand," he said.

Caitlyn studied his green eyes for a time, drinking in the last time she would see the man she loved. "I'll miss you."

"I know." Alex opened his mouth to say something else, but he seemed to hesitate.

"What is it?"

"Nothing. I just wanted to make sure you knew that there were other people who cared for you."

"I know," she said.

"Goodbye, Caitlyn."

Caitlyn balled her fists and fought back another onslaught of tears. "Kiss me. I want to know…"

Alex placed his warm hands on her face and shook his head. "I'm sorry, Caitlyn, but I won't. I love you, but I won't give you this false impression to take away from here. We were never what you wanted us to be."

Caitlyn closed her eyes, and her chest trembled. "I understand." Tears ran down her face anew, but Alex wiped them away with his thumbs. She felt his lips touch her forehead.

"Goodbye, Caitlyn," he said again.

"Goodbye, Alex."

"My wife, please." His words echoed in her ears as the mists faded away.

Caitlyn stood from her seat and turned away from everyone. The tears still streamed down her cheeks. "Terra, he wants you," Caitlyn said as she left the house. The warm sun beamed down on her. *Goodbye, Alex.*

Terra watched impassively as Caitlyn pulled her hand away from the sword and stood. "Terra, he wants you," the changeling said. Terra reached out and touched the Guardian's Blade without hesitation. She waited patiently as the white mists descended.

"I'm sorry, Terra," Alex said as he stepped from the fog to her left.

The half-angel didn't turn to look at him; she just lowered her head. "I know."

"I didn't mean for any of this to happen. I just wanted us to be happy together."

"I know."

Silence hung thick in the air with Terra's gaze fixed on a point on the floor a few feet ahead of her. Alex's leather boots entered her field of vision, and she could tell he was facing her.

"Won't you look at me?" he asked. Pain was thick in his voice.

Terra's gaze slowly rose, and she met his eyes. Alex's brows drew down and he took a step forward.

Alex placed his hands on her shoulders. "What's wrong?"

"You're dead, Alex. You're dead, and I feel nothing. Just hollow."

Her husband wrapped his arms around her. "I know. I'm sorry, Terra. I…"

"Why did you just go get yourself killed?" she asked. "Why did you put yourself so far removed? Not even the Life Wardens can bring you back."

"I wouldn't ask them to," Alex said. "It's not supposed to work that way. Josh told me that you were captive on the Realm of Science. Are you all right?"

Terra nodded. "I am. I guess. I don't remember much of coming home. I knew when you…"

Alex suppressed her words when he planted his lips on hers. Terra kissed him back, and she began to feel a distant ache where her heart used to be. She relished feeling the emotion after days of numb emptiness. *Pain is all that's left for me.*

"Hey, don't think like that," he said, breaking their kiss.

Terra frowned at him. "No fair, reading my mind."

Alex smiled. "One of the perks of the job. That, and I can do stuff like this." He turned away from her and waved his hand.

The mist faded away to reveal a sandy beach. The sun hung just above the horizon, and the sky was awash in reds and oranges. Surf crashed against the sand, and Terra smiled.

"It's beautiful," Terra said. She looked about and saw an elven city in the distance. "Where is this?"

Alex shrugged. "I don't know. It's from one of the other Voices. They understand that our end is coming and have shared many of their memories with me. None of them are bad people. I feel bad about removing all of us from the sword."

"If you didn't, would I still be able to see you?" Terra asked.

Alex shook his head. "What we're doing now is similar to the way the blade connects to the wielder. If I didn't remove all of our Voices, then all of you would go insane. I'm only saying goodbye this way because it'll be over soon."

"I understand." Terra looked out at the sunset and grabbed Alex's hand. "May we stay a while?"

Alex kissed Terra's cheek. His lips were warm, and she felt the lingering sensation long after he pulled away. "Of course."

The half-demon and half-angel watched as the orange ball of light sank into the ocean. They leaned back and stared into the night sky as stars began to emerge. "I love you, Terra," Alex said as he squeezed her hand, "and I always will."

It's time. Terra bit her lip as the stars began to waver. *I will not cry! Not in our last moments together.* She knew Alex must have heard the thought, but he had the grace to say nothing about it. "I love you too, Alex. Forever."

Alex stood and held a hand out to his wife. She took it and was lifted to her feet. He kissed her again, and Terra was momentarily confused by the salty taste in her mouth. She opened her eyes to see tears running down his face.

"I love you," he whispered.

"I love you too."

Alex angrily wiped at the tears running down his face and sniffed his nose. "I need to talk to Jessica now."

Terra nodded, unwilling to say those final words. "I'll miss you, Terra."

"I'll miss you too, Alex."

"Goodbye, my love."

"Bye," she choked out. Terra blinked, and she was back in the living room, touching the wooden blade. She looked up at her daughter, a young woman after only two weeks. "Daddy wants to tell you goodbye."

Jessica nodded and stepped forward, laying her hand on Alex's sword.

Jessica stood before Alex on the beach. It felt like early morning, and the sun was rising behind them. "Hello, daddy," she said.

"Hey there, little one," he said with a smile. "I guess I can't call you that any more. You look like you're almost a teenager!"

"Yeah. I guess I do." Jessica kicked at a shell in the sand. "Daddy?"

"Hm?"

"It's not fair."

Her daddy took a deep breath and took her hand. "I know it's not, baby." They walked down the beach hand-in-hand for a time, neither one of them speaking.

"I wish I could have known you for longer," Jessica said.

"Me too, Jessica." Alex knelt before her, taking her other hand. "There are things... things I would have told you and helped you with that I just won't have the chance to."

Jessica nodded. "I know. You did it though. You were able to save everyone."

Alex shrugged. "Yeah, I was, but I wonder if it was worth it. I think I'd have rather stayed home with you and Te- Mommy."

"I wish that could have happened."

He squeezed her hands. "It would have been nice. But there are a three things that I have to tell you now, Jessica, before I'm gone."

"What is it?" Jessica asked, her brows drawn down.

"First, I think Josh is a good man, and that he'll help take care of you. He feels like he owes me a debt, but that's not true. He's not very confident in himself, and he doesn't always think things through, so you'll have to help him see just how strong and smart he can be."

Jessica nodded. "I will."

"Good. Second, I think some people meant for you to become the next Guardian, not Josh. And I think they're going to be extremely angry about it not going the way they wanted. I want you to be careful and be on the lookout for dangers to him and to yourself."

"Okay."

"Third, I need you to be strong for Mommy. She's lost a lot in her life and will need you to help take care of her."

"I can do that, but I think something's wrong with Mommy."

Her father's gaze flicked between her eyes. "What do you mean?"

Jessica thought about it for a moment before answering. "I don't really know. It's hard to explain. It's like she's coming apart. She'll just stare off into the distance for a time, and then come out of it with no memory of what happened while she was staring."

Alex nodded his head. "She's really upset, baby. I wouldn't let that bother you too much. She just needs to you be there for her and help her see that she has reasons to be happy again. Okay?"

"Okay, Daddy."

Alex leaned forward and wrapped his daughter in a tight embrace. "I love you, little one. Before you were born, now, and forever."

"I love you too, Daddy. Bye."

"Bye."

Josh stood in the EDF's Section Five lab under Cheyenne Mountain. Doctor Montoya and Director Strom stood facing him. He had told Jessica to stay

331

behind on Dae with her mother while he ran this final errand. He had gotten a Fyrian Recall Device to allow him to teleport back to where Caitlyn was waiting on him.

I'm still not sure how I feel about being Jessica's protector.

<I'm sure you'll figure it out,> Alex sent into his mind. <All I know is that you need to protect one another. Something's coming, and ancient forces tried to manipulate my daughter into becoming the Guardian.>

I wonder why? What's so bad that they would need to make a little girl into a warrior?

<I think they're called the Outsiders. Fenris, the spirit of Yggdrasil on Caine, showed them to me once. You and Jessica should ask him for more information on them.>

We will.

"Well, that completes just about all of the final checks," the doctor said. "Thank you for returning the armor to us. After you disappeared in that battle, we had begun to worry."

"Yeah, no problem. It wasn't mine to keep. Doctor, Director," Josh said with a nod as he turned to leave.

"Wait," a woman's voice called. Josh turned around and saw a woman's face on the computer terminal behind the armor.

"Aia?" Josh asked, astounded. She smiled at him.

"Doctor," the Director said. "What's going on?"

Doctor Montoya shrugged. "I'm not certain.

That's the AIA, Artificially Intelligent Algorithm, from the Prometheus armor on the screen. It appears that she wanted to say something."

Aia looked at Montoya. "That's right. You're letting my pilot abandon me. This places him in undue danger, something that is contrary to my core programming."

Josh shook his head. "Aia, you have to stay here. You don't belong to me."

The screen turned from blue to red. "I don't *belong* to anyone," Aia snapped.

Director Strom crossed her arms. "You belong to the EDF. You are a computer program."

The screen seemed to zoom out, and Aia's posture matched that of the director's. "And you're just a talking sack of meat." The Prometheus armor closed and powered on of it's own volition. "I'm going with him."

"No, you aren't," the director said.

"Ma'am," Doctor Montoya interrupted, "if I may. The AIA system is fully integrated with the Prometheus prototype. She can't be removed without having to completely rebuild the system. We deployed this prototype knowing full well there could be some glitches and that it would be considered a loss. Why don't we just let her go?"

Margaret stared at Inigo. "Have you lost your mind? That's billions of dollars of R&D you're proposing we let just walk out of here!"

The armor's weapons systems came online, and Josh stepped between the two EDF members and the suit. *I'm pretty sure she won't hurt me.*

Montoya lowered his voice. "Margaret, do you really think you could stop her if she wanted to go?"

"I can still hear you," Aia said. "And the chances of me escaping unharmed are almost one-hundred percent. I can tell you right now, that the chances of you surviving a confrontation are minimal."

Margaret Strom, Director of the Earth Defense Force, was not a stupid woman, and she knew when to back down. "Fine," she said. "But you will not return to Earth for any reason. If you are damaged, then too bad."

"That's acceptable," Aia said. The Prometheus suit opened back up, and Josh glanced at Doctor Montoya and the director.

"Go," Director Strom said.

Josh climbed back inside the armor he had only just exited and bade the doctor farewell. He was going to say goodbye to the director too, but he felt like it would be rubbing in that Aia and the Prometheus suit were coming with him. In a crackle of electricity, he disappeared from the EDF base and stood in a clearing in front of Caitlyn.

"I thought you were giving the armor back?" the changeling asked.

Josh shrugged. "They decided to let me keep it."

"You must have been very convincing."

"Yeah," Aia said, overriding the suit's speakers, "I was."

Caitlyn smiled at hearing the AI's voice and opened the golden portal back to Dae. "Time to get going."

"Niles Wester," Theodore Thelonius said from atop the Architect's seat in the Control Cluster, "you are found guilty of abduction, wrongful imprisonment, inciting anarchy, abuse of power, and conspiracy to commit treason, the punishment for which is mental wiping. After your mind has been scoured of all memories, you will be put to work on the asteroid belt. Have you anything to say in mitigation?"

Niles spat at the man.

"Very well." Theo turned to the men he had enlisted to replace the Praetorians. "Take him away."

The two armed men lifted Niles from his seat and began carrying him away. They were stopped by the CEO of Atlas Labs. "Hard work, out in the belt," he said with a snide smirk. "Not that you'll mind, I suppose, seeing as you'll be nothing more than a senseless hulk."

"You betrayed me!" Niles shouted.

Marcus held up his hands. "Betrayed you? I did nothing of the sort. That infers that I was on your side at some point. I only answered the questions I was asked." He lifted his hand and pointed across the room at the collection of witnesses. "She betrayed you."

Cheryl Black raised her hand and waved at Niles. Her testimony had been a key part in his sentencing.

"I just can't believe *why* she would have kept a private copy of all of your conversations," Marcus said with a shrug. "Oh, I know!" He leaned close and whispered into Niles's left ear. "It was to get your job."

Niles tried to whip his head around to slam his forehead into the man's nose, but he was too slow, and Marcus stepped away. "Fiesty!" Marcus looked at the two guards and stepped out of their way. "Let me not stand in the way of your punishment."

"I heard mental wiping is excruciating," Marcus called as Niles was dragged away. "How dreadful. Good luck in the mines!"

Niles shouted obscenities until the elevator closed.

"I find your conduct unbecoming of one of your station," the Architect said. Marcus turned to see Theo standing behind him.

Marcus held up his hands and shrugged. "My apologies, Paragon. I just never could stand that man."

Theo nodded. "Indeed. Thank you for your assistance in this matter."

"Happy to be of service. Have you received my bid for the repairs to the station?"

"I have. Everything seems to be in order. Tell your crews to get to work," the Architect said as he turned to leave.

"As you will," Marcus said. *Got rid of a couple obnoxious men. Received a few billion credits.* The CEO of Atlas Labs nodded and put his hands in his pockets, whistling a merry tune as he left the Control Cluster. *A good day for profits.*

Eternius seethed as he soared over the planet Earth. *She lied to me, again!* As soon as the fighting on Earth had finished, Ureon vanished without a trace. The newly reinstated Keeper of Fate had scoured the Realm of Balance for the woman, but she was nowhere to be found.

Maybe she has returned to Bara, Eternius thought. Using his Traveler's Pendant, the angel opened a portal to the Amphitheater of High Seats in the City of Spires. Eternius flew through the portal and immediately felt like something was wrong. He looked all about but did not see anything of out of the ordinary.

"What is going on?" he muttered. Then it dawned upon the ancient angel. He was alone on the Realm of Good. There wasn't another angel anywhere, and the colors seemed off. Eternius's gaze drifted skyward until it settled on the Source.

The great ball of light that helped sustain the Nine Realms usually shone a pure white color, but Eternius noted several darker spots on the Source's surface. He launched himself into the air to commune with the sphere, but an invisible force blocked him from touching it. Eternius swore and battered against the transparent barricade, but nothing he did seemed to bring him any closer to the source.

I have to find help. Maybe Fenris knows

something of what has happened. Eternius attempted to use his Traveler's Pendant again, but it would not work. Panic began to build in the Keeper of Fate. He flew to the Gateway Arch as quickly as his wings would carry him and tried to open a portal to Dae. When that failed, he attempted Earth. He tried each of the Realms in succession, even Death and Evil, but it was all for naught.

Eternius turned back to the City of Spires. *I'm trapped here. Trapped in a dying Realm with no way out.*

She materialized in the woman's room in the dead of night. She held the mind spike loosely in her left hand. She knew that to use it too many times on the same people could permanently damage their minds, but she didn't care. If this one failed her, there would be others she could use.

A man stirred beside the sleeping woman, and the intruder paused. *She was supposed to be alone. No matter. A single elf could not stop me.*

She crept along the wooden floor, being careful to not make any noise. The intruder stood over the sleeping woman and smiled. *Too easy.* She touched the tip of the mind spike to the woman's head.

"It's time you give another one of my prophecies, Silvia," Ureon whispered as she began implanting the false memories.

Alex sat at an imagined table in an imagined chair and talked to the other iteration of himself that was imprinted on the Guardian's Blade. The both looked at the holographic images that represented their surroundings. Josh was checking in on Jessica after returning to Dae with the Prometheus armor.

"You know, I think that kid'll do well."

"Yeah, he's got a lot of potential."

The two of him watched Josh bid their wife a good night and leave their home. The new Guardian walked across the street and entered his house. He walked into the bedroom and set the blade down on the dresser.

<I'll take care of them for you,> Josh sent into the blade.

"I know you will," Alex said. "Thank you, Josh."

<You're welcome, Alex. You going now?>

"Yeah. Be good, kid."

<I will.>

Alex looked across the table to his other self. "You ready?"

"Yeah." He reached across the table to shake Alex's hand. "It was fun, Me."

Alex laughed. "I guess it was. Goodbye."

This concludes the War of the Realms Trilogy.

The Nine Realms will return in Fall 2015.

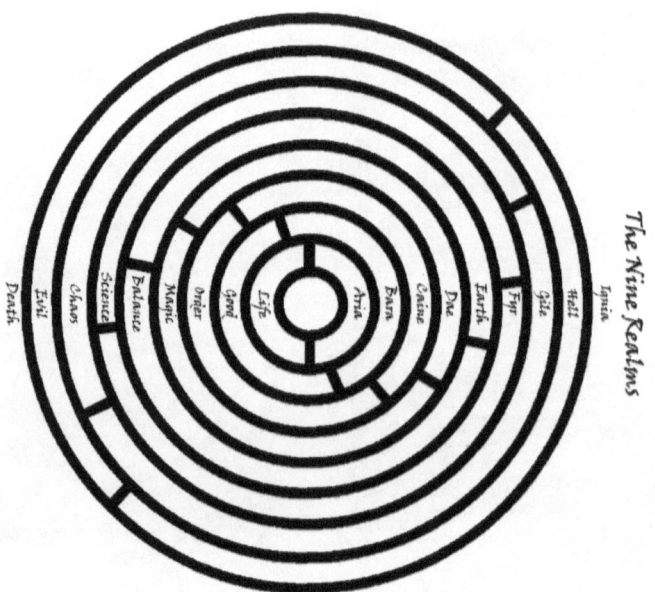

The Nine Realms

Ignia
Hell
Gate
Fyr
Earth
Dae
Cacine
Barn
Aria
Life
Scent
Gnei
Order
Magic
Balance
Science
Chaos
Evil
Death

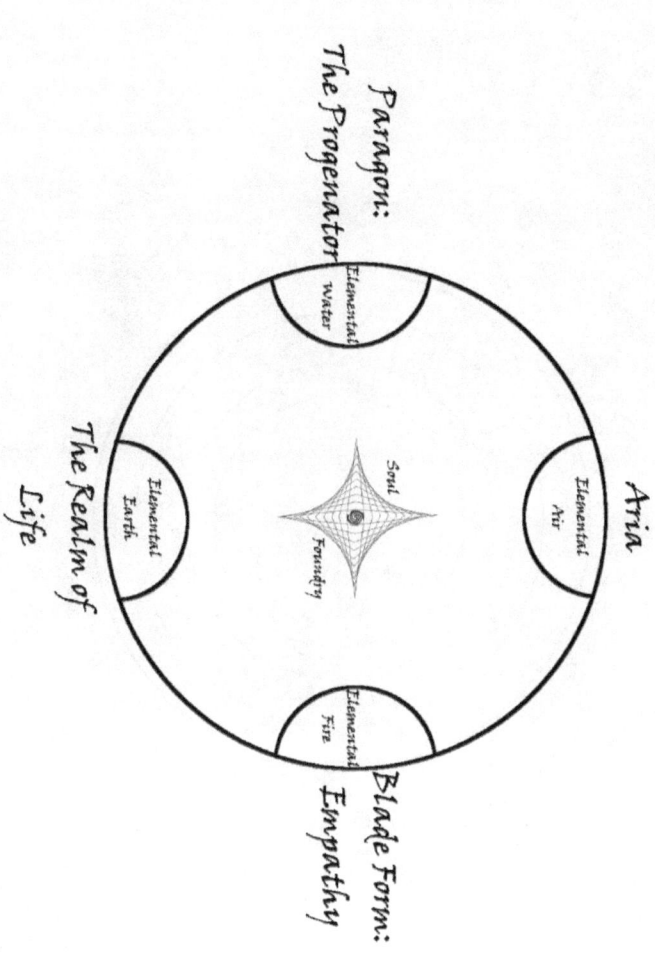

Paragon:
The Progenitor

Aria

Blade Form:
Empathy

The Realm of
Life

Elemental
Water

Elemental
Air

Elemental
Fire

Elemental
Earth

Soul

Foundry

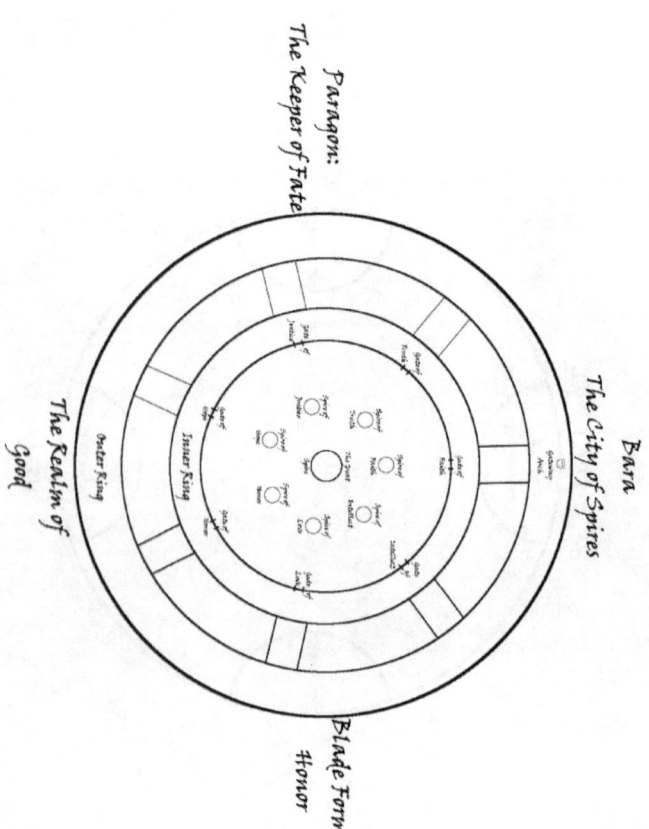

Paragon:
The Keeper of Fate

Bara
The City of Spires

The Realm of
Good

Blade Form:
Honor

Outer Ring

Inner Ring

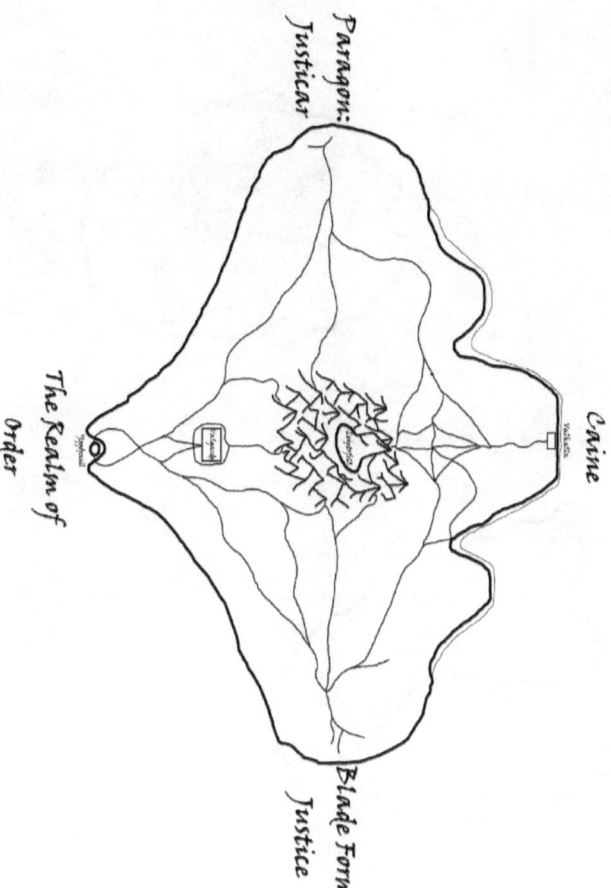

Paragon: Justicar

Caine

The Realm of Order

Blade Form: Justice

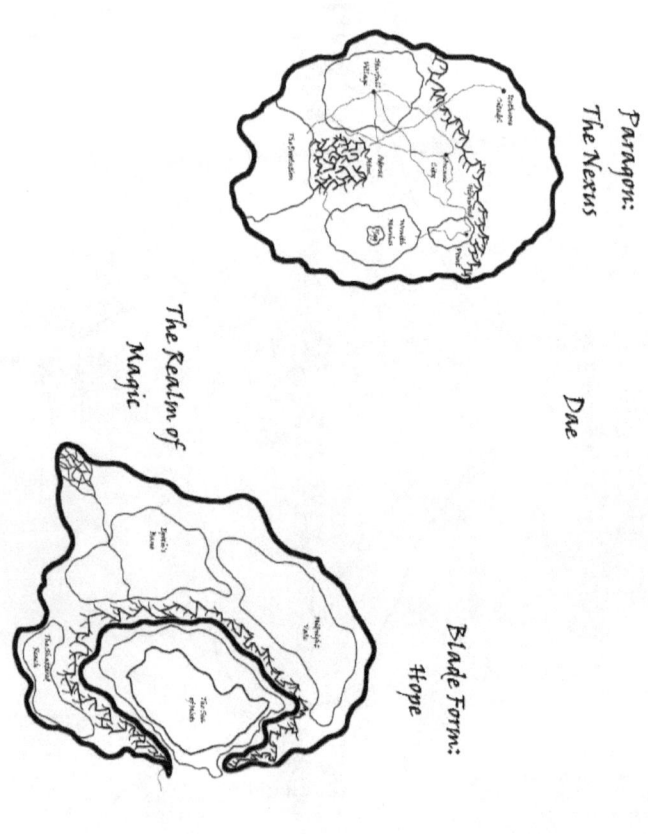

Paragon:
The Nexus

Dae

The Realm of
Magic

Blade Form:
Hope

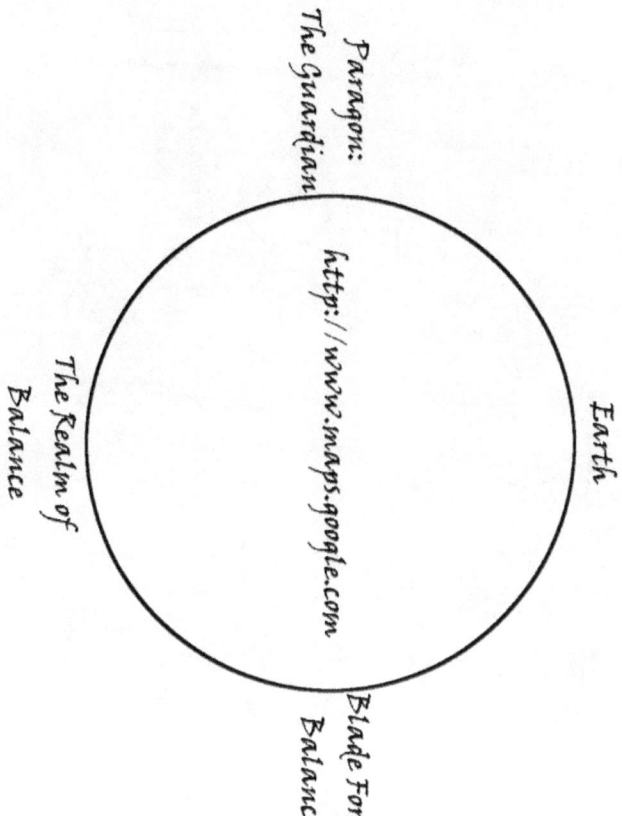

Paragon:
The Guardian

http://www.maps.google.com

Earth

The Realm of
Balance

Blade Form:
Balance

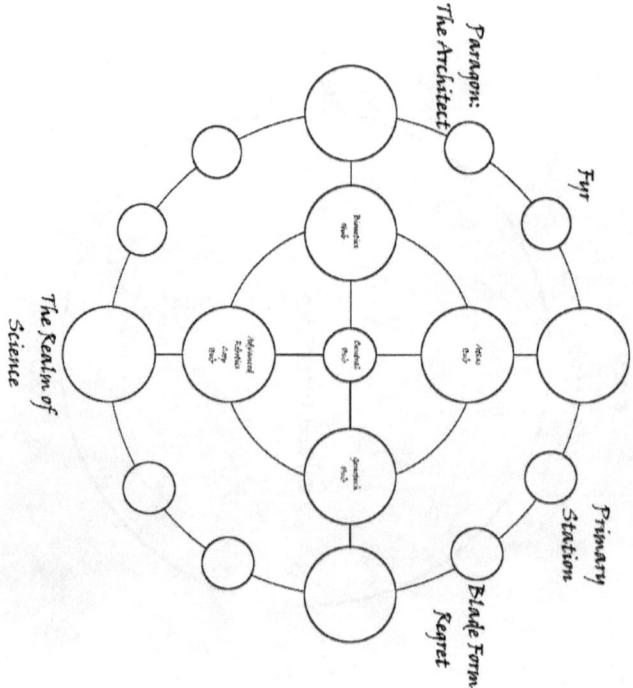

Paragon:
The Architect

Fyr

The Realm of
Science

Primary
Station

Blade Form:
Regret

Gile

Mutable and ever-changing, the strongest
wills and minds control the landscape,
causing mountains and lakes, buildings
and cities to appear and vanish on a whim. — Blade Form:

Paragon: Little is know of Gile and the Effect that   Torment
The Voidwalker   call it home, and the Effect are more than
                willing to share what they know,
                        for a fee of course.
                        The Realm of Chaos

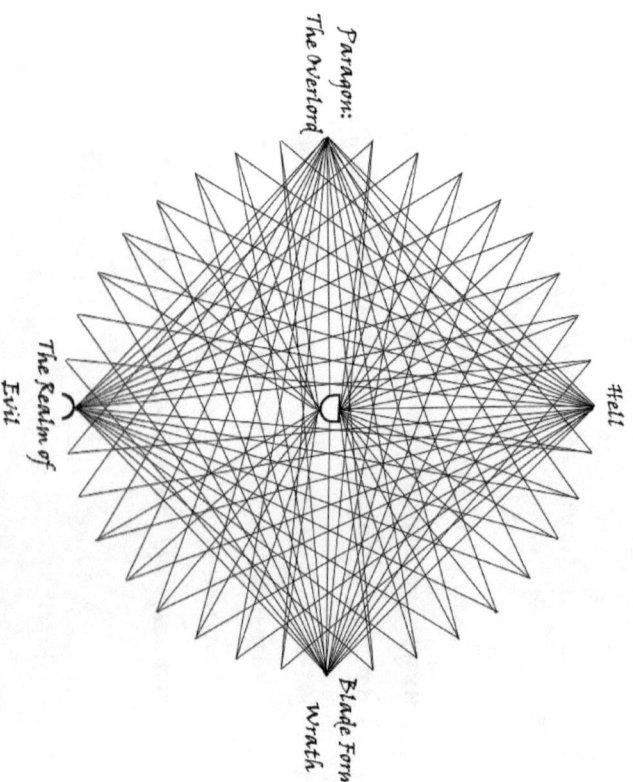

Paragon:
The Overlord

The Realm of
Evil

Hell

Blade Form:
Wrath

Igvia

Paragon:
The Reaper

Blade Form:
The Soul
Ripper

Igvia is enveloped in
impenetrable fog.
Due to this, very little
is known
about the Realm of
Death.

This map only covers
the area in the
immediate vicinity of
the Gateway Arch.

The Realm of
Death.

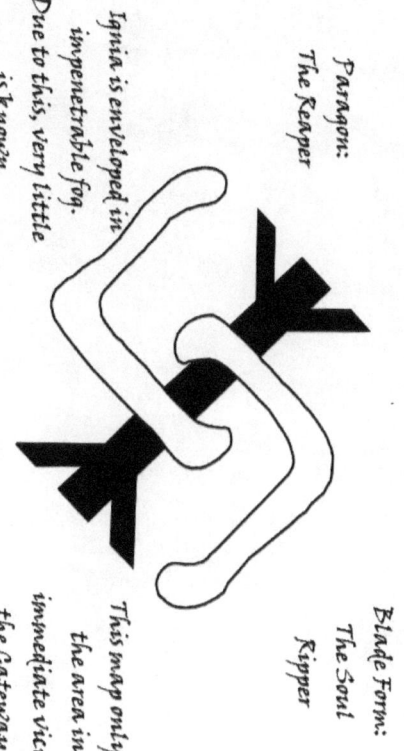

Acknowledgments

Thank you to everyone who helped make this book a reality. You know who you are.

About the Author

Mark Cole is an Operations Specialist in the United States Coast Guard and is currently stationed in Mobile, Alabama. He lives there with his wife and two daughters.

If you have any questions, comments, or just want to tell Mark how much you loved his story (Aren't you so sweet), feel free to contact him at mcthew@outlook.com or www.facebook.com/mcthew

www.ingramcontent.com/pod-product-compliance
Lightning Source LLC
Chambersburg PA
CBHW030553180626
46816CB00005B/1521